A fearless debut
team and how far
their bod

"*We Loved to Run* jumps
second—it's blistering, it's unputdownable....an ode to ....
running itself, and all the contradictions that lie within giving yourself over to
something you hate to love and love to hate. Every line is visceral and poetic,
brutal and psychologically astute. And she perfectly portrays the fraught,
complicated family of a team. What can I say? It's perfect: troubling in all the best
ways." —**Marisa Crane, author of *A Sharp Endless Need***

"Propulsive...Whether or not you've ever been in their shoes, the six teammates
at the heart of this novel, and the torturous, rapturous experience of racing
together, are made vivid through Stephanie Reents's exquisite prose."
—**Leah Hager Cohen, author of *Strangers and Cousins***

*We loved running because it was who we were, who we'd been in high school,
who we hoped to be in futures we couldn't yet imagine. Strong and fast. Fast and
strong.*

At Frost, a small liberal arts college in Massachusetts, the runners on the
women's cross country team have their sights set on the 1992 New England
Division Three Championships and will push themselves through every punishing
workout and skipped meal to achieve their goal. But Kristin, the team's star, is
hiding a secret about what happened over the summer, and her unpredictable
behavior jeopardizes the girls' chance to win. Team Captain Danielle is convinced
she can restore Kristin's confidence, even if it means burying her own past. As
the final meet approaches, Kristin, Danielle, and the rest of the girls must
transcend their individual circumstances and run the race as a team.

Told from the perspective of the six fastest team members, *We Loved to Run*
deftly illuminates the impossible standards young women set for themselves in
spite of their own powerlessness. With startling honesty and boundless empathy,
Stephanie Reents reveals how girls—even those in competition—find ways to
love and defend one another.

Stephanie Reents is the author of *The Kissing List*, a collection of stories that
was an Editors' Choice in *The New York Times Book Review*, and *I Meant to Kill
Ye*, a bibliomemoir chronicling her journey into the strange void at the heart of
Cormac McCarthy's *Blood Meridian*. She has twice received an O. Henry Prize for
her short fiction. Reents received a BA from Amherst College, where she ran on
the cross country team all four years; a BA from the University of Oxford as a
Rhodes Scholar; and an MFA from the University of Arizona. She was a Stegner
Fellow at Stanford University.

We Loved to Run • Stephanie Reents
Hogarth • Hardcover • 08/26/25 • $29.00/$39.00C • 9780593448069

WE LOVED TO RUN

WE LOVED
TO RUN

A NOVEL

STEPHANIE REENTS

HOGARTH
London / New York

Hogarth
An imprint of Random House
A division of Penguin Random House LLC
1745 Broadway, New York, NY 10019
randomhousebooks.com
penguinrandomhouse.com

Hardback ISBN 978-0-593-44806-9
Ebook ISBN 978-0-593-44808-3

Printed in the United States of America on acid-free paper

randomhousebooks.com

2 4 6 8 9 7 5 3 1

$PrintCode

First Edition

Book design by Debbie Glasserman

[Book Team credits, to be modified/inserted by PE]

The authorized representative in the EU for product safety and compliance is Penguin Random House Ireland, Morrison Chambers, 32 Nassau Street, Dublin D02 YH68, Ireland. https://eu-contact.penguin.ie.

PART I

/ /

LIKE A THISTLE
IN A SOCK

WARM UP

WE HATED A LOT OF THINGS. A GRADUAL HILL IN THE SECOND MILE of a cross country race. Two hard workouts in a row. The little packets of Lorna Doones in our brown-bag lunches that Assistant Coach picked up from the college cafeteria: like vanilla chalk. Big toenails that were a tad too long. When our coach said, *Here's where you make your move.* Inner-thigh friction. Holes in our socks. Our mothers' *Shouldn't you take off one day a week?*

We hated our coaches. We hated them for encouraging us to have a love-hate relationship with our bodies, for telling us on some days that we were strong, and on others that we were fat. Only they didn't say it that way. They said, *You've lost your lean,* which meant a gain of a pound or two, a half-percentage point of body fat. As punishment, we had to be the rabbit. We had to run as though something dangerous was chasing us. Though we hated being told what to do, we loved it, too, our emotions some-times not much more evolved than those of sulky thirteen-year-old girls who not-so-secretly longed to be loved the best in the whole wide world, who couldn't take one bit of criticism without totally losing it.

There were six of us. Two seniors: Danielle and Harriet. Three juniors: Liv, Chloe, and Kristin. And Patricia, an exceptionally talented sophomore who wanted to transfer. You'd find more runners in the 1992 Stanzas (the stupid name of our yearbook). But we were the core, the top six, not that you could tell from studying the photo. We looked just like everyone else—healthy and young—but we were the fast ones, even if this was invisible.

We hated our coaches but we also loved them, especially Coach, with his British accent by way of Uganda. He wore a heavy gold watch and made track suits look elegant. Who knows how he ended up at Frost, a tiny college in a tiny corner of New England? We loved Coach for loading us on a van and ferrying us to the running shop in a neighboring town to pick out shoes. We never knew when it was going to happen, which made it even better. Kristin and Patricia were always giddy with excitement because when they'd decided to come to Frost, they both thought they'd sacrificed the freebies that the Div 1 coaches had dangled in front of them. But it turned out that Coach had a slush fund from a generous alum, and he could buy us new shoes once a season. He played songs by a German band, Trio, whose most famous song "Da Da Da" was unknown to us but quickly became our favorite, the anthem of our parties: "I don't know you, you don't know me."

We hated running, and we loved it. We spent so much time trying not to think about our bodies that we were always thinking about them. Thinking about how they were not hungry or not injured or not fatter or weaker than the body of some other girl. Running was the glue that kept us together, but it was also a truth serum, drawing out feelings we'd rather not have. Danielle secretly envied Kristin for being so effortlessly beautiful: Princess Di in denim. You weren't supposed to be fast with boobs as big as hers. Kristin was in awe of Harriet's self-control, the fact she'd never eaten a cafeteria dessert, not once in three years. Liv wished she could speak her mind as effortlessly as Danielle did. Harriet wanted to trade places with Patricia, not forever, but maybe for a couple of months, just to see what it was like to be from rural New Mexico. Patricia didn't want anything the girls on her team had, except for maybe Kristin's black cowboy boots and Harriet's nose ring, but her parents would lose it if she came home with a pierced nose. She was mostly happy with the way she was, even though a lot of things at Frost told her she shouldn't be.

Chloe and Kristin were always hammering on easy days. Patricia took the intervals out too fast. The pack could have let her go but never did. We took the bait. There was no shame in running as hard as you could and then puking. There was no shame in grunting, spitting, farting, leaving skids of snot along your arms. Danielle cried after NESCACs, a year earlier, but there was no shame in that, or at least not too much. We'd run our hardest, but it wasn't enough to carry us to Nationals. Emotions did not behave predictably under physical duress. We loved each other, too, the love as dark and sticky and intense as blackstrap molasses. We'd stand at bathroom doors, sentries, turn on the taps full-tilt, sweep the hair off each other's foreheads, stroke each other's backs while a stomach clenched and released. Danielle regularly threw up after she drank too much, sometimes preemptively. It was an effective way to head off a hangover. We shared tampons, the treats our moms sent us, clean socks, joy and shame and deodorant. We were friends like that.

We loved running because we loved repetition (breathe, stride, breathe, stride, breathe, stride), getting lost in thought, the endorphins that flooded our brains after several miles and swept away obsession and weariness, all that seemed dire and tragic in our college lives, and narrowed our focus to covering each kilometer of the 5K cross country race as swiftly as possible. We loved it because it was who we were, who we'd been in high school, who we hoped to be in futures we couldn't yet imagine. Strong and fast. Fast and strong.

We loved winning, but we didn't always love what was required: cross training, pool workouts, the flotation belts that we wore while running in place in the deep end, serious stretching, form drills, walking backward uphill, cool-downs that were more than five minutes and warm-ups that were more than ten. Chloe really hated lifting. Harriet did, too, though she put on a good show by doing high reps with almost no resistance. She wanted to like lifting because Professor Witt, an old-school feminist who taught WAGs, swore by weight training. Women could be just as strong as men, Witt claimed; they just needed to get over the social stigma of muscles. Whatever, we thought. Witt had never run a mile in her life.

We also hated rest days and easy laps between 400-meter repeats, not because we hated resting, but because it was never quite long enough to recover. Anticipating a workout was always worse than finishing one. Fartleks—which the men pronounced *fartlicks*—could make us puke. (We growled when the men urged, "Go tits out, ladies!") We hated that word *ladies* more than we hated the word *tits*. *Tits* could be thrilling in the right context. We hated running on rainy days until the moment we were drenched, sucking water from the end of a hank of hair. On hot days, sunscreen stung our eyes, but we could skinny-dip in Puffer's Pond, and we did, especially if the men were doing a separate workout, and we expected an ambush. We liked the men's team, though screwing them could feel like making out with your brother. It could be nicer than that, too. It depended on how you felt about someone else's bruised toenails, bony hips, rock-hard thighs.

We loved to run, and we hated it. To run, you had to be willing to accompany yourself on long lonely journeys. You might know the time (90 minutes, two hours, 45) but not the route. Maybe you knew the route—through a shady residential neighborhood, through the park with a hill that looked like a camel's hump, onto the trail just beyond the tennis courts, and then—up, up, up—the foothills opening in front of you like another world: the old military cemetery, the firing range, the corral where several weary horses shifted from hoof to hoof and ambled to the fence wondering whether you'd palm them an apple. Even if you knew where you were going and how long it usually took, you could never anticipate what you would see along the way. Back home in New Mexico, Patricia saw rattlesnakes in late May and early June when they were coming out of hibernation. They draped themselves across trails, seeking a sunny spot to warm their cold hearts, and Patricia hurdled right over them. Chloe saw a fox at the northern edge of Central Park that might have been just a skinny dog. Liv got lost in cornfields in southern Illinois, where her dad's family was from. Danielle was chased and bitten by bats, not once, but twice over the course of two weeks just before sophomore year. She was running along the soupy Seekonk River in Providence. It was not a joking matter, even though there was something inherently absurd about being bitten twice in a three-week stretch. Was she cursed? If you mentioned it, you were courting Danielle's wrath.

We sank to our ankles in mud, we slipped in snow. We got heat stroke in the summer, mild frostbite in the winter, but those were just minor hazards. The real obstacle—underneath the sharp pain in a hip, the mechanical clicking of a knee, the weird way that teeth ached from huffing in winter air—the real obstacle, unchanging and always there, was the desire to stop, and the knowledge that we couldn't. We could never stop because if we did, then we would know we could. If you stopped once, you might stop a second time. You might never run again.

THE BODY DOES WHAT THE BODY WANTS

Kristin

"NO SWEAT," COACH TELLS THEM, THOUGH AT 3:30 ON A DAY AS MOIST as a wet washcloth, Kristin and her teammates are drenched by the time they line up, shoulder to shoulder, three layers deep, waiting for Assistant Coach to raise his arm in preparation for dropping it with all the glee of a man bringing a hatchet down on a chicken's neck.

What a jerk, Kristin thinks, not that she really means it—she's always a little angry right before a time trial, and this one's even worse than usual because it's two miles on the track because Coach just wants *to see where you are*. She hates running more than one mile on the track. Moments earlier, Chloe asked, "What's our pace?" and Coach's eyes widened before he laughed. *You decide.* Someone groaned, expressing the team's communal dread. It's 90 degrees with what feels like 90-percent humidity, the sky low and smudgy. The air smells like a parking garage. She feels the flicker of a headache.

"Let's go, girls!" Danielle says, "We can do it."

"Yes, we can," Liv says, sounding far less sure than Danielle does, before snapping her gum.

Kristin ignores both of them. This is the fourth day of preseason; the fourth day she hasn't slept well despite being totally wiped out from six-milers in the morning followed by lifting with intervals in the afternoon. She keeps waking up at 2 a.m. in her empty dorm room, convinced someone is tapping on her door. It's midnight back in Boise, where she's from. "Who's there?" she asks feeling her way around the body-sized duffle bag she still hasn't unpacked. Could it be her friend Eli, come to persuade her to take a moonlit stroll? She wouldn't mind Eli showing up in the middle of the night, though not for the reasons he'd probably want to be there. The hallway, lit by ghoulish fluorescent tubes, is empty, except for a pair of strappy pink sandals way down at one end. All week Chloe has made a point of edging her out at the end of every run, even in the morning when they're barely awake. And all week Kristin has been deliberately ignoring Chloe, telling herself it doesn't matter, it's just practice. Chloe's just desperate to take back the top position after being sidelined with a stress fracture at the end of last season. But Kristin has no intention of giving her back that spot. She's the one who qualified for Nationals last year, not Chloe, and she'll win when she needs to win, which, she has decided, is right now: at their first time trial.

"Get set," Assistant Coach calls out.

They freeze, which always reminds her of red light/green light, a game she loved as a little girl because she was faster than everyone else. She could cover so much ground behind someone's turned back. She sucks in a deep breath, and then there's something that doesn't belong in her mouth. "Sorry," she says. "Just a second." Stepping off the track, she clears her throat, spits, does it a second and a third time to dislodge whatever's there.

Ugh.

"Are you OK?" Danielle asks.

Assistant Coach laughs nervously.

"Sorry," she says again. "I swallowed a bug." When she returns, she slips into the cozy inside spot, bumping Chloe out of place, which has a domino effect on everyone else, who are squeezing as close as they can to the inner lane. "What the—" Chloe says, frowning.

"Sorry, sorry," she says because she should have gone back to the third lane where she was before, but too bad, it's too late now. Assistant Coach raises his hand, impatient to get the show on the road. "On your mark."

She goes out hard, leaving behind all of her doubt. That always happens. She's thinking, and then she's not. Chloe's right on her shoulder, pushing while Kristin pulls, both of them locked into something that they know and love and hate. Kristin surges— why not? Her legs are OK—and Chloe sticks. Of course she does—she's used to being the fastest on the team. As they're coming around the curve and heading into the backstretch, Chloe uses the momentum from the second lane to whip by Kristin. "Space!" Kristin screams as Chloe steps in front of her.

"Sorry," Chloe says.

Fine. Now Chloe pulls and Kristin pushes, her eyes fixed on the surprisingly delicate orange-and-black butterfly tattoo on Chloe's right shoulder that Chloe got this summer. So out-of-character for Chloe, whose socks always match her shirts. But they're all a little different from who they were last spring—for better, for worse. Kristin shoves the thought away. She's far away from Boise, even farther from the Sawtooth Mountains. She doesn't need to go there. She just needs to keep moving forward. If she stays where she is—in the outside position—she'll have to work a little harder, but whatever. That's what training is all about: choosing the harder thing, owning it. Chloe shifts into something a little faster, and Kristin goes right with her. If she can just hang on . . . the body does what the body wants to do, except when it doesn't. The two of them—Kristin and Chloe—no three, suddenly Liv is following like a shadow, Kristin can smell her Trident bubblegum—pull away from the pack. The straightaway shoots Kristin forward after the sticky curve, and she rides the current. She feels good, each stride as easy as a breath, as miraculous. Assistant Coach calls out a surprisingly fast quarter-mile split, and from somewhere behind them comes Danielle's voice: "Go, girls." For a moment Kristin's occupied with Danielle's generosity. The only thing Kristin is capable of screaming during a speed workout is *"Track!"* They blaze through the third and fourth laps, though on the fifth Kristin's legs start to tighten. "Your arms are bunching up," Assistant Coach yells. "Use your arms. Drive your arms." Her irritation flares again.

When Liv squeezes through the gap that is cracking open between her and Chloe, Kristin realizes that she's slowing down, and suddenly she's two or three steps behind Chloe, a step behind Liv. Just like that, just like that, just like that. Now five. Now six. You blink and you're in no man's land, the front runners abandoning you, the pack behind you watching, smelling opportunity. She's not going to lose, not after what happened this summer, not after almost getting lost.

She's fast. It's not quite a thought. It's like her heart beating and blood surging through her veins, something that happens beyond her consciousness. If she stays with them . . . she imagines being tied to Chloe. Isn't that one of Danielle's visualization exercises? Imagine there's a string tying you to the girl in front of you. It's already taut. Any more tension, and it will snap.

She has to keep moving. Step by step, she wills herself to loosen the tension, to make up for lost ground. She has a hundred meters, not a lot of time. Fifty. She swerves to the outer edge of the second lane, the painted white line rubbed away into a ghost of itself, and bursts forward, her arms pumping, her chest tightening into a knot, the string loosening, and she crosses the line a breath or two in front of Chloe and Liv.

Instead of stopping, she keeps running, hardly breaking stride. Look at her. Look at her go! As she's coming around the top of the first curve, she finds herself running for other reasons— because she can, because she's OK, because she's fast and strong. "Repeat after me," Danielle is always saying. "I am so fast. I am so strong." Her lungs burn like she has breathed in gasoline, but when someone behind her yells "Stop!" she thinks, Why should I? She could run another mile. Maybe not at this pace, but close enough, though once she's finished this lap and come back to where Coach and Assistant Coach are standing, with their clipboards and stopwatches, one of them will surely step into her path to interrupt her little rebellion, and instead of swerving, she'll slow down and do whatever they tell her. Though why should she, she's wondering again, except that it's habit. Well, screw that. She's going to stop doing what other people tell her to do. This thought lasts until Danielle catches up and wallops her on the back, just hard enough to convey a hint of irritation.

"Ow," Kristin yelps in pretend pain.

"Oh my god, Kristi," she cries, "what are you doing? Did you forget where the finish line was?"

"I just . . ." Kristin starts. "I just . . ." She considers what she can plausibly tell Danielle. "I just felt good," she lies. "I felt really good, and I wanted to keep going."

"What part of *Stop!* don't you understand?"

"I—" Kristin says, still searching for an explanation for something she doesn't even fully understand. Danielle's bangs are pushed high off her forehead and her mascara is smudged, but her lips are a perfect pink heart. How does she do it? Kristin watches them soften into a smile as the pack shuffles closer.

"If you do that again, Chloe will kill you," Danielle says. "And then I will have to kill Chloe, and then our team will be seriously fucked." She's grinning now.

"I'm sorry," Kristin says, and she really is. It's not cool to keep running as though the workout didn't end. If Chloe ever did that . . . but she beat Chloe. She beat Chloe, and she kept running.

THE CAPTAIN

Danielle

IF YOU CAN BELIEVE IT, YOU CAN ACHIEVE IT.

Well, that's not absolutely true, which Danielle knows from studying psychology. The behaviorists say what we do is the result of years of unconscious (or conscious) conditioning. Take Pavlov and his ringing bells and salivating mutts, or frat boys (who aren't really frat boys since frats are totally illegal at Frost) whose mouths start watering as soon as the chapel bell rings nine times on Thursday nights. Conditioning plays a role—the way her heart hammers the moment Assistant Coach pulls into the parking lot of their away meets. Or how when the gun goes off—bam—they're all running like dogs.

What's that poem? Your mom and dad, they fuck you up. They don't want to, but they do. One of her psych professors recited it when they were discussing Freud. Harriet runs because she's still rebelling against her mom, who made her quit cross country when she developed a serious eating disorder in her junior year of high school. Harriet's mom even had to lock her running shoes in the liquor cabinet, which Danielle can hardly believe. Harriet's still too skinny. And Chloe, an example of the drama of the gifted child if Danielle ever saw one, is forever trying to win her parents' love by pushing herself to be the best. Poor Clo Clo, who's actually the opposite of poor with her Central Park West address and her private girls' school pedigree. Chloe's parents haven't come to a single meet. Not one. Not even when they were racing in the Bronx, and her parents could have hopped on the subway. They're just too busy, Chloe insists.

Your parents obviously shape you, though not in the way that Freud said. She doesn't believe all that stuff about children's sexual attachment to their mothers, their murderous rage at their fathers. She's not suffering from penis envy. Unexpected boners? No thanks. It's bad enough having boobs. As far as she's concerned, Freud's biggest contribution to psychology was discovering the unconscious. It's so weird—the possibility that you can feel something, believe it with your whole heart, without ever knowing exactly why.

Maybe they love to run for reasons beyond what they actually understand.

It's the first Saturday before the semester officially begins on Monday. This means brunch at Duck, Duck, Goose, a tradition that Danielle started sophomore year. Everyone loves the place, an old mill that sits on the rocky banks of a river—even Patricia, who hates the taste of coffee, and Kristin, who's afraid caffeine will interfere with her race-day rituals. At Duck, Duck, Goose, no one's on a diet, no one requests Equal or skim milk, and everyone eats the muffins, even Chloe, after she breaks hers into a million little pieces, even Harriet, though only after confirming that everyone else has ordered one. Harriet will always be recovering from a competitive eating disorder.

Danielle feels good. This is her second year as captain, her last chance to make her mark. She's never been the fastest, not in junior high when she went out for cross country just cause her best friend was doing it, not in high school when she kept running because she liked the camaraderie, and certainly not in college. But she has been the most dedicated. She likes to think this is why the team chose her—because she believes in them. She believes they can go to Nationals this year, not because she'll be out in front, leading her girls to victory, but because she's going to make sure that each and every one of them reaches her potential. Though she's aware that some of her psych professors would take her to task for this, she believes in the power of positive thinking the way some people put their faith in God. Visualize; realize. Lay a base; build; peak. Do the work. Reap the rewards.

Run hard enough, and you can do almost anything. You may even forget what you would rather not remember.

Harriet's holding forth at the far end of the tables, looking happy. Her face is fuller than before, maybe from a semester of drinking kir royales. Danielle wasn't exactly supportive when Harriet announced she was skipping track to spend the spring semester in Paris. Runners didn't go abroad. A small part of Danielle believed Harriet was leaving to punish her. But now she thinks it was a good idea for Harriet to get away from Frost, from her mother. Her dirty-blond crew cut has grown out, her curls springing up insistently. She looks pretty, Danielle thinks, though Harriet would strenuously object to her use of that word. *Pretty shitty?* Danielle can't help but remember freshman-year Harriet with her big hair and a floral dress that did nothing to disguise that she was scary skinny, and her mother flouncing around in a cloud of Calvin Klein Obsession, loudly complaining about the lack of air conditioning. They both lived on the same hallway of the same freshman dorm. Harriet, still a Southern belle, was an alien among their mostly East Coast crew, but within a few weeks, the two of them were doing late nights in the hallway, cozy in a nest of pillows and blankets, wired from too much diet Dr Pepper. Back then, they were both boy crazy, but then Harriet discovered feminist theory, and the patriarchy, and it was *phallus this* and *phallus that*. They once argued for several days about whether heterosexuality was compulsory. Another time it was about whether Andrea Dworkin's proposition that a "normal fuck" by a "normal man" was inherently violent, which, of course, Danielle found ridiculous. Though they've drifted apart, Harriet knows Danielle better than anyone else, even the Darlings, her beloved roommates.

Liv and Chloe start to crack up and Danielle can tell from the sly close-lipped smile on Harriet's face, the tiny chin tuck, the pause, that she's pleased with whatever she just said. This is Harriet: she likes holding forth, which Danielle usually enjoys until the occasional times when she doesn't. Harriet is telling them about buying a bra in Paris, how the saleslady actually cupped her breasts to decide which size she needed.

Chloe starts barking like a seal, which sometimes happens when she laughs too hard. Patricia giggles.

"I was like 'Madame, *s'il vous plait* get your hands off my tits,'" Harriet says loud enough for everyone in the café to hear.

"How do you even say *tits* in French?" Liv asks.

"Teets," Harriet says, "Les teets."

"Oh, come on," Patricia says. "You're kidding."

"I'm dead serious," Harriet says.

"And then did she bring you le training bra?" Danielle asks.

"Ooh la la," Harriet says. "Harsh."

Everyone laughs, even Kristin, who has been unusually quiet

since they sat down. Danielle's been wanting to catch up with her one-on-one. Kristin was always a bit of a mystery to Danielle, who put a ton of effort into trying to make Kristin one of the Darlings in Kristin's freshman year but failed. Danielle had started to wonder whether Kristin was one of those girls who wasn't good at being friends with other girls. Danielle doesn't like girls like this.

"Oh my God, Harriet is so ridiculous," Danielle whispers to Kristin.

Kristin rolls her eyes.

Something shifted between them last year when Kristin came to Danielle's house at the last minute for Thanksgiving. Kristin, Danielle, and her mom spent a whole day in the kitchen with mugs of hot mulled cider and flour everywhere, making pies. Kristin's secret super power was weaving a perfect lattice pie crust, just the way her grandma had taught her, and somehow she wound up telling them about her parents' divorce when she was a baby and how her dad just disappeared. "That's so sad," Danielle's mom said. "Your dad's really missing out." Kristin said she wasn't sure whether her dad didn't want to see her or whether her mom had made it impossible. Something clicked, and Danielle thought she finally understood why it wasn't easy for Kristin to get close to other people.

"I feel like we haven't had a chance to hang out," Danielle says.

"I know," Kristin says. "I've been so exhausted. All I've been doing apart from going to practice is sleeping."

"Totally," Danielle agrees. "I always come back to school thinking I'm in shape, and then Coach's workouts the first week absolutely kill me."

"I'm actually looking forward to classes starting," Kristin says.

"Me, too," Danielle says. "But how are you? How was your

summer?" Danielle knows a little from the postcards they exchanged all summer. This was her idea. Last spring, she bought them all fountain pens, tiny boxes of disposable ink cartridges, sheets of stamps. She showed them how to load the cartridges and hold the pens properly and warned them not to loan them out since the nibs would bend to their particular writing style. Of course, Chloe complained because she was a leftie, but they kept in better touch than they normally would, and Danielle enjoyed reading between the lines of what they wrote to discover what they were really trying to say.

Kristin twists her silver ring with its eye-shaped turquoise stone. There's some story behind it—her mom found it in the crook of a tree on a hike. "It was fine. My mom drove me crazy. I drove her crazy."

"Why?"

"Oh, you know, same old, same old: she complains about working too much but then she works all the time. I hardly saw her. But it was fine. I ran. I worked. I hung out with friends. I learned to play pool."

"You learned to play pool?" Danielle says, attempting to steer the conversation to something that will draw Kristin out. Never mind that Kristin hardly ever asks Danielle questions. It's Danielle's job to be the older sister. "You're turning into such an urban cowgirl!"

Across the table, Chloe lets out another bark, most certainly for show this time since it always gets a laugh.

"That haircut," Kristin whispers. "She looks like the girl version of Michael J. Fox."

Danielle giggles, then stops. "Poor Clo Clo."

Kristin's lips twitch as though she's about to say something else but doesn't.

"I hope Clo Clo stays healthy this year," Kristin says, though her tone of voice suggests the opposite.

"We all need to stay healthy. And focused."

"I am so focused this year. I am so determined."

For a moment, Danielle can't believe what she's hearing. This is not Kristin. Is she mocking Danielle? These are the exact words that Danielle uses the night before meets when she tries to get her girls to visualize having their best races—all while contending with Harriet's sarcasm, Patricia complaining that she didn't come to college to join a cult, and everyone else being their usual sullen selves.

"Is Kristin actually drinking coffee?" Chloe screeches.

Kristin shrugs. "What can I say? I worked at an espresso bar this summer. It was kind of inevitable."

Chloe is smiling idiotically. "Did Jed teach you?" she teases.

"Who's Jed?" Harriet asks.

"The guy from the coffee shop," Chloe says. "The guy Kristin was dating."

"We weren't dating," Kristin says.

"I thought you said . . ."

"We weren't dating," she says again, her voice rising slightly.

"But you said . . ."

Danielle is surprised she can't remember Kristin mentioning Jed. That's totally the kind of thing she usually picks up on.

"Maybe they were just fucking," Harriet says.

"Harriet!" Danielle cries.

"What?" Harriet is always pleased with herself when she can work *fucking* into a sentence. "There's nothing wrong with fucking, or with the word, *fucking*. Say it loud and say it proud: girls like fucking."

"Can you please stop?" Liv says, which surprises Danielle. Liv usually doesn't take the bait. "Everything is not fucking."

"What do you and Henry call it? Making love?" Harriet smirks and swats at Liv's arm. "Having intercourse?"

Liv turns bright red. She's been dating Henry for a year, and they've become the campus couple: highly visible, completely committed, and pseudo-married.

"They call it the vertical cha-cha-cha," Chloe says, letting out another bark.

Kristin's chair scrapes backward. For a split second, Danielle is afraid she's about to leave in a huff. It's happened before. It can be hard for girls to get along, the potential for hurt feelings endless; it's even harder to get along with girls you're competing with.

"A toast," Kristin says, raising her cup. "We're back, and we're at the beginning." Her hand trembles as she lifts her coffee higher. There's a pause as she moistens her lips. "Here's to our best season yet!"

If Kristin is teasing Danielle by proposing a toast, no one else is picking up on it. They're all standing, all of Danielle's girls—women, she hears Harriet saying in her mind—standing together. Bursting with optimism, she smiles at Kristin, whose expression seems blank until she notices Danielle's gaze. Then her face reassembles itself into something warm and recognizable.

"Here's to sticking together and pushing each other—" Danielle declares. This is a contradiction, but she doesn't give it a second thought because it's the nature of cross country. "Here's to training smart and running every race like it's our last one."

"And here's to going all the way to Nationals!" Liv says.

"And to no injuries!" Chloe adds. "Especially no stress fractures."

"Hear, hear!" Danielle says, because really, she should be kinder to Chloe, even though she also finds herself thinking it's the essence of Chloe's personality to toast herself.

"To freedom from the patriarchal gaze!" Harriet cries out, throwing her arms wide. "To the lesbian continuum!"

There is laughter.

"To kicking some ass," Patricia says, and then they're all leaning in, reaching thin arm toward thin arm, delicate wrist toward delicate wrist, the space between them closing as their paper coffee cups meet and touch, barely making a sound.

"To us," Danielle says.

THE RABBIT

THE FIRST WEEK OF SCHOOL, COACH TOLD US TO MEET HIM IN THE wrestling room. At *three on the nose.* Danielle was the one who relayed this information.

"*Mon Dieu,*" Harriet said. Her semester in Paris had changed her. Our first week back, as we schlepped back and forth between the gym and campus twice a day, she kept stopping and demanding that we appreciate some aspect of Frost—the grassy greens where students sprawled in happy suggestion of deep intellectual discourse or tossed Frisbees back and forth with so much panache it was easy to see how we earned our reputation as intellectual jocks, the view from the war memorial, and even the ivy spidering across the austere brick buildings. She kissed everyone on the cheek three times, even guys on the men's team. In her satchel, she carried around a wedge of brie and offered everyone slivers with their saltines, the only cracker dispensed by the cafeteria. It was all *trés trés trés* you know. She simultaneously loved and hated Frost more intensely.

"*Mon doo doo,*" Patricia replied.

Harriet rolled her eyes. Danielle laughed. "You're funny. Were you this funny last year?"

"No one let me talk last year," Patricia said.

"It's not like we taped your mouth shut," Kristin said. "Or did we?"

"No, you just ignored me," Patricia said. "And you mispronounced my name." For a whole year, everyone on the team called her Pa-TRISH-ah instead of Pa-TRISS-ee-ah, even though she always corrected them.

"We just didn't know how to say it correctly," Liv said, smiling sweetly. "It was nothing personal. Do you want a piece of gum?"

Patricia shook her head.

We were in the locker room changing into short synthetic shorts that were yeast infections waiting to happen. We'd already snipped out the built-in underwear with a pair of tiny silver eyebrow scissors that Danielle kept in her locker for just this purpose. (Patricia insisted on using a Swiss Army pocket knife.) We were supposed to wear gray tees courtesy of the athletic department, but they were too new and stiff with chokey collars. Plus they said *Property of Frost*. We were philosophically opposed to being considered anyone's property. We would not change our last names when we got married, if we even got married at all. Although who knew? It all seemed so far away, a hypothetical that held little allure, except for Liv and Henry, who might as well have been married, they spent so much time together and talked about everything under the sun, like what it would do to Henry's relationship with his dad if he became an investment banker, whether he would be forever separated from his blue-collar family. When he returned to campus, he'd start the process of applying for jobs on Wall Street. Every fall a crop of guys donned blue blazers and yellow ties (which made them look young and old at the same time) and headed to the college inn, where they met with only slightly older guys wearing blue blazers (but no ties) and answered questions about current events and solved weird story problems, like calculating how many bricks would be needed to cover the entire surface of the Empire State Building. Liv was afraid she was going to lose Henry after graduation.

Harriet was wearing a white T-shirt with a scoop neck that was flattering in some way that was hard to put into words. This was also new. She'd cared not at all about clothes, claiming that fashion was a way of controlling women's bodies, and yet she'd brought back a few nice things from Paris—the flattering white T-shirts, a couple of sheer scarves, Doc Marten boots in burgundy, and even a long flowing skirt with tiny winking mirrors embroidered into the patchwork fabric. Harriet, much to her fashionable mother's chagrin, had sworn off skirts at the end of her freshman year. Now, she was exploring her femme side (not to be confused with feminine). "I shouldn't have eaten an apple at lunch," Harriet said, nibbling at her lips, a nervous habit. Was that pink lip gloss, too?

"I hope that's not all you ate," Danielle said. "You have to eat."

"I ate," Harriet insisted.

"Do I have to eat?" This was Chloe from several lockers away, slightly muffled as she searched for a jar of Vaseline. She was mysteriously afflicted with inner-thigh friction, even though her quads were no thicker than three umbrellas.

"You have to eat, too," Danielle said without glancing up from the socks she was putting on. "I have a cheese stick. Do you want a cheese stick, Hairy? Do you want a cheese stick, Clo Clo?" She made a point of carrying snacks in case of emergencies.

There was a Chloe on every team, someone who demanded extra attention while simultaneously exuding strong personality B.O. that repelled others. Danielle had started out with goodwill for Chloe, because, well, Danielle's goal in life was to understand everyone, but then Chloe had pulled an elaborate prank on Danielle two years ago—when Danielle was a sophomore and Chloe a freshman. And after that, Danielle had done her best to ignore Chloe until Chloe's injury last fall—and her melodramatic meltdown—stirred Danielle's inner mom again.

And let's face it: we needed Chloe. She was annoying but she was fast. Teams were a lot like families. You didn't get to choose them. You played the hand you were dealt.

"Did you eat lunch?" Harriet asked.

"Of course I ate lunch." Danielle scowled.

"I had . . ." Chloe started, but no one was paying attention to her.

When we weren't withdrawn and sulky in the lead-up to practice, we could be mean-spirited and snarky.

"Why are you wearing a tank top?" Harriet asked Danielle.

"It's eighty out," Danielle said, blowing her bangs off her forehead before automatically smoothing them down again. She was growing them out but they weren't yet long enough to tuck behind her ears.

"You know exactly what's going to happen," Harriet continued. "This always happens the first week back. He gives us a few days to get back into the swing . . ."

"Maybe it won't," Danielle interrupted.

Harriet continued, ignoring Danielle: "He gives us a few days to get back into the swing of things and then, when he can't wait any longer, he sinks his claws into us." Harriet punched Danielle lightly on the arm. This is what Harriet did when she was annoyed with Danielle, and also to express affection.

"I think you're being a little melodramatic," Danielle said, but no one was listening because Chloe had leapt onto a bench in nothing but a pair of white jockeys and a graying running bra and was hunched over, pinching a roll of fat. "Look at my stomach," she wailed. "I wish I'd trained harder this summer."

"Seriously, Chloe," Liv said. "That's nothing but skin."

"I am so fat," Patricia joined in but without much heart. She was so tiny guys liked to pick her up at parties and toss her into the air, and people often mistook her for a Frostie's younger sibling visiting for the weekend.

"We have to stop this," Harriet said, even though she was last one to take her own advice. "Listen to yourselves. Look at yourselves. This internalized self-hatred is ridiculous."

We all rolled our eyes internally, and yet when we got going like this, it was a landslide, one girl's self-criticism setting off another's, a foot of unstable ground becoming two, then five, then fourteen, rushing down the slope, burying everything beautiful and living in its path. Suddenly, everyone was sucking in their stomachs, eyeing their thighs. Too much here. And here. Not enough there. Oh my god, it was disgusting. Squeezing whatever we could. Pinching. Breasts, bellies, buttocks. If there had been a mirror, it would have been worse. In this mood, it was traumatic to see yourself. It was like looking through the wrong end of binoculars.

We slid down the hallway in our socks, because there was no point in putting on our shoes yet. There was almost no point in wearing any clothes at all, because once we got settled in the padded, unheated wrestling room, with blue mats that traveled halfway up the walls, we'd strip down to our running bras and tiny shorts, we'd take as much off as we could without taking it all off. We wanted to be as light as we could without completely disappearing. We wanted to *almost* not exist.

"These dudes must really like to throw each other around," Patricia said. She chucked a shoe at the wall, and it bounced back.

Chloe copied her. Danielle said to knock it off, it was time to start stretching, and we reluctantly did, a sloppy choreography of noses to knees, heels to buttocks, fingers to toes. We were ridiculously stiff, except for Patricia, who was naturally limber, and Liv, who made a point of working on her flexibility. The door yawned open and in sauntered Coach with Assistant Coach in tow. Each step they took across the wrestling mat sounded like a bare thigh being pulled from hot vinyl.

"Good afternoon, ladies," said Assistant Coach from deep within his hooded blue sweatshirt.

"Hmm," Coach said.

Coach and Assistant Coach couldn't have been more different, but we found reasons to hate each of them: Coach for having trained Div 1 runners, for expecting our unwavering obedience, for saying *Just Do It!* without a crumb of awareness or irony. ("It's an advertising slogan, dude," we'd heard the men complain, though we'd never dared to voice it ourselves.) And Assistant Coach because he'd gone to a liberal-arts college like ours—the kind of place that prided itself on producing intellectual jocks— but turned into a weird loser who still wore nylon short-shorts and sweatshirts, often with the hood concealing his face. The rumor was he had triple-majored in history, philosophy, and math, but couldn't get into a decent law school.

When they reached the center of the room, we rose and lined up. Just like that. Never mind *Question Authority,* our school's informal motto. We lined up without even being asked. "I told you," Harriet whispered to Danielle, and Danielle just shrugged. No one enjoyed waiting to step onto the scale. Assistant Coach inched the weight across the ruler, finding the perfect balance.

"One-oh-nine pounds," he called out.

Patricia sprang from the scale and did a little victory dance.

"Child," Coach said without looking up from the mysterious

notes he took on a yellow legal pad. She stopped immediately.

Then it was Harriet's turn. She paused before mounting the platform. It couldn't have lasted longer than two or three seconds, but it felt like an eternity.

"Just go," Danielle hissed. "You're fine."

"One-nineteen," Assistant Coach announced, and suddenly, Harriet seemed to balloon before our eyes, becoming something big and grotesque, like one of those inflatable snowmen that people put on their front lawns during the Christmas season. She blinked back tears. She was up a pound. It was time to give up brie immediately.

Danielle was next; her number seemed tragic as well, but it was hard to tell with her. A giant, she could seesaw two (or three!) pounds with no ill effects.

Our humiliation continued. Brandishing his calipers, Assistant Coach squeezed our slack triceps and abdomens and the tender parts of our inner thighs because the scale on its own was a clumsy instrument. Fat weighed less than muscle, and there were height differences to take into account (Patricia was 5'3", Danielle 5'11".)

"Ow," Chloe yelped as Assistant Coach bit into her arm with his fat-measuring instrument. We knew he was doing us a favor by trying to press our flesh as thin as possible, but it still hurt.

The door opened. A bearded guy with big glasses stuck his head in, took in what was happening, and quickly retreated.

"Twelve percent," Assistant Coach said.

Coach kept scribbling.

We hated them for making us feel bad about run-of-the-mill changes resulting from water weight, too much lunch, or spiritual malaise. Harriet's lunchtime apple. A handful of dry-roasted peanuts. We hated them, and yet we scorned whoever couldn't keep the weight off. Weak, we thought. Gluttonous. Lazy.

Coach scanned his clipboard as Assistant Coach looked on. Suddenly Kristin's arm shot up. "I'll be the rabbit," she said.

This wasn't how it worked. The rabbit didn't volunteer. The rabbit was the one who'd gained the most weight. Coach was nice that way. He wouldn't come out and say, "You've fattened up." Instead, he chose you to lead the workout. We'd all been there one Monday or another, been the rabbit charged to lead the team.

Coach laughed.

"I want to lead," she said. She'd been quiet during this whole ordeal, so quiet she almost disappeared. She was sitting a bit apart from us, picking at a callus on her big toe. Did she somehow know she was going to be chosen? She didn't appear any fatter than usual. Her boobs were always big, almost pornographically so. It was a wonder she was as fast as she was (and she was, she was really, really fast, and strong, she could take it out and keep it going) because she didn't have the kind of body that was typically built for speed. But looks weren't everything. Weren't we, women at one of the best liberal-arts colleges in the country in the final decade of the twentieth century, supposed to know that, if we knew anything at all?

"Well," Coach said.

We held our collective breath, waiting for Coach to restore order and announce that no, actually someone else had earned the responsibility for maintaining pace. This was one of Coach's twists—the rabbit took it out, but didn't scamper off after the first half. She kept it going. She was responsible for making sure we hit our target pace. If you gained a little weight or faltered in a race, Coach made you the rabbit. He put you back out in front of the pack. He wanted to trick you into believing you belonged there.

"Then it appears that Kristin will be our rabbit for today." It was impossible to tell from his expression whether he was as surprised as we were. "We'll do mile repeats." He eyed Assistant Coach, but only for ceremony, since he had already plotted out every workout that we'd run for the next six weeks. "Four, starting at a 6:20 pace. Each one ten seconds quicker. Which means . . ."

". . . we should bring it in at 5:50," Kristin said.

We usually hated ourselves for our ability to finish Coach's sentences, but Kristin sounded happy.

"Let's go," Kristin called out. Her big toe was bright red and angry where she'd been picking off dry skin. "Time to do some speed."

LET'S DANCE

Danielle

THERE'S A TEAM PARTY.

She brings her own bottle of wine. A decent chianti, not as good as the stuff that her dad buys but not swill, either. He has taught her to appreciate the difference. She and her dad are two peas in a pod: both of them tall (he's 6'3"); both athletes; both leaders (he was the captain of the crew team in college); both of them lousy with optimism. Is this a flaw or a gift?

She doesn't bring a wine glass, though she should, because plastic cups are to gulping what wine glasses are to sipping, and if she's going to cut down this year, she needs to practice appreciating each sip. Her friends already tease her about her preference for wine, but nothing good happens when she drinks hard alcohol. And beer? She doesn't like the taste. The only time she has it is when she's too drunk to care, or when she runs out of wine before she's ready to stop. That's when she tends to drink gin and vodka, too, when her superego is drowsy and her id seizes the opportunity to pursue pleasure to the fullest.

It's the Friday of the first week of school, and they can party because there's no meet tomorrow. Next Friday, the girls' team will gather in her room for a guided meditation before their first meet of the season, and the Friday after that, they'll do a team dinner, and the Friday after that, they'll eat together in the cafeteria and then they'll come back to her room and French- braid each other's hair. (She's still mulling over what they'll do with Harriet and Chloe's hair, too short to braid—she'll come up with something special.) It's all planned out, an activity for every single Friday of the season, even the ones when they don't have a meet the next day. The girls are still like puzzle pieces scattered across a table, and her job is to make sure each and every one of them finds a spot and they come together into something beautiful. The whole is bigger than the parts.

The couch where she's sitting smells of spilled beer and something feral. Last year, the cross country boys had a guinea pig that disappeared after Christmas. This year, she wonders whether they have a cat. Or a kitten. A kitten would be more their style.

Chloe comes through the door with her roommate, both of them wearing odd black masks with beaks, like crows. All Danielle knows about Chloe's roommate is that she's an artist and that she's painting a mural on the side of one of the social dorms. Danielle can't imagine what Chloe has in common with her roommate, who seems artsy and cool, whereas Chloe—well, Chloe is Chloe, cursed with her only-child personality and her new dorky Dorothy Hamill wedge cut. Liv and Henry appear, their elbows hooked like a courting couple from the previous century. Adorable, though Harriet says it's heteronormative, this constant performance of devoted monogamy. But it's sweet, she thinks. Liv's so much happier since she got together with Henry. Danielle uncorks the bottle of wine at her feet and pours herself a bit more. Though she's told herself she won't drink the whole thing, who knows?

Finally there's Harriet with her posse of short-haired girls, all of them in combat boots and Spandex shorts. She shrugs off her sweatshirt, revealing what looks like a halter top.

"Dani," Kristin cries, suddenly appearing. "Da Da Da Dani. There you are!"

She plops down, and Danielle gets a big whiff of something that reminds her of her dad. "Is that—" she shouts over the music. Kristin raises a jelly jar of amber-colored liquid. "I drink coffee *and* whiskey." While she laughs, she sways back and forth until she crashes into Danielle, sloshing gasoline-scented liquid on both of them.

"Oh my god, you're drunk," Danielle says, still sober enough to make this pronouncement. "What time did you start drinking?"

"I'm sorry," Kristin says, petting Danielle's wet spots and then her own. "I'm just happy." Kristin spills more of her drink on the jean jacket that she wears everywhere. On the left pocket, there are three pins: a red B for running varsity at Boise High, a tiny golden mouse, and an Idaho potato pin that everyone teases her about. "Is Harriet smoking?" Danielle looks up, just as Harriet takes a cigarette expertly between her fingers, gestures dramatically, and takes a puff. Danielle thinks, simultaneously worrying about the team and Harriet's obsessive tendencies. That worry is immediately replaced by another. As Harriet is passing the cigarette to the girl standing next to her, not anyone Danielle recognizes, she puts her arm around the girl's neck, leans in, and kisses her. Not on the cheek. And not briefly. Even though Harriet came out sophomore year, she's never had a girlfriend. Just crushes. Is Harriet . . . ?

"Harriet's making out!" Kristin screams before suddenly

standing up and yanking at Danielle's arm.

"What?"

"Let's dance!"

Danielle drinks the last of her wine, then pushes herself up off the couch and starts to sway, letting the music enter her body, letting it move her. Does Harriet actually have a girlfriend? Kristin's facing her, dancing with her, which she's never done before. Danielle smiles as a wave of optimism and determination surges through her: she wants it all so badly and maybe she'll have it if she works hard enough and pulls them all together. "What I Like About You" comes on and they're lip-synching the lyrics, passing compliments back and forth, Kristin's riding the wave of feeling and music with her, she's flowing around her, touching her here and here and here, and now Danielle sees they're encircled by others, by Harriet and the girl who she just smooched and the other girls who are a blur of bodies grind-grind-grinding and the cross country boys doing jerky little robotic moves, hilarious and beautiful, and at some point, Kristin leaps onto a coffee table, which makes her a little taller than Danielle, and for a second Danielle wants to cry because she's always the tallest, and it can make her feel left out, like a freaky mutant giant freak, always stooping slouching hunched, and Kristin grabs Danielle's hands and pulls her close, and they're dancing together, they're undulating like they're one body. It's so weird and wonderful. And powerful. She loves it, this coming together. But then Kristin pulls away, their connection broken, because maybe it's too weird, too intense, but she's just grabbing something from the floor. It's a plastic bottle, and Kristin tips it into her mouth before tipping it into Danielle's, and Danielle sputters after taking a sip, and then the heat is sliding down her throat and spreading through her stomach, and the wave rises, lifting her ever higher. She sees Kristin take another swig, and something clicks.

"You should be careful," Danielle shouts into her ear.

"What?"

"You should be careful," she shrieks again. "You're gonna feel like shit."

"I'm gonna be the best," Kristin screams back. Her teeth shine in the dark, and she's smiling stupidly. "I'm going to beat Chloe."

Oh, Danielle thinks, suddenly more sober than she'd like to be. She can't beat Chloe. Chloe is the fastest, and Kristin is the prettiest, and Liv has a boyfriend, and Harriet is the smartest, the most ambitious, and Patricia sees through the bullshit, and Danielle cares the most. She is the most responsible. Doesn't Kristin know that she can't be the fastest and the most beautiful, that each of them needs something to keep the score even? Poor Chloe. Her idea of a thrilling Saturday night is prank-calling guys she likes. She always has hopelessly impossible crushes on boys who don't even know who she is. What will she have if she's not the fastest?

Kristin slumps against her, her breasts a pillow between them. Is this what it's like for men? Kristin smells like Herbal Essence shampoo and rubbing alcohol. She's going to be wrecked in the morning. But for now, there's nothing to do but keep dancing. As long as they keep moving together, maybe Danielle can keep Kristin from falling down.

RABBIT REDUX

Kristin

"YOU'RE THE RABBIT," COACH SHOUTS AT KRISTIN ON THE THIRD OF eight half-mile repeats around the playing field at the edge of the woods. "You're the leader. Maintain the lead."

It's dusk, and they are flying around the empty lacrosse and soccer fields. This is the second week she's volunteered to lead the workout, the second week that Coach has given her the chance. Why Coach should deviate from his tried-and-true approach is a mystery, except that last week she hit every split perfectly. Maybe he senses how determined she is, how much she wants to be the best, even though right now she's not where she's supposed to be.

She tries not to think about the quantity of whiskey she drank on Friday, the French fries that Danielle fed her at the end of the evening to soak up the booze. *Do you want to have the worst hangover of your life?* Definitely not part of her training plan, but Danielle would know because Danielle's an expert drinker.

Chloe and Liv have edged in front of her. She wills herself to pick it up. It was a shock when she first got to Frost and discovered that she wasn't the fastest. She'd always been out in front, even when she was a little girl first discovering how much she loved to run. Back then, it was track. It required no team, no special equipment. She could just take off—in a skirt, short-shorts underneath, just in case she wanted to hang upside down from the monkey bars at recess—and run around the block of her elementary school. She was fast—faster than the girls who were a year ahead of her—Robin Boyd and Shelley and Melody Dayton—girls who teased her and called her Road Runner because of how much she loved to run and hinted at weird things about her teacher, Mr. Gray, things she didn't understand then and still doesn't really. Mr. Gray skated with all of them at Skate City, holding their hands, all of them little girls, wobbly on wheels. Most boys were still the enemy with a capital E. She couldn't imagine skating with one. If a boy liked you, he hid in the alley after school and punched you and tried to steal your coat. They didn't scare her. She delighted in venturing into unpaved alleys just to show them. The moment they sprang out from their hiding spots behind the metal trash cans, she was off, her arms pumping, her chest burning, her heart thrumming with excitement. Glancing over her shoulder, she caught snatches of their faces, like shriveled apples, rotting with useless determination, as they fell farther and farther behind. She whooped in victory, and then kept trotting all the way home. Even then, she was a feminist (with a capital F), inspired by her mother since women still earned only 70 cents for every dollar earned by a man, and where was the support for working families, never mind single-mom situations like theirs?

This was why Kristin got into sports. They were what she did instead of coming home and letting herself in with a key whose secret location on the front porch would be switched by her mom every three to six months so that unlocking the door often involved trying to remember the latest spot (underneath a corner of the sisal rug, inside the rusty watering pot, behind a pair of bronze frog bookends that sat pressed together with no books between them because her mother couldn't abide anything of her ex-husband's in the house, but they were also too valuable to give away). Kristin wore a metal ERA bracelet that her mother had brought back from the Equal Rights Convention and penned a series of stories called "Land of Ladies" where women were in charge of everything. Mr. Gray made smiley faces in the margins and joked, "Women should be in the kitchen baking chocolate chip cookies." This made her laugh so hard that Melody called her an epileptic turd.

"Focus, babe," Danielle says from behind her. "You got this.

Does being fast matter? She pushes the question out of her head, for now, sucks in a mouthful of air, and surges by Chloe and Liv to where she belongs. Of course it matters. That's why she's decided to be the fastest, the strongest. If she's the strongest, then nothing bad will ever happen to her again. The magic is back, and she is flying. She knows exactly what 5:30 pace feels like. This is her gift, her genius. Some people have perfect pitch, a photographic memory—Kristin's body knows exactly how fast it's running. She doesn't know how she knows—just that she does to within two or three seconds, and she can tell almost immediately when she has clicked in.

In the dying light, things materialize out of nowhere, like a magician pulling a rabbit from his hat. There's the goalie box, a pine tree, a couple walking hand in hand. Coach and Assistant Coach yelling at her to pick it up. And then they're gone. Sweet illusion of speed. That's one of the reasons why she loves running at dusk. Another: the scent of the grass damp with the creeping darkness and the sun's last warm tendrils. Up the hill from the fields, the campus is lit up, and the science building, with its asymmetrically placed octagonal windows, looks like an abstract pumpkin.

She flies around the final turn, everything falling into place, and they float toward the finish line, as though each step is not a battle with gravity. The moon peeks out over the tops of the trees, lighting their way. Eli thinks it's cruel for one person to lead the workouts. "What if you're not feeling it?" he asks, stroking his new goatee. "That's the point," she answers. "When you're not feeling it, you have to do it."

"That is like totally wack," he says. And while she can appreciate his point, she knows no other way. Why would she give in to what she feels? If she did this, she might never run again.

"Two forty-two, forty-three, forty-four, forty-*five!*" Assistant Coach calls out as they gallop by. She has pulled them back to where they are supposed to be—at 5:30 pace for a mile.

Danielle's at her side. "You did it. How are you feeling?"

Danielle's complete sentences are a miracle. This is why she's captain—her ability to put together a thought immediately after finishing an interval. Her never-ending encouragement. Kristin is amazed by her reserves of positivity. "I'm OK," she says, trying to tamp down her anxiety about the first half of the repeat—how she drifted so far off where she was supposed to be and didn't even know it. If she thinks too much, she might jinx herself.

"You pulled it off," Danielle continues, ever the cheerleader. "Way to be strong."

"I really shouldn't have to pull it together." The whine in her voice takes her by surprise. Given the chance, she can be such a baby.

"Oh god," Danielle says. "Don't worry. It's one repeat on one day. Seriously. Don't give it another thought."

"I won't," Kristin says, though her eyes sting. Thank goodness it's dark, and they're both in motion, their gaze trained on the ground two or three feet in front of them. "It's one day," she repeats.

"Dude, this is a recovery lap," someone from behind them yells.

"Seriously," says another voice. It's Chloe's.

Danielle laughs. "Roger that."

"Roger who?" someone says.

There's more laughter, and it pushes Kristin forward into the growing darkness. She doesn't know how fast she's running, except that she is moving farther away from everyone and everything, and from one moment to the next, she's doesn't know exactly where she is until she's there, and then she's lost in the dark again. A hand closes around her heart and squeezes.

"Kristi, slow down." Danielle's voice tries to yank her back. "It's a recovery lap."

She almost got lost this summer. If she keeps surging into the darkness, and then finding herself, she'll be able to put it all behind her. The dark presses in on her, and it feels like she's trapped in her sleeping bag in the Sawtooths, and she wants to scream but she can't find her voice, it's lost in her body, but she keeps moving, and up ahead are Coach and Assistant Coach, two barely human-shaped shapes against the trees in the distance. When she reaches them, she can rest a moment, her hands on her knees, breathing hard until the rest of the pack catches up.

"Hammer queen," someone yells, an accusation, though Kristin hears it as a compliment. She's going to keep hammering for as long as it takes, even if it's the rest of her life.

SEPTEMBER 12: MAINE INVITATIONAL

AT OUR FIRST MEET IN MAINE, WE'D DONE OK, WHICH WAS NOT OK, based on Coach's silence, the fact that he would not meet our eyes when the race director announced that Frost had placed second out of ten teams, but instead stuffed his hands deep into his tracksuit pockets and glowered.

It was the first meet (for fuck's sake, we all thought in our own ways), and we'd done everything right: jogged half the course as a warm-up, joked about how much *fun* it would be to race on a 75-degree day. As part of the warm-up, Chloe jumping-jacked. Liv dutifully stretched. Heel to butt: quads. Nose to knee: hamstrings, a grim expression on her face. Patricia was fiddling with the little ceramic foot that she wore around her neck on race days that left a tiny bruise permanently tattooed at between her collarbones. She also had on two layers of shirts over her singlet. There was something lucky about the number of articles of clothing she wore to warm up in, and while we didn't understand it, we didn't question it, either, because we were all a little superstitious, all susceptible to race-day rituals. Danielle and Harriet, their heads drawn together, were talking last-minute strategy. Or rather Danielle was talking strategy and Harriet was humoring her. Then Harriet jogged off to the porta-potty to pee and came back bitching about the inequities. The guys just dropped trou wherever they damn well pleased, while we had to piss into a hole with poo piled up like soft ice cream. This was one of her familiar rants. Danielle faux-groaned, checked her watch. "Six minutes, ladies."

"Women," Harriet responded.

We circled.

"Aren't you going to sing your song?" Chloe asked Kristin.

You put your left leg in, you pull your left leg out, you put your left leg in, and you shake it all about.

"I don't really feel like it," Kristin replied.

No one moved until Danielle windmilled her arm into the middle of our huddle, her hand palm down, a fresh pink manicure for today's race—one of her rituals. Harriet's hand came next. We went in order of class year—Patricia was last. And then we each brought in our other hand—until we'd made a tower of our limbs, all of us connected to the pole of our collective power. That was a team: stronger than the sum of its parts.

"We can do it," Danielle said with conviction, and then we joined in, chanting, "We can do it, we can do it, we can do it, we can do it," faster and faster until the words ran together, and Danielle's voice boomed, "Go Frost!" Our hands rose in the air.

"Go Poets!" yelled Assistant Coach, hovering right on the edge of our circle.

Danielle took the spot on the line, just like she always did, and we formed a little triangle behind her, a wedge. At 5'11" she was a giant, and she'd use her size to carve a path for us and make sure we didn't get trampled in the initial crush. Coach was always reminding us to pull one another along, that it was easier than way.

All you need to do is stick together. Like a thistle in a sock. Coach pronounced it THEE-sil. *When you stick, you don't think. You just go.*

"On your mark."

At those words we froze, along with everyone around us.

"Get set."

Elbows out, one arm in front, the other cocked back.

We'd scored 63 points, a mere five points behind Clapp, who scored 58. Scores were tallied by adding the places of the top five runners on each team, the lower the score, the better. That's why the fastest and slowest runner were both crucial, why the spread mattered. You could put four girls in the top 15, but if your fifth went out too hard and faded, or if she stopped to pee in the woods because she wasn't one of those gross girls who let it trickle down her leg, then you were sunk. We had to pull together. We had to beat each other, though we could never admit how badly we wanted this. And we had to keep this up week in and week out, not because any of these early meets would help us qualify for Nationals—that didn't happen until NESCACs, the penultimate meet of the season. We had to win to convince ourselves we could win, and because each race was a chance to get faster and stronger, to test our will against a clock.

On the drive home, Assistant Coach at the helm of the van, Coach riding shotgun, the windows fogged with the heat of our bodies so that it looked like we were driving nowhere, we sat with our bag lunches untouched on our laps, the miniature cans of cranberry and apple juice also unopened (which meant plummeting blood sugar, the first flickers of headaches). The yawns began with Chloe and spread to Patricia and Liv and Danielle and Harriet and finally Kristin, until we were all yawning, big face-tingling yawns, eyes closed, mouths stretched open, teeth bared, highly contagious, all of us trying to suck more oxygen into bodies that were starting to rebel, trying to wake ourselves up, trying to keep our heads from imploding.

And then Coach glanced back. He looked straight into our open mouths and saw our pinkish white stubbly tongues and our pearly beige molars and our waggle-flabby tonsils, and he smelled the sad breath of girls who were always hungry (except for Patricia and Liv) and liked feeling that way (except for Danielle). And he roared at us, and Assistant Coach swerved, narrowly missing a car going the other direction (not that any of us saw this, because we couldn't see anything), overcorrected and almost ran off the road (not that we could see this either, but as we slid this way and then that on the vinyl bench seats, jostling each other, we sensed that we were no longer moving in a straight line). Assistant Coach later told Danielle he thought that was it, we'd all be pushing up daisies, but somehow, thank God, he'd managed to put the wheels back on the blacktop. The two of them met every Monday morning in the campus center. Danielle bought the coffee, Assistant Coach the treats, always some kind of muffin. He was a talented baker. He'd gone to Sawyer, which was to Frost what Harvard was to Yale and was only three years older than she was. What they talked about: the last race, the coming one, the art of coaching, whether Danielle should postpone grad school to coach for a year. ("YES!" he shouted, practically leaping out of his chair and spilling both their coffees, his black with two sugars, hers lightened with milk—whole. "But what if I never make it back to school?" she asked. "Then you are meant to be a coach," he said.)

Assistant Coach would be handsome, if not for his extreme dorkiness, the pornographic short shorts that he wore everywhere. His brown hair stuck up in the back as though he'd just rolled out of bed, which Danielle knew was impossible. He was too tightly wound to be a late sleeper, and he was cramming for the LSAT in all his spare time. After the race in Maine, Assistant Coach said that Coach was disappointed in Kristin for not making a bigger move in the last mile of the race. She was in eighth place, and she could have picked off two girls and probably three and nearly caught up to Chloe, who placed third.

"But you know what," Assistant Coach said, "Kristin is on fire, and Liv is, too, and Chloe, well, Chloe's already burning."

Danielle struggled a little to hear Chloe complimented. "What happens when you have to coach someone who you don't actually like?" she asked.

He shook his head. His impossibly long legs bumped the table. He said it was easier not to like the people you coached. "You think I like you?" he said.

She almost didn't get the joke.

Midweek, we were supposed to be taking things easy because we'd run ladders the day before, and the day after we'd do mile repeats. We'd done an easy five through Apple Valley, a new neighborhood where most of the driveways ended in trees, and where the houses that had been constructed were still dark, empty shells. Danielle had asked Chloe to lead the run, but Kristin kept shooting out in front until someone would yell, "Slow down!" And then Chloe would return to the lead, slowing us down to a more comfortable pace, and then the whole thing would happen all over again. We were all getting testy, even Danielle, and no one was talking, even though the whole point of an easy run was to chat.

We just coming up through the woods when she suddenly the pack stopped, and Kristin screamed. She was back in the lead. Of course, she was back in the lead.

"What?" Harriet said.

"Oh my God," Chloe said.

"I think I stepped on a rabbit," Kristin cried out. "I think I killed it."

And then we all saw it: a rabbit huddled in the middle of the path. A tiny rabbit, maybe just a baby, with white-speckled brown fur, delicate whiskers, closed eyes, its ears both flopped over. It was hardly bigger than a mouse.

We'd never seen a rabbit in the woods. We'd seen squirrels by the dozens, including the white demon with red eyes that we fled from because we were sure it was rabid. We'd spied deer, been amazed by how quickly they could freeze and nearly disappear into the trees. We'd smelled skunk, and Patricia said she'd smelled a porcupine and Chloe had objected and said porcupines don't smell, and Patricia said, "How would you know, Miss Chlo? You're from the big city." After being bitten by a bat twice the summer after freshman year, Danielle was now always on the lookout for them, and Kristin claimed she'd spotted a fox, but Harriet said it had probably just been a coyote. We'd come across wild turkeys, big clumsy birds whose melted-wax features made them seem just a few generations removed from dinosaurs.

We formed a circle around the baby rabbit.

"Did I kill it?" Kristin asked again.

"Whatever you did, it's dead," Chloe said. She barked out a laugh. "Dead as a doornail. Maybe if you'd been running slower . . ."

"Yeah," Patricia said. "Maybe if you weren't so focused on getting out in front of everyone."

We didn't disagree.

"Oh, come on," Danielle said, ever the peacekeeper. "I don't think it's dead. I don't think you even stepped on it."

"I didn't kill it?" Kristin sounded relieved.

"Of course not," Danielle said. "I think it's asleep."

But was it? Danielle wasn't going to get close to it, not with her small animal phobia, and Kristin wasn't, because she still convinced that she was to blame, and Chloe was all talk and no action, and Patricia had no patience this kind of nonsense—she saw dead animals all the time in the desert—and Liv, despite many fine qualities, just wasn't a leader, and so it was Harriet who nudged the creature's body with her toe. The bunny's bent ear straightened, its eyes slivered open, and it hopped just once, a pathetic sideways drunken hop, before freezing again, its ear crumpling in slow motion.

"It's definitely not asleep," Harriet declared. "It's injured." Because she had the most experience working with small animals in the neuro-psych lab, we believed her. Never mind that the experiments she undertook sometimes seemed cruel, like dropping rats into open fields and measuring their anxiety levels or observing their behavior on hot plates. She nudged the rabbit again with her toe.

"I don't think you should . . ." But Danielle's words were abruptly swallowed by screaming, high pitched and excruciating, the sound conveying such an unbearable amount of suffering we couldn't listen without beginning to suffer ourselves. We glanced away from the bunny into the woods, looking for what we weren't sure—a girl pinned down by Bigfoot?—but the sound was right here at our feet, even though the baby rabbit looked exactly as it had before, barely moving, almost invisible against the dirt path.

The next thing we knew, Harriet had a rock in her hand.

"We need to kill it," Harriet said as soon as the screaming stopped. "That's the kindest thing we can do."

"Don't," Kristin said unexpectedly. "It's vulnerable, Harriet. Please don't hurt it."

"But it's suffering," Harriet said. "I'll just dispatch it with a good hard blow."

Where did she learn such language, we wondered.

"How do you know it's not just resting?" Danielle chirped.

Harriet gave Danielle a withering look. "Let's see—because it just screamed in pain?"

"Dispatch it," Chloe said, jogging in place because one of her rules was that she never stopped on training runs. "Dispatch it."

Patricia laughed.

"Why are you laughing?" Kristin demanded.

"You know what they say about rabbits," Patricia said. "If I were superstitious . . ." Which she was, but no one pointed this out.

"Don't!" Kristin sounded hysterical. It was as though she thought Harriet was threatening to dispatch one of us. "Don't, Harriet. Please don't. Just leave it. Please just leave it. You're just going to hurt it more."

Ignoring her, Harriet pulled back her arm, and the next thing we knew Kristin had lunged at Harriet. She grabbed Harriet's arm and started peeling back her fingers while Harriet whipped her arm back and forth, trying to break Kristin's grip. Suddenly Kristin let go of Harriet and shoved her, and they both went crashing to the ground, and for a moment, they were a blur of thrashing legs and arms, kicking and slapping. We had chosen cross country because it was not a contact sport. Thrown elbows and mild shoving at the beginning of races was as aggressive as we liked to get. Even Danielle, who should have been doing something, was frozen. And then Harriet screamed.

"What the fuck! You bit me!" Harriet said, rubbing her hand.

Kristin said nothing.

"She bit me," Harriet said, crab-walking away from Kristin as though she feared Kristin would attack again. "You bit me."

"Kristin!" Danielle cried.

Harriet was back on her feet with another rock in her hand. Or maybe it was the same one.

Kristin made a strange noise from where she was still sprawled on the ground.

The rock streaked through the air before thudding to the ground far short of its target.

"Dude," Patricia said. "Your need to work on your arm if you're going to go around dispatching rabbits.

Harriet didn't bother translating *shit* into French. Chloe went to Kristin and offered her a hand up. Then turning on her heels, Chloe started running, and gradually everyone followed, with Kristin, Danielle, and Harriet bringing up the rear.

What on earth was wrong with Kristin? On the run back, she kept repeating that she was sorry—she was sorry, sorry, sorry, so sorry—while Harriet, who had yet another rock clenched in her fist, occasionally raised her arm and pretended she was going to hurl it at Kristin.

Liv finally interrupted her. "Sorry for what? Stepping on a rabbit? Or attacking Harriet?"

"Ouch," Patricia said. "*Mon doo doo.*"

We laughed.

"She didn't step on it," said Harriet, who was obviously going to have the final word. "It was already injured."

Kristin apologized again. "I wasn't trying to bite you—" but Harriet interrupted her. "*S'il vous plait* shut up already. I'm fine."

We understood how to run. Was running away so different? The action was exactly the same: put one foot in front of another. Gradually, the screaming faded in memory, crowded out by other sounds—lawnmowers, stick-and-ball teams calling out commands to each other, the wind complicating the leaves, and the ragged sound of our own breathing.

JUMBO JUBILEE

Kristin

"COME DANCING" IS BLARING FROM ELI'S ROOM AS KRISTIN STANDS outside his door.

It's Sunday night, and she's ecstatic because she beat Chloe for the first time ever at a meet just outside Boston. She knew if it was going to happen, it had to be on a course like yesterday's, a course with lots of crazy hills where she could take advantage of Chloe's one weakness: not the uphills, where she's like a monster truck, plowing over anything in her path, but the downhills, where Chloe has a tendency to slow down and catch her breath. Kristin flew by her on every descent, she made Chloe work extra-hard to catch her on the flats, and then she did it one final time on the final hill that funneled them straight into the finish line. For the past day she has been floating.

She knocks again, this time harder. It's always the Kinks with Eli, his music the soundtrack of Kristin's freshman year when he lived a floor below her and his tunes flowed up the pipes of the

VAX, the internal electronic mail system they had on campus. The first couple months of school, Kristin woke up early every morning, never sure where she was. Fighting back tears, she dressed in the dark, trying not to wake up her roommate, Yvette, a night owl who'd gone to boarding school and whose favorite words were *jaded* and *scandalous*. Everything surprised Kristin: her homesickness, the sophisticated questions other kids asked in class, the parties four nights a week, the kegs of free beer. She missed Friday-night pizza with her mom, always from one of two places in their neighborhood, and going to Blockbuster with her friends and, more often than not, leaving empty-handed because they'd already watched *Harold and Maude* a dozen times. Those were her high school friends: kids who loved Cat Stevens and love affairs that didn't involve sex.

Eli was her first real friend at Frost, even though he hated *Harold and Maude*, calling it schlock that did a disservice to the sexual needs of old women and teenage boys. He was smart and funny with a kind of no-bullshit attitude that reminded her of her mom. And he was also totally in love with her, at least that's what Danielle claimed every time she bumped into the two of them roaming around campus, deeply engrossed in conversation. But it wasn't like that. They were just friends.

Suddenly the door swings open. "Dude," he says, "look at you."

What? she's thinking, because as far as she knows she looks the same as always.

His eyes sliver with pleasure as he takes her hand and twirls her under his arm. "Come dancing," he sings along with the Kinks. He's wearing skinny jeans and a tacky Hawaiian shirt, the outfit quintessential L.A.

"Are we going for a walk or what?" she asks.

"Just a sec," he says, disappearing into his room to turn off his boom box.

On the way out, he says hello to half a dozen kids. "Is being friendly part of your job?" she asks. Last spring, he shocked her by applying to be a resident counselor in a freshman dorm. Kristin can think of nothing worse.

"Wasn't I always friendly?" he asks.

"Yes, but now you're friendly squared. And that," she says, pointing to his spiffy new goatee, "makes you look like a friendly dad."

"Ouch." He mimes burying a dagger in his chest. "I was hoping it would make me look debonair."

"A debonair dad," she teases.

He groans again as they head out on their Walk and Talk, which eventually will end at Mert's for ice cream. Kristin is dying to gloat a little about beating Chloe—heaven knows she can't show she's bursting with happiness in front of her teammates. That'd be like coveting a friend's boyfriend or farting loudly or casually mentioning you lost ten pounds without even trying. But Eli has launched into a description of his summer internship, the psycho intense lawyer he worked for who gave up coffee and booze for six weeks before each and every trial, sure it made him sharper.

"I just don't know if I still want to be a criminal defense lawyer," he says at last.

"Why not?" she asks. "I thought that was your plan."

"It makes me feel a little morally squeamish," he says. "Like are you a bad person for representing bad people?"

"But you don't know," she says. "Right? Isn't that a point of a trial?"

"That's generous," he says. "If you're very good criminal defense lawyer, you know exactly what your clients have done, and you know exactly how to get them acquitted."

"Better than slinging coffee," she says.

"Oh, come on," he says, "You, Kristin, helped bring Boise into the late twentieth century. How does it feel?"

She rolls her eyes. How does it feel? While Eli was trying out something he actually might want to do someday, she was earning $3.25 an hour as a barista at Boise's first espresso shop. This is one of the differences between being raised in a fully staffed family versus a single- mom situation.

"You introduced your brethren to the pleasures of mochas and lattes," he continues.

"It's more like I helped macho men get super caffeinated before they went out bar- hopping," she says, telling him about the guys in cowboy boots sauntering into the coffee shop and grimacing as they slugged back teeny-tiny espressos and claimed she'd really put some hair on their chests.

"Were they real cowboys?" Eli asks. He's peering at her seriously. "Or just urban cowboys?"

"I don't know," she says. "All I know is that they were wearing cowboy boots."

She suddenly wishes she hadn't brought up cowboys. She doesn't want to think about the way they sauntered in. Or strutted. Or the boots they were wearing. Or the blisters they got from hiking in those boots. She doesn't want to think about the coffee shop, period.

Eli knocks into her.

"What?"

"You didn't hear what I said?"

"No," she says. "Sorry. What did you say?"

"I suggested," he says in his parody of a professor voice, "that donning cowboy boots does not make one a cowboy and posited that perhaps one must also be employed with cows . . ."

She lets herself laugh. It feels like opening a window, airing out a stale room.

". . . navigating one's land and managing one's cows from the back of the animal once known as equus ferus caballus."

"Or in a Cessna," she says. "Sometimes ranchers do their surveying in a Cessna."

"Oh, you Idahoians, you've really come into the modern age."

"Idahoan," she says.

"Idahoer?"

"Ha ha," she says.

"Idahaha," he says.

Eli threads his arm through hers, and they walk in perfect step, their shoulders bumping every so often because she's never quite mastered walking in a straight line. It's a nice evening, and there are lots of students out. When they're a block away from Mert's, Kristin spots Danielle with Harriet and the Darlings. It's easy to tell it's her. She towers above all her friends.

"Kristin," Danielle screams as the distance closes. "Kristi, Kristi, Kristin!"

"Da Da Dani," she calls back, unhooking herself from Eli and hurrying forward.

Danielle hands her ice cream to Harriet and throws her arms around Kristin. "We won!" she says. "But we missed you at the party last night."

They won, but she has forgotten all about her team's victory, which is like gazing at a photo of a forest and focusing on a single tree.

"Do you want to bite me again," Harriet teases, with a tiny flare of her nostrils. Her tongue darts out, and she licks Danielle's cone suggestively.

"Harriet," Danielle scolds.

Kristin's face gets hot. "I'm sorry," she says for the millionth time. And yet her fury is close, like a splinter just under the surface of her skin. All she needs is to picture the bunny's pathetic hop, and she can feel something festering inside her.

"It's fine," Harriet says, punching Kristin lightly on the arm before taking another bit of Danielle's ice cream cone. "It was actually kind of hot."

"Ha ha."

"But we really should have killed that poor rabbit. I'm still mad about that."

"Can we agree to disagree?" Danielle suggests.

"No," Harriet says, "that's literally impossible in this situation. When what's at issue is an action, you can't agree to disagree. You got your way, and I didn't."

"It's not a competition," Danielle insists.

"Don't be obtuse," Harriet says hotly. And then they're off.

"You bit Harriet in a non-sexual context?" Eli asks after they've said goodbye and drifted on. "Because of a rabbit?"

"Don't ask," she says, and he doesn't, he just lets it go, which is unlike him, and to repay this kindness, she treats him to ice cream and gets herself a small scoop in a cup because that way they can trade bites.

On their way back to campus, the news finally bursts out of her. "I beat Chloe," she says stopping and waving her spoon at Eli for emphasis.

Eli laughs. "Is that good?"

"Is that *good*?" There's a swagger in her voice that she can't help. "It's great. Chloe was the top runner last year."

"But I thought you beat her last year."

"Nope," Kristin says. "She was out with a stress fracture."

"Well, great," Eli says, although she can tell his enthusiasm is for her benefit. "Does that mean you're the top runner on the team?"

"I'm the best," she says, and she's back in the final 100 meters of the race, barreling toward the finish line. Knowing exactly where she is and what she'll do to get there—the feeling is magic, like suddenly leaping off the ground and swimming through the air.

FIRSTS

WE WERE 1–1 FOR THE SEASON, NOT THAT ANYONE IN THE WORLD was keeping track, except for Coach and Danielle, who had made herself a good old-fashioned grade-school sticker chart with all of our meets listed and taped it to the inside of her locker door. Which did we prefer: the winged- shoe stickers or the puckered lips? Our first- and second-place finishes didn't really matter, except you convinced yourself they did, which Danielle tried her hardest to do. "Last year, we weren't even top three in the first two meets." She paused, pretending to think. "I bet we can do even better next week. What if we all agree to push ourselves just a little harder at the beginning of the last mile?" It was possible to win every meet up until the qualifying meet and then fail spectacularly. Our bodies, which were so strong, were also capable at rebelling at any moment. But if we did keep winning every week, if we kept running faster, or if not faster, since every course was different, but harder, it would mean we were getting stronger. And that was all we could hope for: to be the strongest versions of ourselves at the qualifying meet.

Danielle was trying not to worry about what would happen if Kristin permanently bumped Chloe out of the top spot, how that would possibly mess up their team dynamics. Maybe Chloe would be inspired to run harder next week? Just to be sure that Chloe was hanging in there, Danielle invited her out for coffee for the first time ever, which meant listening to her go on and on about her crush ("Code name: Zoo Boy," Chloe whispered in an idiotically excited voice), a guy in her Islamic history class whose eyes were so intensely blue Chloe could only stare at him for thirty seconds at a time before she literally had to look away. When Danielle tried to steer the conversation back to running, Chloe started to complain about the kitchen in the dorm where she was living and how it was becoming totally unusable just two weeks into the semester because someone had left bags of spinach to rot in the refrigerator, and the smell of liquefying greens was a major bummer, like *gag me with a spoon* gross, the kitchen a disaster zone.

"Why don't you just throw the spinach away?" Danielle asked.

"Ugh," Chloe said, and Danielle thought: Here is a perfect illustration of how college students are still adolescents with developing brains.

Chloe ran by the off-campus co-op where Zoo Boy lived. Though morning practices had ended when school started, she was still doing a little extra mileage. At 6:15, Zoo Boy's window (the third from the left on the second floor, which she knew from some casual detective work) was still dark. Indeed, the whole house appeared to be asleep, except for the red of the exit sign and a light burning in the kitchen. She expected that kids drawn to communal living would be early risers, like farmers, real salt-of-the-earth types, but maybe not. Maybe they were just college kids who liked having access to twenty-five pound boxes of chocolate chips. As she jogged in place, she considered making a dash down the driveway to see whether someone was in the kitchen. Wouldn't it be funny if it were Zoo Boy? She pictured him dressed in a pair of blue striped Brooks Brothers pajamas, like her dad wore, the bottoms too short and showing his ankles, the start of his calves. She wondered whether Zoo Boy slept in socks, like she did; whether he ever accidentally forgot to put on a pair before climbing into bed; whether, as he was lying there, hoping his cold, bare feet would eventually get warm, he wished that there was someone to say *I'll get you a warm pair of socks, honey.* As Chloe was considering this, she bent over and picked up a pebble and tried to toss it at Zoo Boy's window, but it only went as far as the roof. She waited a moment and then threw another, but it also missed its target.

We discussed (on an easy run) whether, if you gave a guy a blow job, you had to add him to your list.

"What list?" Patricia asked.

"You know, the list of the guys of you've been with," Chloe said.

"How would you know?" someone asked.

"That is so rude," Chloe said. Everyone knew that Chloe was only a single drunken hookup away from being a flaming V. If you didn't remember having sex, did it count? Or were you still a virgin?

"What about lapping up on clitty?" Harriet said.

Kristin gave her a look. The rest of us giggled.

"You're all so heterosexist," Harriet continued.

"What about anal? Does that count?"

"Gross."

We changed the subject.

Patricia kissed a girl who lived in the German House; it wasn't bad, but it wasn't different enough from kissing a boy to make her question her sexual preference. It was just another thing, like going to a super-selective East Coast college, that seemed vaguely disappointing. Her parents had pushed her to go to Frost because they thought it would broaden her horizons. Ha. Frost felt smaller than the pueblo where she had grown up. Leaving the land of enchantment—where she felt like she was running on the edge of the world, the horizon a hundred miles wide—had made her perpetually disenchanted? To cheer herself up, she took the bus to Boston and went to a Georgia O'Keeffe exhibit at the MFA.

We discussed (on a cool-down after intervals) whether if you got a drunk with a guy, you were asking for it.

"Asking for what?" Harriet said. "What is this, the Middle Ages?"

"Or the 1960s," Patricia added.

"I would never leave a friend alone at a party," Chloe declared. "Or a bar."

Have you ever been at a bar, someone asked.

"Friends are important," Danielle said, looking at Harriet.

"Speed is important," Kristin said.

"Women have a right to party," Harriet declared. "They have the right to wear short skirts and tight shirts and shake their asses. They have the right to sleep around, if they want to, and none of this gives men the right to rape them."

Chloe sighed. "I think you're being a little unrealistic. And besides, I'm not talking about rape, I'm talking about—" She slowed and made bunny ears. "—crossed wires."

Harriet socked her on the arm. It was a little harder than her usual love tap. "That's rape, Chloe."

We changed the subject.

Standing in front of the full-length mirror on the inside of her armoire door, Liv blew a big Trident bubblegum bubble until it popped and then punched herself in the stomach. To her image, she said, "You cannot be pregnant," and buried her fist in her stomach again. "If you are pregnant, I will kill you." She had never punched herself before.

Also a first: she'd averaged 6:30 miles in the last race. Kristin and Chloe had both beaten her, but she'd stayed within striking distance. Henry had taken a Peter Pan bus to Boston to see her run. She'd managed to get in the zone; the moment the gun went off, her mind quieted and her body became an animal. It was like sex in a way, except there was nothing wrong with the before part of sex, her desire for Henry as delicious as Henry himself, his beautiful body, his broad shoulders and smooth pecs, the divot at the base of his neck, his happy trail (his term), leading down to a tangle of soft hair, the smell of talcum powder and something else, a scent she never knew before she started sleeping with Henry. And sex itself? Like being a tree bursting into flowers.

Another first: she'd had sex with Henry without a condom.

She wasn't sure why she'd done this.

After they had sex without a condom, when Liv went to take out the sponge (which she always used as back-up contraception because a well-meaning peer educator drilled it into her that condoms weren't one-hundred-percent effective—that they could fail in any number of other ways, that sperm was sneaky and aggressive, driven by a biological imperative that cared little about the

fact that Liv was just twenty-one and Henry twenty-two), the
sponge wasn't where it usually was. She went deeper, beyond her
knuckle to the base of her pointer finger, feeling helplessly
around.

"Babe," Henry said sleepily, "you coming to bed?"

She was standing behind the door of his armoire, trying not
to look at herself in the mirror as she hunched over, attempting
to fish out the sponge, which wasn't like a sponge at all, but rather
a white plastic doughnut. She was flushed, her chest blotchy.

"Yeah," she said, "just a sec." She kept her voice light. Somehow, telling Henry that she couldn't find the sponge seemed
more personal than what they'd finished doing just moments earlier. She didn't want to tell him, and yet as she kept wiggling her
finger around, touching parts of her body that she hadn't known
existed, she grew more panicked—both about the possibility that
Henry pushed the sponge so deep that she'd never be able to find
it and the equally embarrassing task of telling him. She couldn't
just return to bed, not with a sponge stuck inside her. Not to
mention that if her sponge was not in place, did this mean it failed
to do its job?

"Babe?" He sounded tired and happy. She heard him yawn.

"I have a problem." She was still hiding behind her armoire
door, humiliated.

"Are you OK?"

"No," she said. "Not really. Promise me you won't laugh."

"What happened?" he said.

"You have to promise," she insisted.

"All right," he said.

"Say it."

"All right," he said. "I promise."

"You promise what?"

"I promise I won't laugh." He laughed while he said this.

"I can't find the sponge."

"What?" he said.

She couldn't bring herself to say it again.

There was silence.

"Well," he said at last. "Do you want me to try to find it?"

She was sort of surprised by his offer. It was terribly unro-
mantic, terribly personal. Liv closed her eyes while Henry probed
her most private parts with his finger. "Umm," he said. "Can you
spread your legs a little more? Like this. But you know I don't
mean it like that." She had no idea what he meant. "I just . . ." He
trailed off.

They decided to go to the ER, which was itself a trial because
Henry had to borrow his friend Eric's car, but when they knocked
on Eric's door just down the hallway a girl they didn't know answered and explained she was visiting from Lincoln and Eric had
let her crash there. Then they traipsed across the dark quad to
Dickinson, where Eric's girlfriend lived. "Henny Penny," a
bearded dude called out when they entered the first-floor hallway.
A party was spilling out of someone's room and kids sat in tight
little circles drinking beer from cans and passing around joints. It
was 1 a.m. on a Wednesday night.

"Come join us." The bearded guy did something with his
arms that looked like swimming in slow motion.

"Do you know him?" Liv whispered to Henry as they stepped
over a body in a pink sweatsuit. Was that Danielle passed out in
the middle of the hallway? With a meet just days away? She
looked again. It couldn't be.

"He was on my freshman hall," Henry said.

When they got to Eric's girlfriend's room, Henry said he'd
just creep in and retrieve the keys from Eric's pocket. Liv found
this odd. What if they were having sex? But Henry went in anyway and when he came out a few minutes later, he looked seri-

ously worried.

"What's wrong?" Liv asked, thinking this was the weirdest night ever.

"There were two people in bed," he said, "and they both had breasts."

"How do you know?" She was holding herself up against the wall, suddenly so dizzy with fatigue she felt drunk.

"I touched them," he said.

"Why?"

"Because it was pitch black, and I was trying to figure out if Eric was actually there."

Liv giggled, and Henry did, too. The bearded guy breast-stroked over to them (of course, Liv thought, of course). "Henny Penny," he repeated, feinting a left jab and then a right, all the while holding a smoldering joint between his lips. He pinched it between his fingers and offered it to Henry.

"Bucker," Henry said in a nasally voice that was new to Liv. "You are one very bad influence, dude." He threw his arm around Liv and took a long hit, at least it seemed so to Liv, who had smoked pot a couple times with her beloved roommate Mel, or at least pretended to. She had absolutely no opinion about what other people put into their bodies, and at the same time, she didn't want to besmirch her lungs. Henry coughed. "Have you seen Eric?"

Bucker pointed to a huddle of people at the other end of the hallway.

"Eric," Henry called.

"Dude." Bucker pressed his finger to his nose and scowled. "People are sleeping."

"Oh shit," Henry said.

Liv giggled. Was it possible the second-hand smoke had gotten her stoned?

It turned out Henry knew almost everyone in the hallway, or at least, they all kept calling him "Henny Penny" like the little chicken who thought the sky was falling. Later, she'd ask him how he'd gotten the nickname, and he'd admit he had no idea. It was just one of those freshman things—someone said something funny about you and if it stuck it stuck. For the rest of your life, you had a nickname that meant something only because you'd had it for so long. By the time they reached Eric, who was cradling a handle of Jim Beam in the corner, looking dejected, she'd almost forgotten why they'd been trying to find Eric in the first place.

"What's wrong, dude?" Henry asked.

"Karen likes girls." Eric drew his hand across his nose, and Liv noticed that he was crying. "She likes girls, like like-likes them. She's in love with some girl named Harriet."

Harriet?! Liv wondered whether Henry had touched Harriet's breast, except that Harriet hardly had breasts.

"I'm sorry, man," Henry said. "Can we borrow your car keys?"

Eric dug them out of his pocket without asking why.

"We'll talk tomorrow, man," Henry said. "Make sure you drink a bunch of water before you go to bed."

"Yeah, man. I will."

Henry wrapped Eric in a hug, so that Liv was hugging him, too.

So that was what happened. She probably wasn't pregnant, and yet when the ER doc offered to write her a prescription for the morning-after pill after fishing out the sponge with what looked like tongs, she lied, claiming she was already on oral contraception. The morning-after pill had a reputation for making your body go haywire, and she couldn't afford to miss even a day of practice. Not when she was running so well.

PLEASE, PLEASE, PLEASE

Danielle

"DO WE REALLY NEED FOUR PACKAGES OF SPAGHETTI?" HARRIET ASKS, scowling at the baton-shaped packages as though they're as dangerous as sticks of dynamite.

"We probably need five. Maybe even six," she replies, mostly just to wind her up.

They are at Stop and Shop. If Harriet had her way, they'd buy lettuce, cucumbers, and green peppers, maybe some black olives and garbanzo beans if she were really splurging. And lemons. Since coming back from Paris, she squeezes lemons on everything, even her hair. This is shopping with Harriet: negotiating quantities, arguing over the difference between low-fat and fat-free, sneaking butter into the cart behind Harriet's back. You can't make good garlic bread with margarine, and garlic bread is a staple of their team dinners. Danielle's hosting one tomorrow night before Little IIIs, the race where they meet their biggest rivals. Winning Little IIIs might mean they're good enough to go all the way to Nationals, especially since Sawyer qualified last year. If they can just beat Sawyer . . . Danielle is trying not to obsess about it.

It's good to be spending time with Harriet. Alone. It's different than when they're all together, and she's the captain, and Harriet's the provocateur, both of them playing their roles. After their last weigh-in—because face it, that's what they are, even though they are superficially about choosing a leader for the speed workout—Harriet pointed out that the men's team was never surveilled in the same way. Chloe said it was just because the boys were already so skinny, and Harriet snorted, like what Chloe said was so stupid she wasn't even going to dignify it with a response. And Danielle found herself defending Coach. She couldn't help it. Being captain has turned her into one of Pavlov's slobbery dogs.

Harriet wheels the cart around before giving it a big push forward and leaping off the ground, putting all her weight on the handle. "Careful," Danielle warns. "You're going to flip it."

"American grocery stores are so gross," Harriet says, and Danielle can almost predict what will come next: a disquisition on how the French way of shopping is superior to the way Americans do it. But Harriet surprises her. "Push me?" she asks.

"What?"

Before she can say no, Harriet's climbing in the cart.

"Hairy," she protests, lunging forward to grab the handle and counterbalance her weight, "what are you doing? That's so dangerous."

"Push me, Mom," she laughs.

Danielle sighs. The weird thing is that with her knees pulled up to her chest, Harriet is as small as a child, and if she weren't wearing those ridiculously clunky burgundy boots, she'd have even more room.

"We really need to finish shopping," Danielle says.

"Please," Harriet says, her voice higher than usual, more girl-ish. She raises her left eyebrow—oh, how Danielle would kill to do that—and smiles wickedly. A funny thing happens when Harriet behaves like this—almost never anymore, not since she became *radicalized* (her term)—Danielle feels a little drunk.

"You asked for it," she says.

The cereal aisle is empty as Danielle speeds down it—first walking briskly and then breaking into a jog. She takes the corner a little too fast, barely keeping the cart upright, and clips the potato chip display, sending bags tumbling to the floor. There's a solitary shopper in the baking aisle, so she keeps moving, turning in a wide arc into frozen foods. Harriet makes happy sounds—not quite squeals because she would never squeal. Danielle knows she should stop when they reach the end because then they'll be back in the store's main corridor of checkout lanes and store employees.

"Don't stop," Harriet says, egging her on. "You can do it. One more lap."

She goes for it, heading for fruits and vegetables, ignoring what she is sure are the disapproving looks of other shoppers. Danielle's secret weakness is that she hates getting in trouble. She'll do almost anything to avoid other people's disappointment. They careen into the maze of potatoes and onions, oranges and apples.

They're almost home free when a stern voice says, "Girls! Girls!" A tall man in a red apron steps out from behind a rack of croutons. "This isn't an amusement park."

"Just ignore him," Harriet whispers. "Pretend we're on the lam."

But there is no way Danielle's going to do that. She feels her face getting hot as she starts to apologize. The man cuts her off.

"You need to get out of the cart pronto, young lady," he says, pointing a long bony finger in Harriet's direction. "Do you know how many kids get concussions from playing around in carts?" Danielle's first thought is, Oh no. Then: Please don't lecture him on language. Please, please, please, please, please, please. Harriet smirks as she begins climbing out while Danielle holds the cart steady. "Did you read the sign at the front of the store?" the man continues. "We're not liable for accidents resulting from inappropriate usage of carts."

"It's all right, it's OK," Harriet begins, but Danielle interrupts her before she can finish the chant: you will work for us someday. "I'm sorry, you're totally right. We're almost done with our shopping."

The man harumphs as Danielle hisses at Harriet to follow her to the cheese section. When they're safe, Harriet laughs. "God, what a bureaucrat. *Inappropriate usage of carts.*"

"He's right," Danielle says. "We shouldn't have done that."

"Don't be such a goody-goody, Dani," Harriet says, slugging her in the arm. "You're a very responsible cart driver. That guy just has a stick up his ass."

Danielle grabs a wedge of parm and a couple of balls of mozzarella.

"You're going to be liable for my immodest consumption of calories," Harriet says.

"Very funny," Danielle says.

"Seriously, Dani, don't be upset. That's almost the most thrilling thing I've done in ages."

"Almost?" This is so Harriet: to offer a compliment and then qualify it in some way.

"Skinny-dipping in the Seine was pretty exciting. And lifting weights with Witt. Our mission was to match the men grunt for grunt."

Harriet hates lifting. Danielle's so busy picturing the absurdity of tiny Harriet and big Witt in the weight room that she almost misses what Harriet says next. "Wait, what? You're in love?"

"I might be," she says, frowning as she studies the label on a piece of brie. "God, the brie in this store is so inferior."

"Don't try to change the subject," Danielle says. "Who with? The girl you kissed at the party the other night?"

"Her name's Karen."

"I thought she was dating a guy."

"She was, and now she's not."

"You barely know her."

"I didn't say I was in love for sure. I said I might be."

"But I thought you didn't believe in love."

"I knew you were going to say that."

"Well, you're always going on and on about how love is a so-cial construct."

"True," Harriet says, "though it's not like I ever said that made it any less real. I think Karen might be my soul mate."

Danielle snorts, and Harriet chucks the piece of brie at her. "Shut up," she says, "I thought you would be ecstatic for me. I'm coming over to the dark side. I'm turning into a romantic."

"Oh Hairy," Danielle says, bending over to envelope her in a hug as her heart beats wildly. "You are something else."

SEPTEMBER 26: LITTLE IIIS

KRISTIN KEPT RUNNING THE WRONG PACE. HER SENSE OF PACE, ONCE legendary, was gone. Sometimes it was too slow, but mostly it was too fast. Too fucking fast. It was messing things up for all of us.

Chloe complained non-stop on the ride down. First, she had to pee, having chugged six glasses of water at breakfast because she was worried about being dehydrated and getting cramps. Then, she was feeling carsick because she was wedged into the last bench seat. Was it possible for her to ride shotgun, she called out? Danielle laughed, because if she didn't, she would have probably said something that was not in the spirit of being a good captain. She was secretly hoping that Chloe would beat Kristin today, even if just by a second or two. Patricia was slumped against the window, sleeping. Kristin was listening to her Walkman. We thought she was still embarrassed by the little rabbit episode. Harriet was reading Kathy Acker. She said angry feminist screeds got her in the mood to kick some ass. Liv was staring straight ahead, as she always did, because she was the one who was actually prone to motion sickness, and if she started to feel nauseated on the ride, she would really start to freak out about the possibility that she was pregnant. She could not be pregnant, she told herself. It was highly unlikely, if not impossible. She'd used enough spermicide to kill a whole army of sperm.

The meet was two hours away. This time, the time before meets, was always elastic, like saltwater taffy spinning around a taffy machine, growing longer and then shorter, getting impossibly thin until suddenly we were pulling up on a grassy field and parking in a row of identical cargo vans, and time snapped.

The two teams we were racing that day were our biggest rivals. Why they were our biggest rivals, we were never sure, just that Frost, Sawyer, and Olin were known as the Little IIIs, and our rivalry was historical and permanent, like a family feud, a conflict passed down from one generation to another. Never mind that most of us had also applied to Sawyer, because it was nearly indistinguishable from Frost, and until recently had boasted a better running program, and Harriet had considered transferring to Olin because its campus was slightly more progressive and less preppy.

It was in the mid-60s, an unseasonably warm late-September morning. There had been no frost, and the trees still wore crowns of bright green leaves.

"It's going to be hot," Kristin said as she stepped outside.

"It's perfect," Patricia said.

Kristin ignored her.

Liv was already stretching her left Achilles, one leg bent, the other straight, a palm planted on the painted F, the other on the painted R, as though she was trying to push the van over. The rest of us were milling around, not stretching, because we wouldn't even think about trying to touch our toes until after we'd jogged a few painful, slow miles. We eyed the girls from Sawyer, who had shown up in French braids for the meet. Olin had a few decent girls, but no depth. We barely gave them a second look, except to see if they had dyed their hair for the occasion. It was Sawyer we feared. The Beavers. Suzie was their captain. Built like a tank (for lack of a better word). Fast on the hills. Brutally determined in the last 100 meters. She'd placed fifth in Nationals last year, beating Kristin. She'd allegedly been recruited by Stanford and the real Ivies. We watched Danielle go over, crouch, and give Suzie a hug. Then they talked for a few minutes, both of them nodding almost non-stop, the way girls do when they're trying to be nice.

"What the . . . ?" Patricia said when Danielle returned.

"We hung out a little at a women's leadership conference in Boston this summer," Danielle said. It was odd to hear *women* roll off Danielle's tongue. "She's actually pretty cool. She wants to get a master's in social work and do juvenile justice advocacy stuff."

Patricia gave Danielle a blank look and Harriet snorted. "You're consorting with the enemy."

"I didn't tell her our strategy," Danielle said.

"What is our strategy?" Harriet asked.

The night before, we'd gathered in Danielle's room for a guided meditation. As she turned off the lights and lit candles, we lay down on her wonderfully comfy carpet, throw pillows under our heads, light blankets spread across our bodies. We loved the ceremony of these evenings, the predictability, even if all of us didn't quite buy into Danielle's bullshit. Usually, the point of a guided meditation was to visualize ourselves running the best race of our lives. *You're at the starting line,* Danielle would begin, and she'd talk us through going out hard, using our elbows to create pockets of space, finding a runner ten or twenty feet ahead, making her a target. *When you come through the first mile*, Danielle would say, *no matter what, I want you to whisper*, That was easy. That was easy. That was easy. *Say it at least three times, and each time, make it little faster.*

That was easy. That was easy. That was easy.

I am fast. I am fast. I am fast.

We actually did this. Who knew whether it worked or not, whether we could attribute a good race to Danielle's pop psychology or Coach's magic or the fact that hardwired into our DNA was faster-than-average slow-twitch capacity.

Last night, she'd done something different. After she had us picturing ourselves at the starting line, she told us to take a deep breath through our noses.

We did, because we always did what Danielle told us to do during these sessions. We took a breath, hearing and feeling the air, one breath joining the communal breath, and we felt something cool sliding up toward the tops of ours noses until it stopped, our chests and lungs pressing frantically back.

"Hold it," Danielle had said. "Hold it. Hold it. Hold it."

This was hard to do, but we tried.

"And now open your mouth and let your breath rush out, and as it leaves, let laughter join it. Breathe it in and laugh it out."

For a moment or two, our sounds were fake and ugly. To laugh as we exhaled entailed pulling our lips back into painful grimaces. Then, the sound descended into our chests, and we were wailing. We were supposed to be laughing, but it sounded like we were all crying. Or maybe we were crying. Wasn't it true that things that appeared to be so different, opposites even, always had to meet somewhere?

"Who's making that sound?" Danielle asked.

We all had our eyes closed, and when we opened them, the room had sunk into pitch darkness. "Who blew out the candles?" Chloe whined.

"Our strategy is the same as last week," Danielle said before Little IIIs. "We're going to win."

That was always our strategy: to win by running fast. To win because we wanted it so badly. To be the hound and the quarry. The bow and the bullseye. Danielle threw an arm around Harriet and pulled her into an armpit embrace. Harriet smirked, and then laughed.

"But that's the goal," Harriet countered. "How did we get there?"

"We win by winning," Danielle said. "At every single moment, you have a choice. You can either pass someone or be passed."

"What if you have the lead?" Kristin asked.

"Then you better be really brave," Danielle answered.

Of course, Kristin would try to take the lead, we thought, even though it was a terrifying place to be with the whole pack chasing you. It was rare to win the race from the beginning. Usually someone patient and cunning appeared at the end to become the fastest girl.

Chloe clapped her shoes together. "Can we get this show on the road?"

The course hugged the perimeter of a golf course. Clusters of girls were already out there, jogging it. We had a strange habit of wearing our racing flats on our hands during the warm up, waffle-sole side down, so that at any moment we could drop to all fours and canter like horses. No one was actually limber enough to do this, except maybe Liv, but we liked joking about it. And we liked sharing it as a ritual. Racing flats. Check. Bandannas or ponytails. Check.

"Does anyone have an extra safety pin?" Kristin asked.

"I'll do you," Harriet said, attaching the final corner of Kristin's race number on the back of her singlet. Another olive branch, we thought.

Lipstick. Check. In the tiny pocket on the inside of her shorts, the place you might carry a ten-dollar bill or a dorm-room key, Danielle had a tube of bright red lipstick. She said it was her good-luck charm, and before we warmed up, she'd take it out, and she'd apply some to whoever was game. It was nice to close our eyes, pucker up, and let Danielle dab it on our lips, using her thumb, or sometimes the tip of her pinkie, to get it just so. There was something so tender about it—it took Liv right back to her bedroom in Evanston, the hour before a dance, when her mother would make a big deal of putting a bit of makeup on Liv. Chloe always shook her head, then changed her mind since she couldn't pass up a chance for some extra attention. Last year, Harriet wouldn't have been caught dead wearing lipstick, but this year, she'd started closing her eyes and puckering her lips and letting Danielle perform her girly magic.

We shuffled off, with Danielle in the lead because she was the captain. And then Harriet took over, because she was the other senior on the team. And then Chloe, followed by Kristin, followed by Liv, and finally Patricia, followed by the rest of the team. And when everyone had taken a turn at the front of the pack, we tried to run together, in a straight line, with no one out of step, though we weren't always that coordinated, and someone often drifted a few steps ahead, and when we grumbled, she apologized. We did pretty well today because the course was wide and roomy, except that Kristin kept surging forward.

"Take a chill pill," Patricia said. "Very shortly, you can run all of us into the ground."

"I think we should try something new," Danielle proposed. "Let's pair up. Kristin and Chloe. Patricia and Liv. Harriet and me." She kept rattling off names.

"Right now?" Harriet asked.

"No, I mean in the race. Each pair sticks together. We push each other. And try to keep the pair in front of you within striking range."

"Sounds brutal," someone said.

"Just as an experiment," Danielle said.

"Is this Assistant Coach's idea?" Harriet asked.

Danielle didn't answer.

"Is it Coach's idea?"

"I'm already so tired," Chloe moaned.

"Oh God, Chloe, could you please . . ." Danielle started. Then stopped. "You say that every week. Change the script."

"Change the script," Harriet parroted.

This was part of the ritual, too, the moment when we turned on each other.

Patricia turned to Liv. "You and me. Are we going to kick some ass, or what?"

"Yeah hell," Liv said, offering Patricia her pinkie before blowing a big bubble. She chewed gum right up until the beginning of the race and then she stuck it into the tiny pocket in her shorts.

"You mean 'Hell yeah'?" Patricia asked.

"Isn't that what I said?" Liv asked.

Patricia shook her head.

Then we quieted down. Chloe imagined, as she always did, what would happen if her parents were there, if they could see her run, and Zoo Boy, and her Islamic history professor, who kept telling her she needed to work smarter—*not harder, Chloe, smarter*—if they were all there, if they could just see her, then maybe her feelings—she was good, so, so good!—would last be-

yond the finish line. Zoo Boy would catch a glimpse of her butterfly tattoo peeking out from her singlet and see that she was so
much cooler than her matching socks and shirts suggested. But
none of them was here. She tried to push the thought away. Not
her parents, who had almost never watched her run, not even in
high school when the meets were close by. Not her history professor, who was doing whatever history professors did on Saturday
mornings when they weren't telling students they needed to
work smarter. Not Zoo Boy, who was in her history class but
probably didn't even know her name. Still, she thought, she
would show them.

Danielle was thinking how badly she wanted Frost to win, not
because today's race counted for anything, but because they
needed to prove to themselves that they could, that their first-
place finish last week wasn't an anomaly. They needed to build all
season—she realized Harriet would accuse her of drinking the
Kool-Aid, but it was true. They needed momentum—which
didn't necessarily mean running faster every week since you
could run tits out on a hilly course and still clock a relatively slow
time. Nationals were within their reach; if they didn't get there,
they had only themselves to blame. This was a dangerous thought,
but she didn't care.

Harriet was wondering why she was still on the cross country
team, not an ideal thought to entertain right before a race. She'd
run in high school until she'd gotten too skinny and been forced
to quit by her mom and the school shrink. And then she'd come
to college, and she'd decided to give running another go, both
because Danielle was doing it and she wanted to show her mother
that she was fine. Four years later, she no longer cared about
proving anything to her mother, and yet here she was, giving up
her Saturdays and doing what Coach told her to do. She thought
about the rabbit on the trail—ending its suffering would have

been an act of mercy, but she didn't throw the rock hard enough. *Merde,* was she all bark and no bite? She needed to act on her convictions. Taking a deep breath, she rubbed her hand across her prickly scalp, remembering her long blond locks scattered beneath her on the grass of the freshman quad. *Like sleeping snakes.* She liked that image. "You're a badass," Karen had said to her after they'd been rolling around in bed for hours. She liked that, too.

Patricia thought:lame-ass New England golf course cross country course, lame-ass New England golf course cross country course, lame-ass, lame-ass, lame, lame, lame, ass, ass.

Being fast matters, Kristin told herself. Of course, it matters. If she won, she'd be OK.

When we returned from our warm-up, Coach and Assistant Coach were still sitting in the front of the van, drinking tea (Coach) and coffee (Assistant Coach) from big matching green-and-yellow insulated cups. Exactly fifteen minutes before the race, the doors of the van opened, like a flightless bird spreading its wings, and they got out and ambled over to the other coaches and shook their hands while we went through the motions of stretching. Patricia did the splits. After calling her a show-off, Chloe attempted a clumsy one-handed cartwheel. Liv loosened her fiery red hair, running her fingers through her curls, shaking them out until she looked like a fluffy-maned lion, and then she gathered it all together into a tingly-tight ponytail. Kristin closed her eyes. Harriet yawned.

And then we were at the starting line. Even though the courses were different each week, the starting lines were always the same:

spaces that were too small for the field of runners, and therefore crowded, uneasy, irritable. Moments before, we'd been friends and teammates, joining our hands—Go Frost! Go Poets!—and now we had to tap into something dark and icky that we did not want to name. Some man—it was always a man, never a woman—why was this? Some man in Olin's colors raised a black gun in the air. It was always like this. Some man raised a gun in one hand and brought a megaphone to his mouth with the other. *Runners, take your mark.* The static made the words sound more robotic than human. *Get set.* If we were paying close attention, Coach once explained to us, we could go as soon as we saw the smoke. Light traveled faster than sound. He was always giving us such tips. Start strong, but not too strong. In nine cases out of ten, the leader fades. "You want to spend the whole race being chased by the pack?" he asked. "You like being chased?" We watched for smoke, but truth be told, it was almost impossible to do this without blinking in anticipation of the loud noise, without closing your eyes to protect yourself against the shock.

Bang.

And then we were shooting out like bullets.

KEEP IT GOING

Kristin

BECAUSE SHE HAS PRACTICED—SLAMMING DOORS WITHOUT BLINK-ing, dropping twenty-pound dumbbells in the weight room and watching them thunk against the padded floor—Kristin manages to keep her eyes glued to the gun and gain a fraction of a fraction of an advantage.

The ground feels like a wet sponge. Is she slipping? She second-guesses her decision not to wear spikes.

Others must know Coach's trick, or they are naturally fast starters. Someone is on her right shoulder, someone else on her left. She can't see them, but she can hear them breathing, and she can feel their potential for speed, as though a crank is turning out tinny music, and at any moment, they'll spring. She finds herself listening for the barely audible click of their desire. When it happens, she wants to be ready. She doesn't want to be surprised; not like she was this summer.

Four girls suddenly materialize in front of her. Two from

Sawyer. One from Olin. A freshman from their own team who is running cross country to get in shape for track. That girl always goes out hard and fades well before the first mile. Poor thing.

She pushes extra hard off her left foot. Because of the stress fracture in her right hip in high school, her left leg has become her driver. Her right knee lifts as her left hand swings forward. She's oblivious to all of this except *push, push, push, push.* The words pound in her temples.

She turns it up a notch.

Her right foot, swinging out behind her, catches something, another runner, for just a split second. A sound comes out of her mouth while her arms spread wide to counter gravity, before flinging forward, palm down, in case they need to break her fall. She throws her shoulder backward to catch herself, then tries to re-reverse her center of gravity to keep running forward, and in the middle of all the complex physics that her body's doing beyond the realm of thought or will, someone in a Frost singlet swings by.

Chloe.

Chloe.

Let's pair up.

Kristin's anger consumes her for a few strides, her hatred for Chloe as vast as the high desert outside Boise, but then she pulls her attention back and stares blankly at Chloe until Chloe's butterfly tattoo comes into focus. A butterfly? A flutterby stopping to sip the flowers. This image carries her closer to Chloe, and Kristin suddenly knows that Chloe's advantage is gone. She is lucky. She sits on Chloe's shoulder, letting her do the work. The distance between them and the four runners in front does not change, except the freshman falls a step behind. The toes of Kristin's shoes, covered with broken blades of grass, are wet and green. She forces herself to take a deep breath through her nose, though she's been breathing through her mouth since almost the beginning of the race. This breath is like a drink of water on a hot day. Her shoulders soften, her heart quiets, though her pace remains steady. Feeling refreshed, she and Chloe move up a little closer to the front runners. It's hard to tell whether the lead is slowing, shifting from the turbo-charged start into a pace that will be sustainable for the rest of the race, or whether she and Chloe are making up ground. Chloe glances over her left shoulder, and Kristin takes the opportunity to float up to Chloe's right side, and just as she's pulling even, she swings her arm extra hard, and her left fist kisses Chloe's right tricep and the edge of her back. It's just an accident, she tells herself. Her hands are clenched because this is how she sometimes runs. Chloe says something that Kristin doesn't catch, though they are running shoulder to shoulder. Out of the corner of her eye, she watches Chloe's arms driving back and forth, her hands dangling loosely at the ends of her wrists. She knows Chloe wants to beat her, but it doesn't matter because Kristin is going to be the best.

Be The Best becomes her mantra for a few strides until it reminds her of a waltz—1-2-3, left two three, right two three, and she's thinking about ballroom dancing in high school gym class, and her shoulders start to sway from side to side, *gently, gently like a boat at anchor in a gentle breeze,* Mr. Peters used to say, which sent them into giggles, as their palms grew sweaty and their eyes stayed glued to the floor, ostensibly to avoid stepping on each other's toes, but really because it was too embarrassing to gaze into the eyes of a member of the opposite sex for the duration of a song at 11 a.m. in the brightly lit gymnasium. For a moment, she loses track of Chloe, her attention pulling her away, but now she is reeling it back in, and she casts her eyes forward to the man in a purple sweatsuit calling out numbers. Kristin can't hear him yet, but she knows this is what's happening because one girl has broken away from the lead pack and is quickly approaching him. Kristin wants to hear the numbers before she reaches the man. It will motivate her to push harder, either because she's behind where she wants to be or the opposite: she's ahead. Never mind what happens in the next mile. You never know unless you try, Coach says. But what if you didn't know you needed to try, Kristin thinks. That's how she got lost this summer.

But there's Assistant Coach in short yellow shorts, a silly grin on his face, his eyebrows rising in mock surprise as he spots them. "Poets, Poets, Poets," he calls out in a booming voice. "Go, Chloe! Go, Kristin!" If he would just shut up so she could hear her splits. But now he's yelling for Liv, who she's already forgotten. Liv and Patricia. Danielle and Harriet. The fast ones, plus all the other runners. Her whole team. She doesn't wonder how they're doing until Assistant Coach reminds her to, and then she has to resist the impulse to glance over her shoulder to see how close Liv is. That's the kiss of death. It shows you're scared. That your attention is lagging behind you, like an old poopy dog.

Is she more distracted than usual? Or just more alert?

She took two Tylenols before the race because of the twinge in her groin from the other day. She thinks it's fine. But just in case.

"Five forty-seven," the man calls out. "Forty-eight."

"Go, Kristin! Go, Chloe!"

"Oh," Chloe says.

Or is it "Whoa?"

"Forty-nine," the man says. "Fifty. Fifty-one."

They've come through approximately nine seconds faster than she intended to run the first mile on a very, very slight incline in slightly soggy conditions. If she can keep it going, even though the second miles always feels like you're suddenly carrying a backpack filled with heavy textbooks. If she can keep it going . . .

Keep it going. Keep it going.

It's catchy enough.

Keep it going. Keep it going.

They sweep by the fading freshman who makes a vaguely encouraging sound. If Kristin were a better person, she would respond with something nice, urging her to stick with them. Even though their sixth and seventh runners won't count toward Frost's final score, they're still important because they can displace other teams' top girls, putting them farther back in the pack and adding crucial points to their scores. Instead, she feels a burst of energy as they fly by her and her attention catches on the two girls in front of her, one from Sawyer, one from Clapp, running shoulder to shoulder. The girl on the left, Ponytail, has a butt-kicker stride that is very pretty, but inefficient. The girl on the right, with two braids jittering up and down on her back, has more of a shuffle.

Keep it going. Keep it going.

Chloe is like an anchor at her side.

Anchor. Anchor.

This word slows her down, and Chloe is a half a step in front of her, then a step, and the thought that has been chasing Kristin since August finally catches up: she could have run away. She could have tried, but didn't. Well, the past is gone, and now all she can do is be the fastest on the team. If she gives up now, she'll lose again. If she tries, she'll at least have a chance of winning. If she wins, then maybe she can forgive herself for being stupid. Chloe is getting away. If Kristin's going to try, she has to do it now.

This is what she does: fixes her eyes on Chloe's back; wills herself to drive harder with one leg, then the other; hangs on to this new rhythm by swinging her arms faster. That's the reason for biceps curls. The triceps presses. The pushups. The bench presses. It's not just that Danielle likes to ogle young professors, and Harriet is perfecting her grunt. If the arms lead, the legs will follow.

The body moves, and the mind goes quiet. Sometimes the opposite happens—sometimes the body freezes while the mind keeps racing on. The space between them gets smaller with each step, and Kristin disappears inside herself, flies by Chloe, sets her gaze on the next runner, and begins again. Chloe says something. Or does she? Kristin is so far gone, she isn't sure.

The finish is in a big open field. When Kristin starts her kick, Assistant Coach is on the sidelines, waving his hand back and forth as though trying to get a horse to do something that scares it, screaming at the top of his lungs, "Catch her! Catch her! You've got her! You've got her!" But it's too late, and Suzie hangs on to first place by a few seconds. Kristin's just out of the chute, still trying to catch her breath, when Chloe gallops in, and then a moment later, Liv followed by Patricia. There's not enough time to stumble over to the sidelines and cheer them on.

"Good job," she says to Chloe, clapping her on the back, all of the ill will she felt earlier evaporated.

Chloe's face is red, and maybe angry. Kristin isn't sure.

"You hit me," Chloe says.

"You almost tripped me," Kristin says.

"You know that was an accident," Chloe says. "Swinging your fist into me, though . . ."

"It was an accident," Kristin says. "And if you hadn't tripped me, maybe I would have won."

"Give me a break," Chloe says. "I was trying to stay with you. Remember Danielle told us to stick together."

"It's a race," Kristin repeats. "One of us had to win."

"You didn't win," Chloe spits back.

"But I beat you," Kristin says. She's not going to let Chloe ruin the high she's riding.

"Girls," Danielle squeals, cantering toward them. Her eyes bright, her lipstick smudged, a spot of mud on her chin. "We won. Our team won." She throws her arms around both of them, and Kristin has no choice except to cup Chloe's shoulder. "You both ran so well."

"We won?" Chloe asks.

"You were amazing," Danielle continues, squeezing their arms as she enunciates each syllable. "Ah-MA-zing." "Kristin feels herself being swept into Danielle's excitement.

"We're going all the way, girls," Danielle continues. "If we keep working together, we can do it."

"Do what?" Kristin asks.

"Qualify for Nationals," Danielle scolds. "Have you forgotten why we're torturing ourselves?"

Oh. That's right. Kristin has forgotten all about the team. About Nationals.

She hugs Chloe a bit harder and waits for her to reciprocate. But Chloe drops her hands to her sides and breaks out of the huddle.

"I need to cool down," Chloe says.

"Me, too," Kristin says.

"Girls," Danielle squeals, "for goodness sake, we don't have to cool down yet."

THE TERMINAL

Danielle

DANIELLE IS STANDING NEAR THE SALAD BAR IN THE TERMINAL, SCAN-
ning the room for Harriet. Long and narrow, with floor-to-ceiling
rectangular windows on both sides and a gray carpet that is perpetually stained from food fights and kids with no table manners,
the dining room looks like an airport terminal, which is how it
got its name, though wittier students call it *Terminal Illness* or *Terminal Velocity*. Danielle and the Darlings never eat here. It's rowdy,
and the salad bar is always a mess. Not a place for a civilized dinner. It's also the last place she would expect Harriet to ask to meet
her. Harriet usually hangs out in one of the smaller dining rooms
where the artsy kids linger after dinner smoking cigarettes. It's so
Harriet to have friends who all smoke. Danielle just hopes Harriet will keep her word and lay off the furtive drags until after the
cross country season's over. Not that Danielle wants Harriet to
ever start smoking, but she'll take what she can get.

"There you are," Harriet says rushing up. She does her French kissing thing that Danielle is still not used to. Left, right, left again. Half the time Danielle moves her head the wrong way before the third kiss and messes it up.

It takes Danielle a moment to register that Harriet's not alone, that she's brought Karen along with her. Danielle has been dying to meet Karen. Officially. Their paths have crossed a couple times on campus, Harriet and Karen so close they might have been holding hands moments earlier, but each time Danielle approached them, Harriet just said hey, without stopping and offering to introduce them, and Danielle felt just the teeniest bit hurt, like she was losing Harriet. Even though she also knows that's totally ridiculous. It's not like Harriet is hers to lose, and she also understands why Harriet might want to keep her relationship secret. Frost is such a gossipy place. It can't be easy to be gay, not that Harriet has ever complained about her own situation specifically, but she also has never had a girlfriend. Never been in love. This is another reason she probably needed to go to Paris—to escape their squeaky-clean campus. Or whatever. Their clean-on-the-surface campus.

"Hi," Danielle says way too eagerly. This is what she does when she's nervous: defaults to *mom speak* and smiles in that idiotic way that moms do when they're trying to broadcast enthusiasm. She is so excited to be here! She can't help it! Harriet is finally bringing them all together! Maybe she chose *The Terminal* because she doesn't want to risk seeing any of the other girls from the team.

Harriet raises one eyebrow, then laughs and claps her hands together. "You're here," she says again, and Danielle realizes that Harriet is also nervous.

"I'm here," she says while the three of them stand there awkwardly. Harriet's eyes keep

roaming around the giant room as though she searching for

someone. But who could she be looking for? The Terminal is where the most violent teams eat—like hockey. Danielle hates the hockey team, which is yet another reason for avoiding this place. And she has little affection for the football players—all one hundred of them—who behave like such idiots, pounding their fists on the tables, stringing together chants that sound like threats or distracting themselves from their defeats by daring and double-daring each other to perform such feats as eating fifty pats of butter or downing a whole trayful of glasses of milk. Football is a stupid sport, and Frost's football team sucks, and yet the college still throws money at them. If the cross country team got a tenth of the resources as the football team . . . well, it makes her furious.

"I'm so glad you could join us for the performance."

Danielle straightens.

"It's a Witt production," Harriet explains.

"Here?" Danielle asks, feeling her pulse quicken because The Terminal seems like the worst place for a Witt production, or maybe the best, if what Harriet is going for is spectacle. At the last feminist "happening" that Witt orchestrated, twelve long-haired girls sat on stools on the freshman quad getting their heads shaved while Witt videotaped gawking students. The men were the rowdiest: no shocker there. "Are you and—" She looks at Karen again. She's even smaller than Harriet, and she has two pigtails sprouting off the sides of her head. Until recently, she was dating Liv's boyfriend's best friend. And now she's dating Harriet, if that's what they're doing.

"Oh, sorry, Karen, this is Dani, the captain of the cross country team, otherwise known as the biggest badass. Dani, this is Karen."

"I've heard so much about you," Karen says.

"Don't believe a word of whatever Harriet has told you,"

Danielle says. "But it's nice to finally meet you."

At this, Harriet turns a tiny bit pink before recovering and giving Danielle a playful punch on the arm. Karen grins. She has a dimple, too, except hers is on the right. "It's nice to meet you, too," she says. "I can't believe Harriet's going to do this." She shakes her head.

"What do you have up your sleeve, Hairy?"

"Hairy?" Karen laughs. "That's the cutest nickname ever."

Danielle glances at Harriet, waiting for her object to Karen's use of the word *cute*, and launch into a whole lecture about how demeaning it is to call women cute; just because she's small, that doesn't mean she's not fierce. And just because Karen is small. . . . but Harriet just tucks her chin, looking pleased with herself. Wow. Has being in love softened her, made her forsake her sharp feminist edge? "We're going to take off our shirts . . ."

"We?"

"Not you," Harriet says, "though you're certainly welcome to join us. No, there are women sitting throughout the dining hall who are going to stand up, take off their shirts, and then sit back down and keep eating. When I give the signal . . ."

"Is Professor Witt here?"

"That's who I was looking for. She said she'd be standing in the back. She's going to videotape it. But I don't see her. Do you see her, Karen?"

"I haven't had the pleasure of meeting Professor Witt," Karen says.

"Are you doing this, too?" Danielle asks Karen.

"Oh God, no," Karen answers. "I'm not as brave as Harriet is."

"I really don't think this is a good idea," Danielle says, unable to stop herself. Already her mind is moving to the worst possible outcome. "What if you get in trouble?"

Harriet scowls. "I knew you would say that."

"What if you get suspended?" Danielle continues, unable to stop herself. "What if you can't run?

"Don't be such a worrywart," Harriet replies. "No one gets kicked out of Frost. You know that." The pointed look she gives Danielle is like kick in the shin, and it takes Danielle a moment to catch her breath. Is she really bringing up *that* right now? She doesn't want to believe that Harriet could be so cruel.

"You don't even have boobs," Danielle says, immediately regretting how stupid and juvenile that sounds. So mean. What will she say next? My boobies are bigger than your boobies? Which is true, but barely.

"I think her breasts are plenty nice," Karen says, and Harriet blushes again, and Danielle is left to imagine what Karen and Harriet do together.

"There she is," Harriet announces, and before Danielle can beg her to reconsider, Harriet takes one step forward and then another and climbs onto the table at the front of the room that is empty for some reason. Unknotting the gauzy pink scarf that she's been wearing ever since she came back from Paris, she raises it and waves triumphantly above her head. Danielle can't see her expression—whether she wears a giddy smile or has set her jaw in determination. The scarf flutters to the ground, and Karen scurries forward to pick it up, as though this is part of the plan, and then in one smooth motion, Harriet peels her T-shirt up her torso and over her head, and sends it sailing through the air.

It's hard for Danielle to admit she's wrong. That's the problem with taking responsibility for everything. There's so much pressure, and if she makes a mistake just once, she could lose her nerve for leadership. Her gaze is so fixed on Hairy that she almost misses what's happening throughout the rest of the room—the dozen or so girls standing up, unbuttoning their shirts as though they have all the time in the world, pausing for a moment or two in their bras—black, white, beige, and even red—pausing as though they feel no shame about standing in The Terminal in their bras—and then in what has surely been carefully choreographed beforehand all of their arms disappear behind their backs for a few second as they perform the miracle of unfastening tiny clasps without looking—

The murmur in the room grows as Danielle waits for the football team to mutiny or one of the hockey guys to leap up and start stripping. Boys love to get naked. She can almost hear their guffaws of pleasure. They're such oafs. But that doesn't happen. There's laughter, a few "What the fuck!"s that rise from the general din like helium balloons, but otherwise it's shockingly subdued. One of the cafeteria ladies stands next to Danielle and says, "Well, I'll be . . ." And then one by one the girls sit down, disappearing back into the masses of students eating dinner, and Harriet remains on her perch for a few seconds longer. She is so tiny, her ribs look like a coat of armor with buttons running up her spine, her shoulder blades like stunted wings. When she turns, she pushes her flat chest forward and leaps from the table, high on her victory.

Though the worst hasn't happened, Danielle feels something like sadness trickling through her nerves, and she starts to tremble when Karen gently suggests that Harriet should put her shirt back on before they go through the food line, and Harriet readily agrees. Danielle wishes she could understand her own feelings, but all she has is her very own mind, which at the moment is as soft and gooey as Jell-O.

BITCH

ON MONDAYS, WE RAN LONG INTERVALS THROUGH THE WOODS FOL-
lowed by strength training. On Tuesdays, we did speed workouts
on the track. That was the worst. That was the day that Liv and
Henry always fought, because Liv was so spent that afterward she
fell asleep sitting up in the library, so pale she looked like a zom-
bie, and Danielle wouldn't drink and this would make her grumpy,
and Chloe would go back to her room and cry and her roommate
Kay would cry with her. On Wednesdays, we did long runs and
more strength training. Sometimes instead of taking us to the
weight room, Assistant Coach made us do drills: part calisthenics,
part tongue twisters for the body, they made us aware of muscles
we never knew we had. The worst was walking backward down
Memorial Hill twelve or fifteen times, each step a deep reverse
lunge, with Assistant Coach lecturing us on biomechanics and
yelling at us to go deeper. *Deeper. Deeper. Go deeper.* It was frankly
embarrassing how clueless he could be. Thursdays were another
hard day until, at some magical point toward the end of the season, Coach decided it was time to taper. And then it was just a

medium-hard day. Fridays were easy: something short, like Grist Mill, a run of three miles, lots of stretching, an ice bath to treat injuries that you intended to ignore the next day. We usually raced on Saturday, but yesterday we'd had the day off, except not really. Coach made us report to the track at 7 a.m. for a bonus speed workout. Now it was Sunday, and Patricia was complaining about what a bitch it had been to drag our sorry asses out of bed at the ass crack of dawn just because Coach was psycho.

"Can you please not use the word 'bitch'?" Liv said.

"Why?"

"Because it's like a derogatory term for women."

"But I'm not using it to describe a woman," Patricia said. "I'm using it to describe how I feel about getting up at the *ass crack of dawn* when I should have been snuggled up in bed."

Chloe laughed.

"Still," Liv said, "language matters."

"Thanks for the lecture, Harriet," Chloe said.

In response, Liv just shook her head.

"It really bothers me that there's not the equivalent male-gendered word," Liv continued.

Who knew Liv was so uptight?

Patricia pulled slightly ahead of Chloe and Liv.

"Please don't push the pace," Chloe said.

"Jerk," Patricia said.

"I'm not a jerk," Chloe protested.

"I'm not talking to you," Patricia said.

"*Jerk* is totally generic," Liv said. "Could be applied to either gender."

"'Motherfucker,'" Patricia said.

"Also sexist," Liv answered.

"Why is 'motherfucker' sexist?" Chloe said.

"Yeah, why?" Patricia asked.

"Because it's a transgressive act with your mother," Liv said. "Have you ever heard anyone say 'fatherfucker'? It's like 'girly.' No one says 'boy-y.' Binary oppositions never just describe differences; one term is always superior to the other."

Chloe shrugged and then scowled. "Can anybody step in for this guy? Anybody? For Mr. Motherfucking March of Dimes?"

Patricia's braids whipped back and forth as she said, "That's so racist."

"What?" Liv said.

"Talking like a Black man," Patricia continued "It's like putting on blackface."

"Oh my god," Chloe said. "I can't believe you. We're a melting pot. What's the big deal? This is how my people talk."

By people, she meant New Yorkers. City folks.

"Just kidding," Patricia said.

"I hate you, Patricia," Chloe said, grinning.

"It's Pa-TRISS-ee-ah, Patricia said. "Can you please stop pronouncing my name the ugly way?"

"Sorry," Chloe whined.

"I seriously love *White Men Can't Jump*," Patricia said. "You can put a cat in an oven but that don't make it a biscuit."

We turned left at the mill. From here, we'd run along a rolling dirt lane with farms on both sides, take another left onto a busy road where we'd have to hug the shoulder to avoid being hit, and then hang a final left and climb through an old apple orchard, finishing through the woods at the edge of campus. It was just the three of us. You could run with whomever you wanted on Sundays. Harriet and Danielle always went off on their own, and the rest of us ran together, though Chloe had made it clear she wanted nothing to do with Kristin. She would have normally joined us, but Chloe was still smarting from Kristin beating her two weeks in a row. She'd been the best last year, but this year,

Kristin appeared to have a slight advantage. It could be painful to be friends (or even pretend to be friends) with your race-day nemesis.

On a day like this when the whole world unspooled slowly and leisurely, we loved to run. During a race, it was a different story; then, we hated running—our guts twisting and our mouths filling with the taste of stale saltines, we would feel like sorry sacks of bones until the gun went off and then ideally our cerebral selves would be obliterated. But today, a week of hard workouts behind us, almost forgotten, we floated through three and a half miles until we hit the old farmhouse at the edge of campus, with its orchards and its long, steep, potholed driveway in the shape of a backward C. It wasn't a particularly hard hill, but it was just long enough to be unpleasant. A long gradual uphill was often much harder than a short steep one. It required sustained mental toughness.

"Ready," Chloe said.

Old gnarled apple trees lined the driveway, their green crowns filled with red jewels. Atop the hill was the farmhouse, its blue shingled siding fading to gray, sheets of plywood nailed over a window or two, and weeds growing out of the rain gutter. It had stood empty for years.

"Ready," Patricia said.

Midway up, the hill slowed us down. Though we were taking it easy, exaggerating the swing of our arms to keep our legs moving, the hill felt longer than usual. Patricia bounded in slow motion. Liv, ever so slightly knock-kneed, egg-beatered her legs. Chloe was getting pushed backward, even though she kept telling herself to lean forward. She wasn't as tall as Danielle, but she was the second-tallest on the team.

"Slow down, you mofo," Patricia called out.

"If I go any slower, I'll be running backward," Chloe said.

"Then run backward," Patricia said.

It was amazing how a hill could undo even the most experienced runner, how it often undid us, even though we'd run the orchard hill hundreds of times, often with Assistant Coach urging us to attack it, his voice getting louder and more insistent each time we raced to its top. Our hearts shifted into a higher gear while our quads firmed up like green bananas.

We were at the top half of the C now, the abandoned farmhouse just 100 meters away.

"Mofo," Patricia yelled out again, and Chloe laughed.

Now that the gravel road was leveling out, we surged forward. Already we were forgetting the climb, how surprising it was, how badly we felt, how we weren't supposed to feel tired on an easy day but always did.

"Hey," Chloe said suddenly, pointing at the house. "Is the window on the second floor open?"

"Weird," Liv said. "Someone probably left it open."

"What if someone's in there now," Patricia said. "Spying on us."

"Did you actually see someone?" This was Liv.

"Maybe," Patricia said.

This seemed about as likely as Rapunzel locked up at the top of the tower unfurling her long hair to let some guy climb up and join her. Patricia suddenly stopped and picked up an apple.

"Are you going to eat that?" Chloe said.

"Why wouldn't I?" Patricia replied.

"It's on the ground?" Chloe said, which was quintessential Chloe. She always ran around the track clockwise, had a separate notebook for each class, made her bed every day because her mother, the author of two biographies that took her decades to research and write, once remarked that making your bed meant you accomplish at least one thing every day. She liked rules.

"And what is so wrong with the ground?" Patricia said, polishing the apple with the bottom half of her ratty T-shirt with "Land of Enchantment" written in fading letters across the back. She took a noisy bite before offering it to Chloe, who looked at it for a moment. "Going once, going twice," Patricia said.

The woods were sliding by as we trotted along the serpentine path. "Wow," Chloe said, after taking a bite. "That's one stellar apple."

Patricia announced she was going to come back with a bag and collect more apples. It was just like gathering pine nuts from the piñon trees that grew around her pueblo. She really said that: *pueblo.*

"You're such a hick," Chloe said.

"That's offensive."

Chloe was always saying the wrong thing.

We were out of the woods now, on the edge of the playing fields where other jocks were engrossed in sports that involved moving balls up and down fields and into goals. Peeling off, Liv said she was heading straight back to her dorm because she needed to do some homework before the team dinner that night, but we knew that she was going to hang out with Henry. Their devotion to each other was a foreign language that we didn't yet speak.

Once Liv was gone, Patricia stopped. "Shall we walk a bit?"

"Really?" Chloe never walked until she reached the absolute end of her run.

"I like to walk at the end." Hooking her right hand around her left elbow, Patricia started doing side bends.

"What if Coach sees us?" Chloe asked.

"And?"

"Well, I don't want to get in trouble."

"You are such brown-noser," Patricia said, now bending the other way. "It's not like he's going to anoint you best on the team if you do everything he says. You've got to make that happen on your own."

Chloe nodded. They were halfway across the fields now, the gym looming above them. *The Courthouse,* Harriet called it, not just because of the white columns across the front, but also because it was where we faced judgments and reckonings.

Suddenly, Patricia took Chloe's hand, lacing her fingers through Chloe's, swinging their arms. Poor Chloe! Her instinct was to yank her hand back. She hadn't held hands with anyone since she was a little girl and instinctively found her mother's hand any time they were walking anywhere—which was all the time in the city. At parties, Danielle and Kristin, or sometimes Danielle and Harriet, sat very close, stroking each other's arms. It was always late, and we'd always drank too much, and things would start to get weird—unlikely people paired off and disappeared; guys rolled around on the floor together or karate-kicked each other. This was the time when something always broke: a lamp, a coffee mug half-filled with wine, a wall, kids' hearts, and once a poor freshman's nose. Danielle called it the witching hour. Harriet said it was when people expressed their true selves. Kristin joked it was why she left parties early. Too much collateral damage.

Instead of pulling away, Chloe found herself falling into rhythm with Patricia, left foot forward, arms swing forward; right foot forward, arms swing back. They were in perfect harmony until Patricia started moved faster, laughing, and Chloe tried to keep up but it was impossible to keep their arms in synch with their legs. Patricia suddenly dropped Chloe's hand, and Chloe felt stupid. She liked to be the one to pull away first because she didn't want to be the one left behind. We'd all noticed this about her.

"Kristin hit me during the last race," Chloe suddenly blurted out.

"What?" Patricia said, stopping and facing Chloe. "What do you mean?"

"She swung her fist into me and hit my arm. On purpose."

"You're just saying that because she beat you," Patricia said.

"No, I'm not!"

"I'm just kidding," Patricia said, and Chloe let out a long sigh of relief. "But that sucks," Patricia continued. "The next time Kristin hits you, you should hit her back."

THE TUBS

Kristin

KRISTIN DRIFTS INTO THE STUDENT CENTER, A YELLOW WEDDING cake of a building. She's been in the library trying to cram in some reading before class. Though she usually allows herself just four malted-milk balls, today she scoops up a fifth and then a sixth from the bin and drops them into the plastic bag, then twists the top and ties it into a knot. If she doesn't do this, she'll eat all of the candy before she's even reached the library steps, with little memory of the pleasure.

"That'll be forty-seven cents," says the guy working the register. He wears a pair of vaguely German glasses and a plaid shirt buttoned all the way up that makes her own throat feel chokey.

She swings her backpack off one shoulder, trying to wedge it between her body and the counter to fish out her coin purse, but it's too heavy and she winds up dropping it on the floor. She counts out the change.

"Hey," the guy says, flashing a sly smile. "I recognize you.

You're the Tubs player of the week."

"Yep," she says.

"That's very cool," he says, bobbing his head up and down.

It's super cool, she thinks. The newspaper chooses an athlete every week, based on their performance in some competition, and the winner gets a gift certificate to Tubs, a nearby ribs joint. She's never eaten a rib in her whole life, and probably never will, but she is legitimately psyched with how she did in the last two meets. Though she didn't win either one, she was the fastest on her team, and she felt the pleasure of her body that went all the way back to the Presidential Physical Fitness Test, when she was ten, and she was determined to beat her record of twenty laps around the school block from the year before. Mr. Gray was standing there, a shiny silver whistle hanging from his neck, and she was wearing her first pair of Nikes, white with a red swoosh, bought with babysitting money, and the shorts that her mom didn't want her to wear because it was April, the first crocuses just raising their tiny purple heads from the half-frozen ground. She remembers the jitters and the goose pimples on her arms and legs and her hair pulled back tight and tingly and jumping up and down at the starting line with her friend Wren. And then she was off, she was off, she was off, her body a best friend she was meeting for the first time.

"A Tubs in the flesh," he continues, planting his chin in his hands and looking up at her. "What's your sport?"

"Cross country," she says.

"Funny," he says. "You don't look like a runner."

She laughs uncomfortably. It's like the dumbest possible thing a person could say, and yet she hears it all the time. At least he's managed to keep his eyes off her chest. Points for that.

"How far do you run?"

"5K," she says.

His squint indicates that he doesn't think in meters.

"A hair over three miles."

"And you run as fast as you can?"

"Well, you run as fast as you can for three miles."

"That's brutal," he says.

"It's something," she says.

"And you like it?"

"Like what?"

"Running?"

"I love running," she blurts out, then is surprised by the heft of her feelings. There it is. She loves to run. Nothing will take that away from her. She shouldn't have hit Chloe in the last race, but she can't dwell on that now. Two steps forward, one step back. Three steps forward, one step back. If she stays healthy and gets enough sleep, she'll keep getting stronger, and it will be four steps forward, no steps back, and then five and six. She just wants to put some distance on the summer. She thinks of the lake, the water so clear, so beautiful. *What kind of bear are you?* The body moves before the brain stops it, both a blessing and a curse.

Swept along by her optimism, Kristin walks into the mailroom. It looks like a bomb has gone off, the floor littered with blue leaflets dropped by students in disgust or laziness, advertisements for a used-textbook company that a handful of enterprising freshmen are trying to get off the ground. "Top $$$$ for used books."

When she first got to Frost, she used to fantasize that maybe her dad would finally write, that he'd say he was waiting until he knew that her mother couldn't intercept his letters, that he couldn't wait to meet her. That hope isn't totally dead, but as she peers through the tiny rectangular window and sees that her box is crammed full, she's not thinking about her dad, she's thinking about how much junk collects when you don't stay on top of it. Muscle memory moves her fingers through her combination. The lock clicks, and she excavates several weeks of mail before turning to one of the high tables in the middle of the room to sort it. Tori Amos drifts in from the atrium where there's a baby grand and someone with a surprisingly good voice is belting out *And if I die today, I'll be the happy phantom.* It's all junk, except for a single letter with her name and address written in blocky letters. No return address. Postmarked Boise, Idaho two weeks earlier.

All at once she is picturing the Chevy Impala, the smell of baked leather and burnt oil, the long bench seat, the way he drove, the triangle of his elbow out the window, maneuvering the wheel one-handed, his eyes invisible behind the mirrored sunglasses. *Woo-hoo, the time is getting closer.* She remembers leaning in the window because he needed to tell her something, and he was suddenly kissing her, on Main Street right in front of the coffee shop, and she felt like his lips were dragging her through the window, and she would have gone wherever he wanted to take her.

Woo-hoo, the time to be a ghost.

Because she's holding this letter, it means he's back in Boise, and the wilderness did not swallow him, and she can finally put to bed her half-hearted worrying, the nagging feeling that she did something wrong when she hiked out of the Sawtooths all by herself, leaving him fast asleep at their campsite. The last two weeks before she returned to college, she kept glancing through the plate-glass windows of the coffee shop, half wishing she'd spy him pulling up, half dreading it.

"Kristin?" someone says, putting a hand on her arm. She jumps.

"Eli!"

"Look at you." His eyes glint. "You won the Tubs award."

It takes her a moment to remember, and then she has to force a smile onto her face.

"Did you get bad news?" He points at the letter.

"I don't know," she says, which is the closest she's come to being honest with Eli since the semester began.

"Walk and talk?" he offers.

"I can't," she says. "I don't have time."

"Are you sure?" he says.

She nods.

"OK," he says. "I guess I'll catch you later." He turns and disappears into the tide of students washing into the mailroom. His purple backpack, slung over one shoulder, is gaping open, his books and notebook just moments away from spilling out.

"Eli, your backpack . . ." And then too quickly she has forgotten Eli and is looking down at the envelope again, turning it over and over in her hands, wondering whether she should open it while knowing at the same time that of course she will because it is not in her nature to resist her own curiosity.

Inside are three pieces of yellow lined paper like from the legal pads her mom uses.

"Hello," it says at the top in cursive. The handwriting makes her pause, first because it's hard to read and second because the cursive reminds her of her grandma and her fourth-grade teacher Mrs. J, who liked to say that cursive was a lot friendlier than print because the letters were all holding hands. Cursive seemed cheerful. Now she wonders if it's deceptive.

How are you, runner girl? Are you winning your races? Are you blowing everyone out of the water? I'm sure you are.

There's an empty line. In that space, her lips start to quiver.

I would have written sooner, but I had to find your address first, which wasn't easy. If I'd known you were going to leave me, and I wasn't going to see you again, I would have gotten it from you earlier in the summer. I came by your house several times right before you left for school, but I guess you didn't hear the pebbles I threw.

Another empty line.

The best stretch of the river has the most boulders. Did I ever tell you this? That's what makes a river worth rafting. The water collides with the rocks and produces turbulence. In fluid mechanics, turbulence is a flow condition in which speed and pressure change unpredictably as an average flow is maintained. That's from the dictionary. Ha. Ha. In my book, turbulence is pure adrenaline. The biggest, baddest rush. Man, you would have loved it, Kristin. At least I think you would have. There's always a risk, but that's the whole point. If only you'd known this about me.

She grabs the table to steady herself.

The Rivers, man! They're God's arteries. The Salmon. The Snake. The Selway. The mighty Payette. You're from Idaho, runner girl, but what do you know of them? What do they mean to you? If the river grabs your paddle, hold fast. You'll need it. If it grabs your body, let go. The only way out of a vortex is to go deeper. If you're drowning, drown some more. Only the deepest currents behave predictably. Those are the ones that will sweep you forward.

Do you understand, Kristin? To escape the hole, you have to first go all the way to the bottom. It's scary down there, but then you're tumbling out. Open your eyes. Find the light. That's the surface. Swim for it. You're not where you started, but it doesn't matter. You're never where you thought you were. Take a mouthful of air. Breathe. Ride the current until it lets you go. Never fight it. It will always beat you, and foolish is the man who thinks he is stronger than nature.

Another space.

Comprende, my friend?

You're crazy, she thinks to break the spell. He's crazy. To think otherwise would make her crazy, and she's not, or only a little.

She looks around the room to remind herself where she is, that she is not alone. Other kids are standing at the grid of mailboxes, twirling their locks, retrieving envelopes that bring them the world, or take it away, depending on their contents. They are, she tells herself, embroiled in their own dramas, even though none of them are visible. The candy sits on the table, forgotten. She rips open the plastic bag and pops a malted-milk ball into her mouth, sucking off the chocolate before her tongue touches the crunchy interior. She eats another, this time chewing it up immediately. The sweetness is soothing. She starts to read again.

When you clambered out of the lake that day, weren't you a sight for sore eyes. So perfect. So beautiful. Every goddam inch of you.

Another empty line. Another.

She pulls her gaze away. The chocolate is gone, and just like that, she's back where she started, back to wanting him to apologize. To say it was a mistake, he's been thinking about it for the past two months, and he's writing because he's sorry, sorry for not listening to her, sorry for playing a stupid game, sorry for everything that happened afterward, sorry for making her doubt just how strong she is. If he says he's sorry, then she'll be able to forgive herself. And if he doesn't? Then it's all her fault.

You disappeared, runner girl. Where did you go?

(Smiley Face)

Where did you go?

(Smiley Face)

I'm sorry you got so cold, but you weren't really in danger of dying. Love, Jed."

Her fist on the table is loud and sharp, like the gun at the beginning of a race. She does not feel the heat of everyone looking at her. She hits the table again. It feels good to do something.

SOMEBUNNY

THIS WAS COLLEGE: CONSTANT TUMULT. WE COULD NOT RIDE A high—which we were most definitely riding after winning Little IIIs and beating Sawyer so resoundingly—without something ruining it. First, it was Harriet's lab paper, for which she'd received her first-ever extension, only to discover that now that the deadline was a moving target, she couldn't bring herself to plant her bony butt in a library chair and finish it. Every night, she would vow she was going to get to the end, but instead, she'd hang out with Karen. She was dizzy with love.

Then, Liv happened to glimpse something in her boyfriend Henry's calendar—the word *London* printed in Henry's neat hand in mid-December with a line going through one week and then the next. Henry hadn't mentioned anything about going to London, and Liv couldn't believe he would keep a secret from her, not when their lives were so mashed up, not when Henry knew everything about her, including the approximate length of her menstrual cycle. (She had still not gotten her period.) A couple days passed during which Liv kept waiting for Henry to tell her about the trip, and then when he didn't, Liv began to wonder whether she really knew Henry at all. Maybe he was bored, and he was going to break up with her. It wouldn't surprise her, not really, since he was already interviewing for jobs for next year, and once he was in New York, where he was most definitely headed since he was a genius at econ, he was going to want to spread his oats and sow his wings. Or however the saying went. And what if she were . . . ? She couldn't think about that.

And the rest of us—Danielle, Chloe and Patricia, the freshmen and the stupid recreational runners—were dealing with the usual stressors: too much reading and endless orgo labs, pangs of homesickness, roommate drama, laundry loads that were forgotten and sat for so long they grew mildewy, lost keys and jackets, morning shifts in the cafeteria, awkward crushes and unrequited love.

Then something happened on Wednesday that threw us all into a tizzy. It was after five, perhaps closer to six, and we walked in weary silence through the long empty halls of the gym and made our way single-file down the stairs, holding fast to the railing because our legs were like red vine licorice, firm only to a point. We'd run five one-mile repeats, one more than we normally did, with just four minutes of recovery after each one. Each repeat was supposed to be ten seconds faster than the one before it, which was the opposite of what our bodies wanted to do.

It was a brutal workout, but Coach said we couldn't rest on our laurels. We'd had a week off from racing, and he didn't want us to forget what it felt like to suffer. Kristin, who'd started out strong on each one but quickly faded, said she wasn't feeling well. We thought little of it at the time; we were too focused on our own misery.

After that, he had us gather in the padded room, which always felt cold, and especially when we were as tired as we were that day, and spoke to us about *potential*. We all had it, he said, and it was a luxury: "The future is a gift that is hard to receive when you are so young, the horizon only visible if you slow down to look." But of course, we couldn't slow down, which was why we needed to put all of our trust in him. And then he described the roads he'd run as a young man, the little puffs of dust that rose behind him and soon sifted back to the ground. In the rainy season, there was mud, and sometimes it sucked off one of his shoes, and he had to stop, go back, pull it out, jam his muddy foot into his muddy shoe, and start running again. The distance in front of him was continually opening, and then closing again, and there was no one to tell him when he'd run far enough. Did we see how lucky we were? How lucky we were to have him there telling us how far we needed to run and helping us realize our potential?

By the time we got to the locker room, it was dark and empty and smelled of fake forest, which meant the custodians had already come and swabbed the floors with Lysol, and we needed to watch for puddles and be careful not to slip. Chloe almost bumped into Liv, who had stopped abruptly and was feeling along the wall for the light switch. We wouldn't get to dinner until well after six, when the line would be out the cafeteria doors, and the salad bar would be ravaged: the hard-boiled eggs mashed up, the baby corn and black olives and spinach gone, the cottage cheese purple with beet juice. We'd probably end up eating Grape-Nuts with skim milk, grilled chicken breasts, brown rice, apples. The fluorescent lights flickered on and then buzzed like flies on the wrong side of a closed window. In our row, Harriet's burgundy Doc Martens stood guard on top of the lockers as we struggled to get out of our clammy clothes as quickly as we could, except for Chloe, who was standing there with a strange expression on her face, not that we noticed this.

"*The future is a gift that you do not know,*" Harriet said, trying but failing to imitate Coach.

"Like, what the fuck," Liv said, thinking of Henry and how the future was like receiving a box that you were excited to open, only to find that it held an ugly sweater and now you had to pretend to love it. The future was unknowable, all right, and as far as she was concerned, that sucked. "What's the point?"

"I don't know," Harriet said. "Maybe Danielle knows."

"Why would I know?" Danielle said testily.

"Because you're the captain, and you have coffee with Assistant Coach every week," Harriet said.

"Assistant Coach doesn't know the plan," she said. "I think he was as surprised as we were when Coach made us run that last mile."

"It's abusive," Harriet said.

"But we did it," Danielle said, switching into her usual tedious cheerleader tone. "It's not like I wanted to run the last mile. I didn't think I could. But then I did. And so did you." She looked at Harriet, and then her gaze swept across all of us. "You all did."

"I did, but I didn't want to."

"But when do you ever want to?"

Harriet punched Danielle lightly on the arm.

"Not you specifically, Hairy," Danielle said, "I mean all of us. We never want to do it. But then we do. That's what makes Coach so brilliant. He knows how to unlock our potential." Suddenly she stopped. "Kristin? What's wrong?"

Kristin had stepped out from behind her open locker door totally naked. We couldn't help but marvel at her curves, her gravity-defying breasts, her eraser-sized nipples, the half-moons of empty space between her waist and hips where the rest of our bodies were ruler straight. None of us wanted a body like hers, and yet we could still appreciate its beauty. She was almost never naked in front of us. She was usually struggling to use the bath-mat-sized towel to keep herself covered up.

Kristin let out a little sob and buried her face in her hands.

"What's happened?" Danielle asked as she moved forward, Harriet at her side. They always managed to put aside their disagreements. We often felt if they'd been co-captains, the team would have been stronger, with Danielle urging us on, and Harriet injecting reality into the situation. Yin and yang. It was important that there was room for us to voice our uneasiness, even if it was purely symbolic, even if we always came around to the idea of doing exactly what Coach told us to do. What other choice did we have? Quit running?

Chloe was standing there like a deer caught in the headlights of a car, like disaster was imminent, and she wasn't sure what to do. Danielle and Harriet shoved her out of the way—perhaps harder than they needed to, we thought. And then they were hammocking Kristin in their arms, lowering her to the bench, sitting so close their bare thighs all touched. When called upon, we put aside our petty grievances and our fierce desires to beat each other, and our real love came racing back. Not just Danielle's. All of ours. We were a team.

"Go get a wet paper towel," Danielle instructed Liv, who scurried off, going the long way around to get to the sink because the rest of us were standing in the center of the aisle in a useless knot.

"Are you OK?" Danielle asked Kristin again.

"I'm sorry," Chloe blurted out.

"What are you talking about?" Harriet said, without looking up.

"I said 'I'm sorry,' " Chloe said. "I'm sorry. I did it. I thought it would be funny."

Now we were all looking at Chloe as she disappeared behind Kristin's open locker and reappeared several long seconds later with a puppet on her right hand. Not just any puppet, but a rabbit puppet. "Somebunny isn't very funny," she said in a strained sing-songy voice.

"Are you serious?" Danielle snapped. "Jesus, Chloe, what's wrong with you?"

Chloe stood there with the puppet bobbing in her right hand and the front of her towel gripped in her left to keep it from slipping down her flat chest. "It was just a joke," she finally said in a small pathetic voice that, under other circumstances, might have made us feel bad for her because it was never nice to be the object of Danielle's wrath. But now we felt she deserved it. We gathered around Kristin; we turned our back on Chloe, who was struck by the profound loneliness of being near people but not with them.

Chloe wasn't stupid. She understood that every prank had an element of cruelty, even when it was as silly as replacing Lindor truffles with cherry tomatoes and wrapping them back up in their fancy papers, retwisting the cellophane ends (which her mother had done once). When you're expecting a chocolate and you get a tomato, it's crushing. There's a moment when you feel so exposed, so vulnerable. She remembered the utterly confusing taste of the sour tomato in her mouth, spitting it out and then furiously scraping at her tongue with her hand. She hadn't yet noticed her mother standing there with her hand pressed to her lips, shaking silently.

Her mother laughed out loud when Chloe hurled a handful of the Lindor cherry tomatoes at her. *IT'S NOT FUNNY, MOTHER,* she'd yelled. But then later, when her mother had brought out the stash of unwrapped chocolates hidden in a cereal bowl in the cabinet, the two of them stood side by side eating them: the astonishing pleasure of rolling a single chocolate around in her mouth, sucking on it, trying not to dent it with her teeth. The soft delicious gooey center. Before each chocolate, they tried to guess its flavor until her mother sighed and said she should get back to work. She always had to get back to work.

We weren't paying attention when Chloe started to cry.

CLAPP INVITATIONAL: OCTOBER 10

Danielle

THERE'S A GUY IN A RED CAP STANDING ON THE EDGE OF THE TRAIL and calling out "Six thirty-two, thirty-three, thirty-four, six thirty-five!" Somehow Danielle's not where she usually is, she's already at the first mile marker. Who the fuck made this course? For a moment she's worried she's taken a short cut from the starting line to the first mile, but no, there are girls out in front. She doesn't glance over her shoulder. That would be a sign of weakness. "Thirty-eight, thirty-nine." And now the guy's behind her, and she's not even silently cursing him and the numbers are climbing and receding at the same time until the only thing she hears is her own breathing. Normally she would think, You're going to pay the piper for going out too fast, Dani, but she's not thinking anything, she's just hurtling through the second mile, picking off girls in front of her, their ponytails wagging like the tails of friendly dogs. She's in the zone, a term she's always found suspiciously mystical and annoyingly vague, like the phrase, "I'll know it when I see it." Totally lame.

The second mile climbs up a hill, then disappears into the New England woods that she used to love but not anymore. Not since the summer of the bats.

The trail narrows, trees on both sides. The girl in front of her—a Silly, Silly Sawyer—that's funny—Silly, Silly Sawyer—Danielle barely registers that she's Sawyer's third-best runner—is suddenly blocking her way, and without deciding what she's going to do, Danielle eases up on her right shoulder, pushing her left without laying a finger on her, until the Sawyer girl is pinned between a tangle of bushes and Danielle, and the girl has no choice except to step off the trail, allowing Danielle to fly on by. And then there's another figure up ahead. What luck! It's easier to keep it going when there's someone to beat. She turns it up a notch, her legs whirling effortlessly beneath her. Pulling closer, Danielle sees that not only is it a Frostie, it's Kristin—What the fuck?!—Kristin went out fast. She should be up with the front runners, not back here. Danielle's best is Kristin's average, but suddenly Danielle's two steps behind her, and it's not because she's running so fast, though she is; it's because Kristin is slowing down.

The path is too narrow for Danielle to pull up beside her. "Hey," she just manages to say. "Keep going."

They tried talking to Kristin after Chloe's prank—she and Harriet did—and Kristin kept insisting that she was fine, she was just tired, she had mountains of work, and she hadn't been getting enough sleep. It had nothing to do with the stupid rabbit puppet. "You can bite me again if it will make you feel better," Harriet joked, and Kristin blanched, her bottom lip quivering, tears leaking from her eyes. It was bewildering.

They're both panting. It's hard to tell where her breath ends and Kristin's begins. If the path were wider, she'd take Kristin's hand, and they'd run like that—just for a few steps, just for Kristin to feel a surge of power, the strength of their camaraderie. Danielle pulling, Kristin pushing. They are so much more than individuals. They are a team, one body with a will of its own. If they can stick together until they're out of the woods, then Kristin can turn it up again. And Danielle will tuck in right behind her for as long as she's capable.

"You're strong," Danielle hisses through her ragged breath. "Keep going."

Kristin steps off the path, and Danielle runs by her, like water finding a suddenly clear way through rocks. This is not Kristin, suddenly yielding her lead, giving up. Danielle wants to stop, but years of running have taught her she can't. Not in the middle of a race. Not when there's so much at stake. She doesn't even look back to make sure that Kristin is there.

Normally she doesn't drink alone. At least she waits until five to open a bottle of wine. That's respectable, though sometimes her dad jokes, "It's always five p.m. somewhere." Her common room is empty, the Darlings off doing whatever regular people do on Saturdays. Half a pot of cold tea sits on the table next to a box of shortbread cookies. She eats one, and then another, though they don't go especially well with red wine. Chocolate would be better. She pours herself more wine, just half a glass. With each sip, her brain get fuzzier, like penciled words being gradually erased on a piece of paper, and her lips turn up into an involuntary smile. Her torso fills with warm stones, and she forgets about her long limbs. It's the kind of wine that makes her feel all the surfaces of her mouth, not just her tongue, and works its way up pleasantly into her nose.

No one answers Harriet's number. "Are you there?" she asks when the answering machine clicks on. "Hello, hello." She pictures two small bodies pressed together in Harriet's single bed, then she shakes the image from her mind because it seems creepy, like thinking about penises during church, which occasionally happened when she was in high school. "Hairy, I really need to talk to you. So call me as soon as you get this. OK?"

Kristin isn't home, either. "Hey," she says after waiting for what seems like forever between Kristin's message and the beep. "It sounds like you need to delete some messages. Listen, I'm sorry you had a bad race today, but remember it's just one race. It really doesn't matter. We all have bad races. The thing you need to do . . ." Suddenly the machine beeps again, cutting her off. She sighs and pours herself some more wine.

She calls Chloe.

"Why are you calling me?" Chloe asks.

"Jesus, Chloe, can't I call you?"

"Sure, but you never do."

"That's true, but I just wanted to see how you're doing."

"I'm fine," Chloe says. "How are you?"

She wants to kill Chloe sometimes. She's like talking to a fourth-grader.

"Well, I just wanted to tell you that you ran a good race today," Danielle says.

"Thanks," Chloe says.

This is just making her feel worse, so she hangs up.

After she's had enough to drink, a walk seems like a good idea. Maybe if Assistant Coach is in his office, they can have a drink together and figure out what went wrong today, even though they've never ever done that before. But there's a first for everything, she thinks brightly. Gathering up her stuff, she makes her way outside. It's colder than it was earlier, so she heads back inside to get her coat, but she has locked herself out, her key forgotten in the backpack that she took the meet today. Shit. She pulls her sleeves over hands. It's still light out, and the campus seems curiously quiet. It takes her a moment to realize it's dinner time and she's forgotten to eat. She crosses the freshman quad and walks quickly to the War Memorial. No one is admiring the view of the playing fields and beyond them the woods, a tapestry of beautiful colors, though Danielle stops to take another sip of wine straight from the bottle, its warmth spreading through her chest now. It's so pretty here.

The gym is empty, Assistant Coach's office dark. Why would he be here on a Saturday night? Why is Danielle? It's quiet, except for the sound of a ball bouncing, the squeak of shoes. The hallways are lined with black-and-white photographs of men in stiff formal arrangements, not quite real. She drinks more wine, happy she has a second bottle in her purse. The swimmers look like they'd drown in the woolen swimsuits they're wearing. The football players all have center parts in their dark shiny hair, and something about their expressions seems bemused, like the joke's on Danielle all these years later. You think Frost wants women? They're wearing belts and dangerous-looking leather boots.

As she continues down the hallway, the uniforms get shorter, more recognizable. The photographs are in color now. Cheeks flush pink, and hair turns from black and gray to red, blond, brown, and shiny black. There's long hair, a handful of afros, especially in the late '60s. But it's all men until 1976.

She's looked at these photos before, but not like she is now, not studying them.

The girls in those early years wear their faces like goalies' masks.

AWOL

THIS WAS HOW WE SURVIVED THE FINAL 400: BY STRIKING TINY BAR-gains with ourselves.

Accelerate with each step, finish strong, and you can eat a spoonful of crushed Oreos and blackberries on your fat-free fro-zen yogurt. Or you can squander twenty minutes in the periodi-cal room reading *People*. Or you can shave your legs twice and slather on lemon verbena lotion pilfered from your roommate. Or you can power-nap.d

Or don't think at all.

Fix the finish line in your sights. Let your head float away from your body. Let your body do its thing. Don't think. Just do.

Or practice magical thinking. Be superstitious. Choose some-thing that has nothing to do with running—a petty jealousy, your psych mid-term, something that you're trying to forget—and tell yourself if you are strong enough to sprint the last 400, then you are strong enough to ignore the jealousy gnawing at your heart or ace your test. Forget every last bit of everything that happened over the summer. Or tell yourself if you beat Kristin in today's practice, you will definitely fly by her in next week's race.

We struck totally illogical bargains with ourselves, and as long as they worked, what did it matter?

In the background, Coach was barking out commands, and Assistant Coach was urging us to empty our tanks, *it's time to empty your tanks, ladies. This is where you shift into a higher gear. Pedal to the metal, ladies.*

The third time the pack caught and swallowed Kristin and then left her behind, Coach pulled her aside, steering her away from the rest of us. We could see him talking to her, but we couldn't hear what he was saying. Danielle wanted to go find out what was happening, but Assistant Coach called her back to the line.

And this was how we choked: by forgetting how to do the thing we'd always done without a moment's thought. It wasn't about being passed in the final half-mile of a 5K race—that could happen anytime, that happened all the time, that was the brutal essence of competition—the scary part was losing control. Doubt worming its way into your head, finding a comfortable spot, and curling up, and on a hill in the middle of an easy run, your arms bunched up like a small child's, and your stride slowed to a shuffle and then crept to a walk.

Our shared recurring nightmare? It's the last 400 on a grassy straightaway, and when we try to kick it in—to fly toward the finish line—nothing happens. Legs like overcooked spaghetti. No matter how hard we try, we can't make our legs work, can't push off the ground. It's like trying to run across a sheet of ice. Like running on air.

Dusk was overtaking the day.

Assistant Coach called us back. "Line up, ladies. Let's go.

Pedal to the metal."

Always ladies.

Also machines.

We fanned out. Coach and Kristin were two dark dots floating toward the stairs as Assistant Coach sliced through the night with his arm, and we lurched forward like a small regiment of wind-up toys, running until our springs had sprung.

After that, Kristin was gone. First one day, then a second.

It wasn't totally surprising. If you were having a hard time—if you were choking, if you'd bonked in a race or your life just generally sucked—then it could be wise to skip a practice. And Kristin had done pretty badly at the last race. Not terribly, certainly. But Chloe and Liv had beaten her by a lot, and Danielle had slipped by Kristin by having the race of her life. Patricia was close enough to smell Kristin's fear, or so she told Chloe. "You play the devil and the devil will bite you back," Patricia said, and Chloe had no idea what she meant. She couldn't wait to tell her parents she was back in the top spot.

Two years earlier, Liv, whose calm personality did not match her flaming red hair, who we loved because she was more Life Saver than Laffy Taffy, all-American Liv who seemed like a model Frost student had weathered some big drama with her roommate Mel. Rumor was Mel had refused to leave their room for three weeks, except to go down the hallway to the bathroom because Liv put her foot down when Mel tried to pee into a bottle. (Have you tried it? We had, on long drives to meets when we were too embarrassed to ask Coach to pull over for a bathroom break. It's difficult to manage without major spillage.) And then she locked Liv out of their room one morning, and Liv had to slash the screen to get back in. She carried Mel to health services. Except halfway across the main quad, she lost her grip on Mel and dropped her.

"Shit," Mel cried out. "That hurt."

It was 10:45, morning classes just out. Liv stood there, waiting for someone to stop and ask whether she needed help. But no one did. She realized that Mel was wearing a long nightgown and furry pink slippers, her hair a tumbleweed around her head from weeks without a shower. Of course, no one stopped. No one wanted to lift you up and carry you when you actually needed it.

"You need to stand up," Liv said. "You need to walk."

"No, I don't," Mel said. "I'm not going anywhere."

No one knew exactly what happened to Mel, only that Liv didn't come to practice for four days after that.

On Tuesday, Chloe looked for Kristin at breakfast. They were both early risers, both solitary creatures. Chloe wanted to tell Kristin she was sorry about the puppet. It wasn't anything personal, or not that personal. She was worried that she was to blame for Kristin's struggles.

Once, when Chloe was in second grade, she had impulsively moved her friend Jenny's chair so that when Jenny sat down, she went crashing to the floor. "Ow, my bum bum is broken," the girl said because *butt* was considered a bad word and *ass* was totally off-limits. Outside the principal's office, where Chloe sat waiting on a floral couch, she wondered whether the principal was going to send her home, and if he did, whether her parents would come and pick her up. Not her dad, of course. He was at work. But maybe her mom, except that she was often too deep in her writing to answer the phone. But instead, Dr. Bright asked her why on earth she'd done it. His question took her by surprise, and she said nothing for the longest time. "Chloe," Dr. Bright ask. He wore cardigan sweaters just like Mr. Rogers. "Umm," she said, "the chair hopped into my hands?"

Would Kristin understand that there was a flawed place in Chloe's heart that kept letting chairs hop into Chloe's hands? And also that she was a little bit mad at Kristin for socking her in the middle of a race? Who wouldn't be?

But Kristin never materialized, which was strange. Chloe couldn't remember the last time she and Kristin hadn't exchanged awkward hellos standing in front of the skim-milk dispenser.

After practice on Wednesday, Danielle and Harriet went to Kristin's dorm on the off chance of finding her there. Grove (aka the Monastery), which is where Kristin lived that year, drew a mix of seriously brainy folks and serious potheads who functioned better with regularly administered tokes and a few who fell into both categories. How Kristin ended up living there was a mystery, except if you took into account that all the rooms were singles and Kristin was an introvert, according to Danielle.

At the entrance to the low-slung brick building, which had once housed the college infirmary, Danielle suddenly felt sick. A long time ago, she had vowed that she would never set foot in the Monastery again, but here she was.

"Dani?" Harriet said. "*Mon Dieu,* you're as pale as a ghost. Are you OK?" She was at Danielle's side, stroking her arm. "Are you feeling sick?"

"Low blood sugar, I think. I just need some food," she said, swallowing the promises she made herself once upon a time. She couldn't change the past, but she could control the present.

Inside, the long hallway was empty, except for the overwhelming smells of pot and air freshener. Danielle had a vague memory of racing up and down this very same hallway on a ten- speed with a wobbly front tire and a bright orange flag on the back. It was some kind of drinking game, the object to get obliterated under the pretense of having fun. That was always the point. Suddenly, she could picture herself climbing onto the bike with B, holding fast to his chest while he stood on the pedals and readied to pump her. And then they were off, weaving back and forth until they collided with a wall. That was freshman year. She sighed.

Kristin's room was at the far end of the hallway. They knew they'd reached it when they spotted the photo of the Tarahumara, a tribe of Indians who lived in Copper Canyon in Mexico and were famous for their long-distance running abilities. As impressive, they ran barefoot or in crude sandals and wore fancy embroidered shirts and white shorts that sort of looked like saggy diapers. The photo, which had been hanging in Kristin's locker last year, had prompted a long discussion about whether it was an example of cultural appropriation. Without knowing a lot more about the customs of the Tarahumara, was this not an instance of exoticizing the Other, Harriet asked? We snickered. Danielle said the same could be said of most art. And Patricia pronounced the Tarahumara cool. "Running barefoot is boss," she said. "I think we should all try it," and for a couple of days Patricia did until Coach ordered to put her shoes back on, or she was going to get injured.

Harriet knocked. "Kristin?" she called out, and then knocked even harder. "Are you there?" She pressed her ear to the door. "Do you hear something?" Danielle listened and shook her head. Then Harriet put her hand on Kristin's doorknob.

"Do you think that's a good idea?" Danielle asked.

Harriet paused. "I don't know. But what if something happened to her?"

A guy in a blue baseball hat emerging from the room next to

Kristin's made Danielle practically jump out of her skin.

"Dani," Harriet said. "Are you sure you're OK?"

Danielle nodded. He was just a guy. He didn't look at them, let alone say hello. That was college: learning how to look away.

The door wasn't locked, which was normal for Frost. We were one big happy family. Harriet pushed it open just a little and peered through a three-inch crack. "Mon Dieu," she whispered, and Danielle felt herself start to shake. "What is it?" Danielle said. "You have to see," Harriet said. Danielle slid her chin onto the top of Harriet's head and found herself peering into a completely empty room. Except for a single red pillow, it didn't look like anyone was living there. There was nothing: not a dresser, not a desk. Nothing on the floors. Nothing on the walls. No books. Just the bed and the standard gray garbage can.

"Did she leave?" Danielle whispered.

"I don't know," Harriet said. "Maybe she never moved in?"

"This is so unlike her," Danielle declared, though as soon as the words were out of her mouth, she thought about how complicated people were, how, as soon as you thought you had someone pinned down, they'd go and do something utterly out of character. Generalizations were essential—she knew that, the brain could only handle so much detail. But they were also misleading.

Harriet and Danielle stepped back into the hallway and stared at each other, and for once, both of those know-it-alls who always had something to say found themselves at a loss for words.

On Thursday morning, before they'd even rolled out of bed, Henry and Liv fought about whether Liv should go to the dean to report Kristin missing. They both knew that Liv was thinking about Mel, about what happened to Mel that day when Liv tried to carry her all the way to health services, but couldn't, and stood there helplessly on the main quad, beseeching Mel to get up and walk, please walk, Mel, please, please, please, you can lean on me, I'll help you, but Mel wouldn't budge. But they couldn't talk about it because they disagreed about the outcome. Henry thought Mel was crazy, while Liv believed that if only Mel had walked to health services, then she could have started seeing a counselor and gotten her shit together while doing the bare minimum to avoid flunking out of Frost, but instead an ambulance rolled up and carried her away to a hospital. The last time Liv saw Mel, she was sitting in a pastel-pink room working on a jigsaw puzzle of a sunset. The old Mel would have mimed sticking a finger down her throat and clearing out the vomit, but the new Mel just smiled pleasantly and invited Liv to help her find all of the edge pieces. Later, she offered Liv some grape juice.

College, Liv had come to believe, was the place where parents sent their kids to fuck up so they didn't have to watch it happen themselves. They thought someone else was watching, just in case their kids really threw themselves into the deep end, but no one was watching, at least no one who knew what to do.

This was reconfirmed when Liv, at Henry's insistence, marched off to see the dean. He offered her licorice tea, listened attentively to her concerns while stroking his beardless chin, and then told her there was nothing they could do since Kristin was an adult and adults had the right to disappear. The difference between "lying low" and "going missing," he said, putting air quotes around the two terms in question, was tricky. But in his twenty years, no one had vanished. He smiled smugly. What about Mel? Liv thought bitterly.

Because it was a small campus, reports of sightings drifted in:

some probable, some harder to believe. The guys' captain might have seen Kristin treading water in the pool, but it was impossible to be sure since the observation windows were steamy, and everyone looked seal-like and the same in a swim cap. A freshman named Grace, who would eventually go on to become captain but at that point was still a sheep trying to distinguish herself from the herd of freshman, claimed that Kristin had been to a performance of Last Man Standing, the improv group on campus. But it seemed highly unlikely that she'd choose avant-garde comedy to cheer herself up. Her tastes, as far as we understood them, ran toward MTV, still a novelty to her since she'd grown up without cable and only got to watch music videos at sleepovers. Other rumors: she'd maybe been at the regular Wednesday-night theater party where the drama kids played a drinking game called "Silly Charades" that involved taking a shot every time one team failed to guess correctly; she was holed up in the sub-basement of the library, writing her first paper for Professor Saunders, a notoriously hard grader; she'd been spotted with her friend Eli, the hobbit, walking away from the bagel shop in town (possible); she'd joined the Zoo crew on one of their full-moon nude bicycle rides across campus (never; it took Kristin a year before she was comfortable enough to change out of her running bra in front of us); she showed up in the faculty dining room with an intriguing young poli-sci professor with a handlebar mustache (we wished—we needed some juicy gossip!).

Then, there was the report from a friend of one of Harriet's friends who thought she had spotted a girl who looked like Kristin sitting by herself at one of the long tables in the Terminal. No one sat alone in the Terminal. Only losers sat alone in the Terminal. Harriet's friend's friend told Harriet that she'd hurried over to make sure the person who looked like Kristin was OK because it was not OK to sit alone in the Terminal—bad things could happen, like football players farting as they passed by your table. And then it became clear why she was there all by herself. Orbiting her spot were dozens of dinner plates and glasses, surrounded by smaller constellations of salad plates and soup bowls, coffee cups and saucers (yes, Frost still had saucers, though no one used them for anything except ashing cigarettes). All were clean. "'Oh hello,' Kristin had said," Harriet told us. "Would you like a bite of chocolate cake?" She waved a fork. "It's German chocolate. My absolute favorite."

"Wait, what?" Patricia said, and Harriet had to explain the whole thing all over again, and then Patricia said, "That's ass-out bonkers."

We had a meet the next day.

Danielle's common room was dark, the curtains drawn, as though we were holding a secret meeting, but it was just that Danielle was too distracted to play her usual role of hostess. There was no tea, there were no candles burning, no soothing words of self-visualization or loud music to get us psyched up. There was just Danielle obsessively picking at her nails, a losing proposition since she was just moving the dirt from under one nail to the tip of another. It was painful to watch. But also mesmerizing.

"What do you think, Hair?" Danielle asked. "Do you think she was actually eating alone in the Terminal?"

"I don't know," Harriet said. "It's probably just a rumor."

Danielle sighed.

"It doesn't matter," Chloe said. "I'm running well, and Liv's on fire."

Liv let out a little laugh before blushing to the color of her hair.

"If the five of us—" Chloe continued.

Danielle interrupted her. "We placed third in the last meet,

Chloe. We went from first in the meet before to third in this one. We won't go to Nationals without Kristin."

"I'm not saying that we don't need her," Chloe said. "I'm legitimately worried about her, too. I'm just saying—"

"We need Kristin," Danielle repeatedly emphatically. "To go to Nationals, we need her."

"Please stop interrupting me," Chloe said. When we were angry, we became exceedingly polite. "I'm just saying that we're strong, with or without Kristin. Isn't Coach always telling us it's not about a single runner? It's about the depth of the team. We can't give up just because Kristin is having a hard time. We still have a shot at Nationals."

"We know what you're saying," Danielle said, her voice rising a little. "But you don't have a lot of credibility right now."

"I'm sorry," Chloe cried. "I already said I was sorry about the puppet. Are you blaming me?"

Danielle said nothing, and the silence that followed was painful. It was as excruciating as standing in line for the weekly weigh-in or realizing midway through a class presentation on Herman Melville and homosocial desire that you weren't making sense, your words tangling around your tongue, tighter and tighter. We had read Deborah Tannen; we knew we had a low tolerance for long pauses; we knew that, as women, we had been socialized to be supportive listeners. But knowing this did nothing to slow our ever-quickening hearts.

Finally, Harriet piped up. "We're not blaming you, Chloe, but I don't think you can really claim that our egos aren't involved. I mean, come on. If you were really all *rah rah go team go,* you wouldn't have played the joke on Kristin. But the fact is you want to beat Kristin. Just like Kristin wants to beat you. And Liv wants to beat both of you."

Liv turned crimson again and opened her mouth to protest

before Patricia interrupted her. "What about me?" Patricia asked.

"You go screaming by me every week," Harriet said, pulling her knees to her chest and resting her chin there. "And who knows what will happen when you're a junior? Who knows who you'll be running down?"

"We need Kristin," Danielle repeated, standing now, her hands on her hips, looming over us as though we were preschoolers. "We have to stick together, even though we also have to push each other. If each of us does her best, then we'll all run faster. Just like what Harriet said." Danielle smiled in Harriet's direction.

Did Harriet let out an inaudible sigh? Did she roll her eyes? It was nearly too dark to tell. Danielle had a special gift for translating competition into camaraderie.

In the meantime, though, it didn't matter if we agreed with Danielle, if we loathed Chloe, if we envied Harriet for speaking her mind: nothing changed the fact that Kristin was gone, and we had no idea where to find her.

THIS AND THAT

Kristin

WITH NOTHING ELSE TO DO, KRISTIN MAKES A LIST OF EVERYTHING IN the abandoned house: broken beer bottles, a wall calendar from 1976, a set of three nesting cast-iron frying pans, an ironing board, four Trojan wrappers and a single used condom, the last item a sight so repulsive that she pulls her sleeve over her hand and picks it up along with the empty wrappers, waiting for the cover of darkness to sneak to the garbage can near the tennis courts and throw them away. An old red couch with busted springs where she is presently sitting and writing her list. A surprisingly nice coffee table shaped like a . . . She studies the table where she's resting her feet. Like a surfboard? Or a coffin? She recaps her pen. What's the point? The point is there's no point. The point was just to take a break, initially for a day or two, though it's already Friday (unless she's lost track), which means it's been three days. First, she totally bonked in the race, then she couldn't finish the speed workout. On Tuesday morning Eli walked her to the house. Where else could she go? Her foot jerks involuntarily, the way it sometimes does when she's drifting off to sleep, though she's not, and the coffee cup, probably stolen from the cafeteria, clunks over, spilling cigarette butts across the table. The smell is immediate: like hot asphalt and burned metal. She coughs. There is mouse poop in the corners, the bodies of wrecked flies on the windowsills. She almost feels sorry for them. It's not nice to be trapped, to see where you want to go without having a way to get there.

Eli has shown up at the back door each of the past three nights. He's got peanut-butter-and-jelly sandwiches wrapped in napkins, Styrofoam cups of salad, apples and bananas. She keeps meaning to tell him that she doesn't like Granny Smiths; they're too tart. He brings coffee in old Snapple bottles, packets of powdered creamer and sugar. She's furious with herself for getting addicted, and yet she's so relieved every time she sees that he hasn't forgotten the coffee. He talks to her in a fake-cheerful voice, like she's a dog or a toddler, even though he's the one who told her she could get into the old house at the top of the orchard through the bulkhead. It was never locked. She could spend the night there if she really needed to get away. When he steps forward to hug her before he leaves, she shrinks back. "I stink," she says, waving her hands in front of her. He has stopped saying, "Look at you," which tells her exactly how she looks.

This is definitely the weirdest thing she's ever done. She thinks it's a hopeful sign that she recognizes its weirdness. Sure, she was struggling before, but she was holding it together, and then the letter came, and she wasn't.

If only she'd just torn up the letter instead of reading it. She could be so stupid. She *was* so stupid.

At the beginning of the semester, she made a deal with herself *à la* Danielle. She ripped a piece of paper out of a notebook and wrote, "I will be fine." But that wasn't good enough. If it were going to be true, she needed proof, so she crossed it out and wrote, "If I'm the best on the team, I will be fine." Then she lit a candle and watched the paper burn. It was better than eating it, which she had also considered.

And it had worked until it hadn't. And she couldn't blame the dying baby bunny, and she couldn't really blame Chloe, though when Chloe overtook her in the last meet, when Chloe sailed by her before the first mile mark, and Kristin's thread didn't hold, when Kristin realized that Chloe wasn't pulling her along, and Kristin wasn't pushing Chloe forward, when she understood that Chloe was in her own world and didn't care how crucial it was for Kristin to be the best, when Kristin understood that she was all alone, then she was back in the mountains right at the moment when she realized she had wandered off the trail. She was hiking in the dark, and the dots on the trees were invisible. Who could she blame but herself?

"Dude," Eli said to her on Tuesday night, "you've got to get your head screwed on."

She couldn't tell him what was wrong. It was too embarrassing. If she told him, the first thing he'd ask would be, "Why did you go backpacking with him? Not that I know what backpacking is." Eli would add that last bit to lighten the mood, because really he'd be thinking, Why on earth would you go off with that creep?

Because she should have known, right? The signs were all there. He showed up at her house in the middle of the night and threw pebbles at her window to wake her up, and she thought it was romantic, but really it was creepy. And he told her to dress

up, because no one IDed a girl who looked as hot as she did, and
he took her to bars and bought her Jacks neat. That was creepy,
too, or was it? Wasn't it sort of cool? Who didn't want to go to
dive bars? But was it also creepy? He showed her how to slide the
cue through the valley of her thumb and index finger. "Feel this,"
he said, inviting her to stroke a callus on the inside of his knuckle,
which was proof of what a pool shark he was, and when she remembered this, she could hear the sound of the cue ball rolling
across the green felt, the bright pock of it kissing another ball, the
cheerful noise of Jed racking, and her own heart jumping frantically around in her chest. And she went backpacking with him,
because she thought it was romantic, like the most romantic offer
she'd ever gotten, but she should have known, right? She wanted
to have an adventure.

"Can't screw on my head until I find it," she told Eli. They
exchanged a smirk. Eli was so cute. Why was she so dumb?

She was running so fast. Shouldn't that have mattered? But then
his letter arrived, and he didn't even acknowledge what had happened, let alone say he was sorry, and she felt lost all over again.
Because really what was the difference between getting lost and
almost getting lost? She'd threaded her way through the empty
spaces between the trees for at least an hour until she came to a
creek. It was barely light enough for her to see that this wasn't
where they had crossed the creek the day before. Without a
bridge, there was no way for her to get to the other side. Unless
she tried to walk across a log or jump from rock to rock.

She was the fastest, and then she read the letter, and she
wasn't. And because she couldn't unburn the piece of paper
where she'd written, "If I'm the best on the team, I will be fine,"
and she couldn't unsee the baby rabbit just beneath her foot or

unhear the horrible sound it made or undo everything else she had done that she now regretted, like hitting Chloe and biting Harriet, she had to think of something else to do, and she asked Eli to help her move all the furniture out her room. Not the bed. It would be too unwieldly to maneuver into the basement.

"What are you going for? Minimalism?" His face lit up with the hint of a smile. Why did she care that he wasn't taller than she was?

"Just a fresh start,"

"May I ask why?"

"You may," she said.

He laughed and stroked his goatee. "Being difficult I see. Why do you need a fresh start?"

"I'm not sure exactly," she paused. "I need to focus."

He looked puzzled.

"I was running really well," she said.

"Tubs Player of the Week," he said in his shmaltzy voice. "I'm still waiting for the dinner invite."

"But now I'm not," she said. "I lost."

"You didn't lose," he said. "Didn't you say you'd finished fourth for the team?"

"That's worse than losing," she said.

He looked confused. "And you think this will help?"

For several nights, she slept under the bed in her empty room, and she thought she was better but then she wasn't. Then she got lost again. The pack kept catching her, even though she was the rabbit and it was her job to stay out in front.

And now it's Friday night, and maybe it's not so funny anymore that she's still hiding in the farmhouse. She tries not to think about how many classes she's missed. With struggle comes strength, she tells herself. In running, pain is the path forward. She'd be lying if she claimed she liked pain's outer edge, but she doesn't fear it, either. She pushes through it. That's what runners do. They meet it, and it makes them stronger.

Eli is at the back door. Shave and a haircut, two bits.

"Dude," he says as he pushes down the fur-lined hood of his parka. "Are you staying dry in there?"

"It's watertight." Not quite true, but close enough. She wasn't out in the worst of today's rain, not like her teammates who she watched plodding up the last bit of hill, as pathetic as waterlogged cats, Patricia and Chloe with nothing over their running bras. "Aren't you a little overdressed?" she asks.

"I really think . . ." he starts.

She gives him the hand.

"No, listen. Hear me out," he says. "This is a ridiculous situation. I'll pay for you to stay in a motel. I mean, my parents will pay for it."

"That's so nice," she says.

"My dad was like, 'Who is this young lady?'" Eli is leaning against door frame, grinning. "He's thrilled to imagine me shacking up . . ."

She interrupts him. "I'm going to be fine."

"I was just joking," he insists. "You know that, right?"

There's no bathroom on the first floor of the house, and she's afraid to venture up to the second floor because several of the stairs are missing their treads. The last thing she needs to do is hurt herself.

"What's pooping in the woods for a couple more days?" she asks, and Eli looks horrified. "I'm joking," she says repeating what Eli just said. "You get that, right?"

And then it's Saturday morning, and her shoes are still wet from yesterday. She went out for a run around noon before it really started raining hard. It's hard to believe that Coach sent the team out in the worst of yesterday's downpour. He isn't cruel, though he can be single-minded. She was psyching herself out, he told her as he led her away from the interval practice on Monday—which seems like ages ago. "It will just get worse, the more it happens. Once you think someone can beat you, they will. Your body begins to believe what it experiences. It remembers." She wanted to glance back at her team and somehow let them know that she wasn't abandoning them. Something was temporarily wrong with her body. She loved to run. Really loved it. I'm sorry, she longed to call out. But sorry for what?

"Kristin." It always sounded more like *Christine.* "The stick only works until it breaks."

How could she explain that she was no longer sure she was as strong as she once thought? She was so dependent on this. When she ran, she felt so good, like she was invincible. Running had given her this, which she imagined to be a gift. Was it so wrong to see herself as powerful, to take pleasure in her body's speed, to trust its capacity to carry her from danger? If only she'd known what was going to happen, she could have run away. She could have easily beaten him, even in the dark, even in bare feet. He had a blister the size of a nickel on his heel from the stupid cowboy boots he was hiking in.

But now she knows: speed is not enough.

I'm sorry you got so cold, but you weren't really in danger of dying.

She can't quite bring herself to believe that.

"Once you find your way back," Coach told her the other day, "you'll be back."

In the kitchen, she strikes a match to light the oven. There is a refrigerator without a door, presumably to keep children from shutting themselves inside and suffocating. A dressmaker's dummy that made her jump with fright the first time she ventured in to see whether the sink worked. Who puts a dressmaker's dummy in a kitchen?

Has she become this kind of girl, the danger-everywhere kind of girl? She'd rather be dead.

"What happened?" Eli keeps asking. "I'm worried."

Yes is braver than no.

Isn't that what she's spent her whole life learning?

Yes was the girl running until she had a stress fracture in her hip, yes was going to college all by herself, with duffle bags that weighed twice as much as she did, yes was trails above Boise, the smell of cottonwoods when the route dipped down into a ravine, yes was choosing Frost when her mom asked didn't she want to stay closer to home, yes was the ERA bracelet and her mom being one of four women in her law school class, yes was the answer to "Is it just you and your mom?" Yes was running on hot days and snowy days, welts on her hips from the cold, yes was the curvy road into the mountains, diving into the lake. Yes is being fearless. Being fast. Being proud of being fast. Not being ashamed.

She doesn't even have the energy to clean up the spilled cigarettes.

Once, in fourth or fifth grade—when the other girls in her class banded together and singled her out for teasing, nicknaming her *road runner*—she pretended to trade places with herself. The Kristin who was becoming self-conscious, who was beginning to see that getting older meant feeling scrutinized by others, left earth for a short vacation, and in her place, her alien self, with a thicker skin, descended. Everything that hurt her lost its sting since she wasn't really there. She was watching from a distance.

Maybe she can do this now: rocket herself away?

She sticks her running shoes in the oven to dry. Her teammates are probably squeezing into the van right now. Are they wondering where she is? Or are they so angry they've forgotten her? She no longer sees the point of running a six-minute mile, which for her is like forgetting how to walk up a set of stairs, like standing at the bottom of a staircase and doing a handstand and thinking that's the way to tackle them. Above her, something small runs back and forth.

"Goodbye," she calls out, willing hope into her voice. "I'll be back when things are better."

PART II

ALL THE BEARS
YOU CANNOT SEE

WEIRDLY ENOUGH, ONE OF THE FIRST THINGS KRISTIN NOTICED WAS his Adam's apple, firm and round, its smooth movement up and down his neck as he drank a glass of water, which he always did before taking his first sip of coffee. He was J. Crew handsome, she thought, but not preppy, with tousled brown hair, a square jaw, and friendly green eyes. He was always wearing jeans, even on hot days, a dark T-shirt, scuffed-up cowboy boots. He came into the espresso bar where she worked, planted himself on a stool at the counter, and made her laugh. When the shop was quiet, which was most of the time because espresso was a newfangled thing in Boise, he told stories about being a river guide and ordered complicated drinks that didn't appear on the menu and that she suspected he was inventing on the spot to give her something to do. They had funny names like the *jitterbug* and the *masochist*. His name was Jed, and he found it scandalous that she worked in a coffee shop but didn't drink coffee.

"How can you possibly be qualified to dispense caffeine if you don't imbibe it yourself?" he said.

It was he who convinced her to tiptoe toward addiction by making herself a mocha, which, of course, she loved because of the amount of chocolate and sugar required to mask the coffee's bitterness. "You've ruined me," she told him.

"Wait until you try an iced mocha," he said, giving her his little half-smile that made her scalp tingle.

She mostly wasn't weird about food, was trying hard not to be like Harriet, very consciously resisting the urge to be competitive about how disciplined she could be, was always trying to channel her mother who had never once gone on a diet while Kristin was a child and teenager, who was slender but not skinny, who had passed on the big-boob gene to Kristin, and still wore clingy tank tops, and even halter tops, because she'd come of age in the '60s and '70s, when a tight T-shirt and flares were the uniform. Kristin's mom's rule was: everything in moderation, including moderation. One Christmas she ate a whole box of fudge with walnuts, a holiday gift from another partner in the firm, or rather his wife. And yet, Kristin couldn't deny that she liked the feeling of hunger.

After she tried the mocha and the iced mocha—Jed was right, iced mochas were divine, especially at the end of her shift before she stepped into the furnace of a summer afternoon—she decided she'd let herself drink one every Wednesday. It wasn't mostly about the calories or her boobs, her child-bearing hips or big husky thighs, but of course the decision was shaped by how she saw herself. It was impossible not to compare yourself to other women, and in college that habit had just intensified, especially because suddenly she wasn't the top runner anymore. She had to work to keep up. She had to *want* to beat Chloe and Liv, and she had to accept that they wanted to beat her. It wasn't like Boise High where her teammates came through the finish line a minute or two after her, and she was always there cheering them on, not because she was such a great sport, or a gracious winner, though that's what people said, but because the second- and third-place runners posed no real threat. When she sensed Chloe or Liv on her heels, when she could hear their footsteps, she forgot, for a moment, that it was a race. Instead, she was being chased. And when she could tap into her terror, she flew from them as though they were angry dogs with spit swinging from their chops. But when she couldn't, when her fear made her feel meek or paralyzed, Chloe or Liv would shoot by her like a bullet from a gun.

Drinking a mocha every Wednesday fit in with her love of rituals and treats. It was a way to brush over what she was denying herself. She would focus on what she was enjoying and would enjoy it more by not ruining it with habit. And anyway, that was the day when Jed came in and lingered. Hardly anyone was taking rafting trips that summer because the rivers were low after a curiously dry winter.

"It's the beginning of the end," Jed liked to say, raising a cup of joe, his muscles rippling underneath his T-shirt. He had broad shoulders and a trim waist. A hint of a strut when he came through the door and ambled up to the counter.

Kristin felt drugged. So far, she had managed to outrun desire. For as long as she could remember, her mom was always saying that she had the rest of her life to fall in love. Kristin often rolled her eyes at this, but she'd seen girls come undone over love, dropping friends and activities, obsessing over what they'd done or should have done. It just didn't seem worth it. Men are a lot of work, her mom always said, which Kristin found hilarious since her mom had been single for the past twenty years. How much work could her dad have been?

Kristin and Jed clinked glasses.

"Come here," he said.

"Come here," he demanded because evidently standing on the other side of the counter from him wasn't close enough. She leaned over, aware he was probably getting an eyeful of her cleavage peeking out of the top of the red apron she tied on every morning. "You've got a little foam here," and he took his thumb and rubbed it along her bottom lip. Then he touched her top lip. He smelled faintly of leather.

She smiled idiotically because she could think of nothing to say.

Kristin remembered the *exercises* she'd done in fifth or sixth grade, pressing her elbows back, drawing in her shoulder blades while thrusting her embarrassingly bony chest forward. "We must, we must, we must increase our bust." Did she do this alone? Or with Jenny, her oldest childhood friend? She begged her mother for a Playtex *Thank Goodness It Fits* bra that had no purpose except to make lines under her shirts, a crucial signal to others that she was wearing a bra, even though she didn't need one. And then suddenly they were there, no longer her future or a possibility, but the present. Nectarines and then peaches. Oranges. Grapefruits that swelled into small melons, like cantaloupes. Of course, her mother would say if they ever talked about it, which they didn't, the metaphors revealed how much she internalized society's way of seeing women. Like treats to be eaten. Her mother wouldn't even let her watch *The Facts of Life* or buy *Seventeen*. At first, her reason (besides the fact that magazines were a waste of money) was that Kristin wasn't seventeen, even though everyone knew that *Seventeen* ("It's Where the Girl Ends and the Woman Begins") was really meant for thirteen-year-old girls who couldn't wait to wear makeup and find their looks (groovy, tough, sleek, chic, creative, confident) and agonize over such problems as having two boys like them at the same time. If only she'd read the magazine, then Kristin would have learned how to tell whether a guy was interested or just friendly as well as "11 Surefire Ways to Ruin a Relationship." (Tip #5: Love him only when he's feeling cheerful and strong.")

"Your legs aren't even hairy," her mother said after finding a razor in Kristin's shower.

"That's because I just shaved them."

"Oh," her mother said. "Well, before that, I mean. I didn't think you had hairy legs."

"I'm sixteen," Kristin said. "Everyone shaves their legs. And I like how it feels. It makes me feel fast."

Her mother was wearing black tights with a long chenille sweater and a pair of tennis shoes that looked old but were not retro or cool. Her glasses sat on top of her head, holding back her messy brown hair. They were always buried there, except when she was reading something with tiny print or using them theatrically—waving them around to make a point or letting them slide to the tip of her nose and squinting through them. When Kristin made a dubious claim, she did both of these things. There were faint purple rings under her eyes and tiny hairs growing out of places on her face where they did not belong. She looked slightly deranged in an interesting way, Kristin thought, like a woman who talked to trees and ran from one place to another. She did not look like someone who cared what men thought. For as long as Kristin could remember, her mom had not been on a date.

She and Jed had a lot to talk about: rivers and national forests, the Sawtooths where Kristin had gone to cross country camp twice in high school. "How does that work?" Jed asked, a faint smile on his face. He had a way of looking amused, which made her talk faster. "Did you run all day?"

Kristin laughed. "Oh no, it was mostly fun. We went for a long run in the mornings. And then we just hung out. The camp was on a lake. We swam and tried not to tip over the canoes. We had spontaneous dance parties."

"Have you done any backpacking?" he asked.

"No," she said. "I'm dying to."

"Rafting?"

She shook her head.

"Kirstin," he said in a voice that suggested she had done something wrong.

"What?"

"It's a travesty that you haven't gone rafting," he said. "It's worse, dare I say it's even worse, than the fact that you are an espresso girl who doesn't drink espresso."

When she tried to interrupt him to defend herself, he clamped his hand over her mouth.

And then he started listing reasons that she'd love rafting (Number 4: You get to see parts of the wilderness only accessible from the river, places no one else will ever see). He'd much prefer to take her over the rich out-of-staters who signed up for his trips. They were nightmares, people who liked looking at nature more than they liked being in it. Sometimes clients on a rafting trip would complain about the weather. They didn't pay for rain. Couldn't they do something about the mosquitos? Where was all the wildlife? Shouldn't they be seeing bears?

He pretended like he wasn't going to let her move his hand from his face. She had to work at it, and when she was finally free, she was almost panting.

The door opened, the cowbell that the owners had hung to give the espresso bar a homey touch clanged, but Kristin didn't look up, she was laughing so hard at the story that Jed was telling about a woman on one trip who had expected bathrooms. "You want me to poop in the woods?" she had said. The next morning, she handed one of the guides a plastic bottle of urine as they were packing the rafts.

"How could she even pee in a bottle?" Kristin asked.

Jed raised his eyebrows and his lips twitched into another half-smile. "You tell me."

"Kristin?"

Kristin looked up, slightly annoyed to be interrupted, and there was her beloved high school biology teacher who got so excited talking about cell division that she punctuated her lectures by saying, "Science is a miracle," which always struck Kristin as a bit of an oxymoron.

"Mrs. D!"

"Your mom told me you were working here," said Mrs. D, her face lighting up with her smile. Dimples appeared in both cheeks. Everyone loved Mrs. D. She was so adorable. "How's Frost?"

"It's great. I'm an English major."

"I thought you were going to do geology."

"I was." She felt guilty admitting to Mrs. D that she was abandoning science for law, but she'd decided she wanted to follow in her mom's footsteps. She might even come back to Boise, where she could practice environmental law.

Mrs. D. scrunched up her nose. "Well, we miss you at Boise High. You still running?" her teacher said, rocking back and forth on her heels.

"Totally," Kristin said. "The women's team is really strong. We should have gone to Nationals last year. We just missed qualifying."

"But *you* qualified, right?"

"Yeah." Kristin blushed and glanced at Jed. His head was bent over the counter, and in front of him was a small piece of paper that he was writing on.

"And how'd you do?"

"I did OK," she said. All American was top 10, and she'd placed 16th. For some reason, she didn't want to tell Mrs. D this for fear she'd sound like she was bragging.

"Well, I hope you guys go all the way this fall," her teacher said. "It's a fall sport, right? I can never keep track."

"Yeah," Kristin said. "Oh my gosh, I didn't ask you what you want."

"What do you recommend?"

"I have to admit that I barely drink coffee." Kristin giggled.

"Good girl," Mrs. D said. "Better not to get addicted."

"Jed drinks lots of espresso drinks." She turned to ask him what he'd recommend, but he had vanished. "Oh, I guess he left."

It was weird. She hadn't heard the bell.

Fifteen minutes later, after Mrs. D had wandered out with a cappuccino (*It's like a latte, except with more foam*) and Kristin was wiping down the espresso machine, Jed popped out of the hallway that led to the bathroom.

He stood for several second before saying "Boo" in a quiet voice.

She slapped him playfully on the arm, just as Harriet would have done. "Where were you?" she asked. "Were you in the bathroom the whole time?"

"Runner girl," he said, giving her a playful slap back, then letting his hand linger on her bicep. "You never told me you were a such a good runner." They were standing so close she could smell that he'd washed his hands with the lemon soap in the bathroom.

"I told you I ran in high school," she said with a laugh.

"But not college. And not that you went to Nationals."

"It's just Div 3," she said.

His hand was still on her bicep. "Don't undersell yourself." He gave her bicep a light squeeze and smiled at her. "I hope I'm never chasing you."

"Very funny," she said. She wanted to ask him if he ran but didn't for fear of sounding nerdy. He finally let go of her arm, even though she would have been happy for him to hold it for much longer. He handed her a folded napkin.

"You should give me a call sometime," he said.

She felt herself blushing.

"Or you can give me your number."

"OK," she said.

For the first time in her life she was paralyzed.

IT WAS SO ROMANTIC.

Jed would come by at night, slipping along the side of the house or coming through the alley, into the backyard, where he'd toss pebbles at her bedroom windows. Sometimes it was very late, midnight or 1 a.m., and she was sound asleep, but other times it was earlier, and she was awake, her ears trained for the sound, which was sharper than a knock, more like a stick breaking. She got up and pressed her forehead against the screen, her eyes searching for the black cutout of his figure beneath the crabapple tree that was covered in hard red fruit that fell and made the patio sticky. Sometimes he wasn't there. Sometimes she was listening too attentively and anything—the tick of a sprinkler, the rustle of the breeze through the trees, a car door slamming—could sound like a signal. Sometimes he came into the coffee shop and said he'd been there, peppered her window with rocks until he was afraid of cracking the glass, or worse, waking up her mom. He'd shake his head and grin. "You were dead to the world, or maybe you were just ignoring me. Huh?"

"Were you really there?" she'd ask because he'd liked to tease her, and it was hard to tell when he was being serious and when he wasn't. She wasn't used to being teased. It made her feel like she was walking around on her tiptoes all the time.

He held up his right hand. On his middle finger he wore a turquoise ring with a thick silver band that had once belonged to his great-grandfather, a member of the Blackfoot tribe. "Scout's honor," he said every time. "Cross my heart and hope to die." And she both believed him and didn't.

But when he was actually there, she dressed quickly, pulling on a pair of shorts and a T-shirt. She was already wearing a bra because she'd read somewhere that if you had big breasts, you needed around-the-clock support. She had failed the pencil test in ninth grade. Carrying her thongs in one hand, she tiptoed past her mom's room at the top of the stairs, not that her mom minded her going out with Jed, though if she ever found out that he came around so late at night, she would have said that he should be taking her out on proper dates. "Don't sell yourself short," she'd say—whatever that meant, because what on earth was she selling?

She and Jed sat in the backyard talking, or they went for walks. It was thrilling to drift around the streets of her neighborhood at night, streets she knew so well from living there most of her life. In elementary school, she'd had a paper route for a year, hanging little white plastic bags of advertising circulars from people's doorknobs. She'd quickly learned which place had dogs that sounded like they would rip your arm off, the houses where the shades were always drawn or the TV was always on, the volume turned way up. She'd roller-skated and biked and run these streets for so long, she knew everyone on her block and the blocks next to hers. She'd saved money for college babysitting their kids or watering their yards while they went on vacation, and yet, everything seemed altered late at night, as though, like Alice, she'd come upon a bottle that said "Drink Me" and taken a sip. Part of it was that Jed noticed all that she'd somehow missed: the red doors and American flags, the horrible little lawn jockeys and corn growing in the flowerbed right outside someone's front door.

"Is this neighborhood patriotic or what?" he said. "You got the flags and the racist statuary, lots of Ford trucks, a few campers, motorboats."

"This is the most liberal neighborhood in the city," Kristin said.

He stopped in front a house where someone had planted miniature American flags along their walkway. "Case in point."

"You can be liberal and patriotic," she said. "The two aren't mutually exclusive."

Laughing, he swerved and bumped her onto someone's lawn. "Just be careful where you tread," he said.

Other times, they climbed straight up Camel's Back, a park at the edge of the foothills, taking the path that eroded a bit more with each snowfall and melt, and they sat among clumps of sagebrush that got more fragrant after dark. The city stretched west, a crazy quilt of umbrella-shaped trees, houses and lit streets intersected by the bright artery of the freeway. To the south was downtown, a tiny collection of buildings, the tallest just twelve stories. There was the Capitol, where her mom lobbied legislators, there was her church, her high school, the domed bank where each deposit she made was written in red ink in her little blue book, the public library where she biked every night in the spring of her senior year because only by locking herself in the stacks could she finish her homework. His Boise wasn't visible from Camel's Back because it was all out west in the suburbs.

"You didn't come downtown?" she asked.

"Nope," he said. "We hung out at the mall."

"Really?" she said. "We boycotted the mall. My mom's very pro-downtown."

To the east was Table Rock, a six-mile slog to the top, and at its base, the old penitentiary where you could wander into the room that had once held the gallows. It was haunted; how could a place that had seen so much brutality not be? Once, out much later than she should have been because of a flat tire, Kristin had pushed her bike by the pen and heard someone crying.

She told Jed this story.

"Do you believe in ghosts?" he asked.

"During the day, no," she said. "But at night, maybe."

He took her hand and started rubbing it, pressing his thumb into the middle of her palm and moving out with such firm pressure, it felt like he was trying to iron the lines that a palm reader would read, turning her into a blank slate. This was only the second time he'd done this. They hadn't kissed.

"What about you?" she said. "Do you believe in them?"

"I think energy just changes forms. So when someone dies, they don't disappear, they just get absorbed into something new. And if they don't, if they can't find the right form for the next part of the journey, that's when they haunt us." He'd moved on to her fingers, tugging on each one, gently at first, and then more insistently, as though with enough force they would pop right off. "My grandpa became a ghost."

She laughed.

"I'm serious," he said.

"What happened?"

"He was an angry man," Jed said. "No one and nothing wanted to absorb that energy. If a dog would have taken him in, that dog would have become a killer. You hear about that happening sometimes—dog just suddenly turns on its owner and attacks."

It was the sort of thing that she would have never believed in the light of day, but late at night, swaddled in darkness, the world seemed more extraordinary. Tragic, too. Some of the stories that spilled out of the kids she went to college with made her feel so ordinary and unscarred.

She waited for him to say more, but he was quiet as he continued to rub her hand. Her body was quaking. She was glad it was dark because she could feel her lips trembling too, and she would have been embarrassed if he'd noticed this. She didn't want him to stop, and then she worried she was being selfish, and she kept expecting him to stop because how satisfying could it be to rub another person's hand? Whenever she was involved in a group backrub, she was only happy if she were giving the backrub first rather than getting one because the thought of having to rub someone else's back after her backrub ended ruined the whole experience.

"He settled in the basement of my folks' house," he said, and at first, she didn't know what he was talking about. Then she realized *he* was the grandpa ghost.

"Oh," she said. "Wow. Is it scary?"

"Only when you forget he's there."

"Why?" It was late, and in a way, she felt like she was dreaming, even though every inch of her body was awake. If someone picked her up and dropped her, she would shatter into a million pieces.

"Because no one likes to be forgotten, least of all the kind of person who everyone wants to forget."

He stopped rubbing her hand but left it resting in his lap. She thought she could feel heat rising from him, as from an open fire, but maybe she was just imagining it. Was he ever going to make a move? He should be the one, she thought, because he was older, not by a lot, she told herself, except that five years was a quarter of her life, and her mother had been married and pregnant by the time she was twenty-five. Maybe Jed was thinking the same thing: that she should be the one to make the first move since she was younger, and five years probably seemed like an eternity to her, and he didn't want to come across like a creep.

She drank her first whiskey in a bar called The Cactus, except the neon S was burned out—so it was The Cactu. She'd drank plenty of beer before—the gold swill that spurted out of kegs at college parties and made you feel bloated. She would turn twenty-one in February, and then she could sidle up to a bar and order her own drinks, but in the meantime, Jed said he knew the bartenders at The Cactu, and all she needed to do was wear a sexy dress, and it'd be a walk in the park. The first sip made her face pucker and her shoulders bunch up. She felt like the cowboys from the rural county outside Boise who moseyed into the coffee shop and ordered double espressos to get ready for their nights on the town and nearly spit them out. She choked down another tiny taste, and another.

"Take her slow," Jed said, his arm thrown over her shoulder. "Do you want a splash of Coke to brighten things up?" He stood close all night, and he enveloped her, embracing her from behind, when he was showing her the correct way to line up a shot in pool.

A juke box was playing "Don't Stop Believin.'"

"No," she insisted. "I want it the real way." Really, though, she didn't want the extra sugar or calories.

"Try your next one on the rocks," advised one of the bartenders, the one in Lee jeans and a muscle shirt that showed off amazing biceps, "with a splash of water."

By end of the night, she liked it better. And now she could say she was a whiskey drinker, not that she imagined this would ever be her drink of choice, but she would drink it every time they went to The Cactu. All four or five or six times. They also went to a no-name bar way out west in a neighborhood of small farms and horse pastures that Kristin didn't know existed. Shiny motorcycles filled the parking lot. "Where are we?" Kristin asked and Jed just laughed.

"I can rub your feet," he said another time as they sat on top of the hill. She had to be up at 5 to go for a training run before opening the coffee shop at 6:30. She was always tired. Her days drifted by like dreams, not unhappily. It was just that nothing seemed real. Not her mother scolding her for being absentminded and forgetting a doctor's appointment, an oil change, the clothes in the washing machine that had to be redone because they got stinky if you left them sitting there for any amount of time in the summer. Not the postcards she got from the other girls on the cross country team. Not the fact that her days in Boise were dwindling, and she'd be returning to college soon. She wanted Jed to rub her feet but she felt self-conscious about how dusty they must be from walking around in her thongs.

Then, as though he'd read her mind, he said, "Don't worry about how dirty your feet are. I like me some dirty feet."

And she scooted this way, and he scooted that way, and above them, the stars were grand, even with the lights of the city, and satellites winked as they moved along their preordained paths.

"Do you ever wonder what they see when they look down at us?" Jed said, working his thumb along the pad under her big toe.

"Never," she said.

He stopped and waved. "I'm just giving a girl a foot rub. Nothing to see here."

He moved up and started manually circling her big toe. When he bent the toe forward, it let out a loud crack. "Did you know you carry all of your stress in your big toe?"

"No," she said.

"Dead serious," he said. "And based on that crack, you are one stressed mamacita."

"Really," she said, being serious now. She didn't feel stressed, just stirred up. A light breeze blew some dust into her mouth, which she tried to spit out.

"Really," he said. "Really, really stressed."

He stopped, and she felt herself hoping he would start again soon, but he leaned over and kissed her. She almost jumped, her eyes were closed and she was so blissed out from the foot rub. His lips were soft, and they smelled of cherry ChapStick. They kissed for a while, gentle kisses, like taking sips of air, not like the way her old boyfriend Justin had sometimes mashed his lips against hers so that their teeth clanged together. And then he stopped and laughed and said "Where was I?" and she pushed herself up and found his face in the dark and resumed their kissing. She couldn't stand it anymore. If she'd gone one more day without kissing him, she would have burst open, the way a very ripe watermelon does just after you plunge in the tip of a knife.

That was when he said he didn't want to have sex with her out there on top of the hill. It was too public. All those satellites spying on them. Maybe UFOs, too. He pressed against her as though he was trying to fuse their bodies. And she just laughed, because she'd only had sex with one person (and only a handful of times). Justin, freshman year. A tall skinny kid who looked like Lyle Lovett, but was from New Jersey, and wrote lots of poetry that

Kristin pretended to understand. She'd been drawn to his pouf of curls, the fact that he'd hiked part of the Appalachian Trail the summer before freshmen year. The sex had happened after six months of dating, after she and Justin had done everything under the sun, including oral sex, which, for whatever reason, didn't count (well, there was a reason, you couldn't get knocked up from having oral sex). They'd had multiple conversations about whether their relationship was serious and what it would mean to have sex; they had conversations about whether they had enough to talk about. Kristin just wanted to see what sex was like, and Justin, in less of a hurry, wanted to make sure it was special. And so once they actually decided they were ready to do it (lovemaking, as Justin weirdly called it) they had to wait for a weekend when Justin's roommate was away since Kristin was in a triple, and hell would freeze over before there was a night when her roommates, one a serious violist, the other a chem major, would both be gone.

So, sex was the last thing on Kristin's mind on top of Camel's Back that night, though later she would think about sex a lot. They were actually kissing, and she really wasn't thinking anything at all. Kissing could be like running. Sometimes you could just be so into doing something so completely with your body that your brain turned off. It was just like that. Just like that. Just like that. So, so, so, so, so. Just like that.

"IS THAT EVEN GOING TO MAKE IT UP INTO THE MOUNTAINS?" SHE asked when she climbed into his car, an old Chevy with a red vinyl interior and a radio with push-buttons.

She had been sitting on the curb at the gas station, waiting for him to pick her up. Because she'd lied to her mother and said she was going camping with her friend Linda's family, she'd left work early, packed up quickly, and walked to the Stinker Station. It was all part of their plan. Jed just shook his head silently when she said she wasn't going to tell her mother.

They were going backpacking together.

"This is an eight-cylinder beast," he said. "This machine could drive to the top of Machu Picchu."

There was a six-pack of beer sitting on the passenger side. It was still cold, she noticed, moving it to the floor. One can was missing.

"What's this," she asked.

"Road beer," he said.

"Are you serious?" she blurted out. "You're not supposed to

drink in the car." As soon she'd said it, she wished she could take it back. She hated how prissy she sounded.

"Relax," he said, putting his arms around her and pulling her toward him across the slippery vinyl bench seat. He kissed her on the neck, then the jaw, slowly pecking his way to her lips. Her whole body contracted into something prickly and delicious. When he stopped kissing her, she felt disappointed. She started to scoot back to the passenger side.

"Oh no," he said, "You're riding right next to me."

It was the first week of August. She'd be heading back to college in two weeks.

He drove with one hand on the wheel as though he'd driven like this his whole life. The only time he let go of her was when they were driving along the edge of a dam, and there was nothing between Kristin and a two-hundred-foot drop into the canyon below except a puny little guard rail. It was beautiful country. The road climbed from the tawny foothills outside Boise, past the dams on the Boise River, to Sandy Point, the little wimming area where Kristin and her mom went once and only once a summer for "a day at the beach." The water was very low after a long, dry summer and looked as appealing as a mud puddle. They kept driving up and up, past the Hilltop Café, a place famous for its cinnamon rolls, where some of Kristin's high school friends used to ride their bikes.

"Have you ever been there?" Kristin yelled over the roar of the open windows. The anxiety she'd felt as they'd left the city was gradually melting away. Jed was a confident driver, and this was an adventure. She wanted to have more adventures.

"Nope."

"Me, either," Kristin said. "We should stop on our way back."

"Definitely," he said, giving her a squeeze.

Lodgepole pines dotted the hillside, and a frothy little creek tumbled over boulders and downed trees just out her window. There was no shoulder on either side of the road. She took a deep breath of air, and she could tell that it was already cooler. In Idaho City, a jumble of tin-roofed mining shacks and old hotels with second-floor balconies, they stopped for gas, beef jerky, and cans of pop. Around town were heaps of white rocks that had something to do with the gold rush, though Kristin couldn't remember the details. It was hard to imagine that Idaho City had once been the largest city in the whole Northwest.

"We've got to fuel up before we really head into the middle of nowhere," Jed said. He got a baseball cap from the backseat and put it on. Across the front were the words "American Pie."

"What's that?"

"What?"

"American Pie?"

"The song." He started to sing. *"Bye, bye Miss American Pie, drove my Chevy to the levee, but the levee was dry."*

She grinned as he walked around the long nose of the car.

"Is that why you have a Chevy?" she asked.

He kissed her. "That's why I have you," he said.

The road writhed back and forth, the trees growing right up to its edge, the mountain through which it had been cut spilling dirt across the asphalt. Every few miles was a sign for a trailhead or a campground. They got jammed behind a silver turd, that's what Jed called the RV in front of them, taking the curves at a responsible speed so that as soon as they came to fifty feet of straight road, Jed pulled into the left lane, coaxing the car with several *C'mon baby*'s as it spasmed with the effort of 55 miles per hour.

They were probably going to die.

"I thought you weren't supposed to cross the double yellow line," Kristin said, trying not to freak out. For a moment, she closed her eyes. If she were going to perish in a head-on accident, she didn't want to see it coming.

"City slicker," he said.

Still later, they passed a sign that said "Watch for Stock." Another said "Wildlife Crossing." Did that include the little squirrels with black tails? One dashed into the road in front of them.

"Do you think we hit it?" she asked.

"Maybe," he said. "Or it hit us," he said, and she laughed. She could be such a worrywart.

Kristin had been camping before, with her friend Linda and Linda's family, but she'd never been backpacking. Her mother DID NOT BACKPACK, mostly because Kristin's father had been a backpacker. In fact, Kristin's parents had spent part of their honeymoon in the Olympic Peninsula. In a dusty corner of the basement, Kristin had found her mom's old frame pack and leather boots with bright-red laces. When Kristin asked whether she could borrow them, her mom sighed theatrically and said, "Ah, I remember backpacking."

She thought it was a shame that her mom had let the fact of her father ruin something that she had clearly enjoyed. But that was her mom. She liked taking extreme positions, and once she had taken one, she did not waver in her commitment to it. That's why Kristin had no idea as a kid what her dad looked like, because when her dad had said he was leaving, Kristin's mom had said, "if you leave, you will not have a relationship with your daughter," and then she proceeded to destroy every picture of her father that she could put her hands on. Kristin was amazed that the pack and boots had survived, but her mom was also frugal, and it would have been difficult for her to toss something she might someday be able to repurpose (for a trip across Europe) or give away. And somewhere along the way, she'd forgotten about them.

When Kristin turned thirteen, she had gotten a handful of photos of her dad from her grandma, who thought Kristin's mom could be a tad bit severe. Along with the photos, Kristin's grandma had also given her a pearl necklace in a blue velvet box, a tiny bag with three loose diamonds that had been in the family, a set of silver, and a Steuben cat. She said her mother didn't have much of an appreciation for tradition.

Her father had a bright, friendly face, wavy red hair and blue eyes, and a dimple in the exact same spot where Kristin had one. In the photo that Kristin cherished most of all, he wore bell-bottom jeans and a purple-striped shirt with a clownishly big collar, and he was peering down at a white bundle that he held carefully in his arm. This was baby Kristin. It was the only picture of just the two of them. She kept all of her treasures in a little room under the eaves of the house that could only be accessed through a small door at the back of her closet. And when she went to college, she took everything with her, except for the silver in its heavy wooden box. Not that her mom would have minded that she had these things. Maybe the photos would have bothered her a bit, but it had been almost twenty years since they split up, and her mom had recently started to talk about her dad a bit more, revealing odds and ends that didn't really add up to a whole person but nevertheless fascinated Kristin. He was a trial lawyer, a great storyteller. He almost drowned in a waterskiing accident when his father accidentally ran over him with a boat. He loved dill pickles, ballroom dancing, and Raymond Carver. He hated Boise, because he'd grown up there, and it would forever seem like a boring cow town, with too many Mormons and Republicans for his taste. Politically and socially backward. Her mom shared her dad's gripes about the political climate, but she also thought Boise was changing, even back in the 1970s before the influx of Californians. She was from an even smaller town in eastern Oregon, with two stoplights, three restaurants (one a drive-in), and five churches, and Boise was the right size for her—big enough to have a summer Shakespeare company and small enough that she ran into friends at the grocery store. She liked the neighborliness.

Where is he now, Kristin wanted to ask whenever her mom said something about her father in passing, but something about that question felt like a betrayal of her mom, so she never did.

They pulled into Redfish Lake Resort just after five. It was a quaint place with an old-fashioned lodge built from rough-hewn logs almost at the water's edge, tiny cabins, and a campground with wooden picnic tables. They sat in the Adirondack chairs in front of the lodge and admired the lake, so still and glassy that the toothy peaks that bit into the sky were also consuming the water.

"I can't believe I've never been here," Kristin exclaimed. A tremendous sense of goodness filled her, like she'd just run six miles. She inhaled deeply. The air tasted like evergreens and lake water.

"And you call yourself a native," Jed teased.

"I know, right?" Kristin said. "I'm a total imposter."

Their plan was to camp in the campground and then take a boat across the lake to the trailhead the next morning. Otherwise, it would be a twelve-mile hike to Alpine, where they would spend the night. It was a shame they had to be back by Sunday night, but she had to work on Monday. As soon as they'd set up their tent and unrolled their sleeping bags, Jed cracked open a warm beer, and she realized he hadn't touched the six-pack on the drive. He was obviously just winding her up when he called it road beer. She was so earnest. To the extent that she had any self-awareness, she knew this was one of her least-appealing characteristics. She was beautiful but her personality was not. She must have looked glum, because Jed picked up another beer. "Catch." He tossed it underhand. Squealing, she caught it. Even warm, it tasted great, and she sipped it slowly as Jed built a fire. He whistled while he arranged the wood into a teepee-shaped structure packed with bright green moss that he'd culled from neighboring trees.

He produced a small metal canister and took out a wooden match. "And now, ladies and gentlemen, I will light the fire with just one match and one match only."

He struck it against the container, and it flared before suddenly spluttering out.

Kristin leaned against the picnic table where the last rays of the sun made a pool of light.

"Must have been a dud," Jed muttered. "And now watch closely, ladies and ladies, as I light this fire with a single match." He lit it, cupping it in his hand to shield it from the wind, but it burned out again. "Shit," he cursed.

Kristin laughed. "Do you want to use my lighter?"

"Sacrilege." He lit another and another and they both died. "Shit."

Having never heard him curse before, she wondered whether he was getting angry.

"When's the last time you used those matches?"

"No questions from the peanut gallery."

She unwound her bandanna from her hair and threw it in his direction.

"Give me your lighter." Though he sounded brusque, he was

smiling. He winked. "This will be our little secret." He tied her
bandanna around his neck. "That's better." The fire started immediately.

"Great fire," she said.

"Great lighter," he said. They clinked beers, and he opened
two more.

They didn't pitch the tent because Jed said it would slow them
down in the morning. The Milky Way looked like a bag of spilled
sugar; there was hardly any space that wasn't stars. "Good night,"
Jed said, giving her a long slow kiss before turning over and pulling his head into his bag. She lay awake, looking up at the splen-
did sky, squeezing her toes, and then rubbing her right foot
against her left leg, and vice versa, trying to warm them. She felt
disappointed, though she wasn't exactly sure why. This was the
first time she and Jed had spent the night together and she supposed she thought he would want to fool around. She did. She
was wide awake, and she had to pee, but she didn't want to leave
the warmth of her sleeping bag. Struggling to get comfortable,
she turned to one side and then the other; through the inflatable
pad that Jed said was like sleeping on a feather bed, the ground
pressed uncomfortably against her hip. She found it impossible to
fall asleep on her back. An owl—deep and sonorous—distracted
her, its call making her contemplate everything that emerged
after dark, everything that stayed hidden during the day. Something rustled, and she wondered whether they should have locked
their food in the car. She wasn't sure whether they needed to
worry about bears. Soon, Jed began to snore. With great reluc-
tance, she withdrew her hand from her warm sleeping bag and
poked him. When nothing happened, she whispered, "Jed, you're
snoring. Roll over." She nudged him again, but he didn't budge.

She didn't think she would ever fall asleep, and as she lay there, trying to talk herself into the idea that Jed's snoring was soothing and hypnotic, that the sound didn't keep jolting her awake just as she was drifting off, she thought about the times she'd been awakened suddenly in the middle of the night: when she was a little girl and a car exploded next door after someone stuffed a burning rag into the gas tank, or more recently, when she and her mother were staying at a cabin in McCall, and Kristin thought there was a woodpecker on the deck, but when she went to the screen door to investigate, she found herself face to face with a stag, the stubs of his newly forming antlers still covered in velvet, his eyes brown and liquid. Nights were always mysterious; in the dorm freshman year: drunk kids coming home from parties, a nasty argument between the "big couple" on her hallway. She'd never heard people in real life hurl so many awful words at each other. You closed your eyes and the whole world rearranged itself. She'd be so tired in the morning. Would she even enjoy the hike to the lake? Of course she would, but she'd be in a bad mood. For a moment, she longed to be back at home in her own bed, the glow-in-the-dark stars she'd pressed onto the ceiling years earlier only glowing for five or six minutes. But then she looked up at the sky, more stars than she had ever seen, and her felt her thoughts skipping around, in a way that made no sense, and—

When she woke, the sun was peeking over the trees, but it hadn't yet reached their campsite, and everything was still bathed in gray. The air pricked her nose, and she started to sneeze but swallowed it. Jed had a tiny pot of coffee going on a backpacking stove.

"Good morning, beautiful," he said. "I know you don't need a cup of joe, but I do."

She rubbed her eyes, then patted her hair, trying to assess how messy it must be. It was 7:30. She couldn't believe she had slept so late.

"Then, we'll get a stack of hotcakes," he continued. "That's the whole point of hiking from Redfish Lodge. You start your day right."

"Luxurious," she said.

"You bet," he said.

Her breath made her wish she'd brought mints. Jed was wearing a red parka and shorts. She'd never seen his thighs before, and she couldn't believe how much she liked looking at them. The words that sprang to mind were *meaty* and *delicious*. He was humming as he poured the coffee into a tiny tin cup. She sat up and yawned.

After breakfast, they threw their packs into one side of the boat and sat on the other. The boat gurgled across the lake in a swirl of gasoline and coffee. Jed had his hand around her shoulder, holding her tightly. Mountains loomed all around them. Whatever uneasiness she'd been feeling earlier was erased by the enormity of the landscape, her sense of being pleasantly swallowed up by it. "It's beautiful," she said, but the words were immediately whipped away by the wind. Jed said something she couldn't hear, and she smiled anyway.

The trail was a series of long switchbacks across the ridge. "Why can't we just go straight up," Kristin said, stepping off the path. She could see the trail fifty feet above her. "It would be so much faster."

"No." Jed grabbed her arm and she nearly lost her balance. "First, you'll wear yourself out right away," he said. "But more important, you'll cause erosion. If one person leaves the path,

everyone will. And then this whole place will be just like Camel's
Back. Nothing more than a city park." He took slow deliberate
steps, digging his toes into the ground and sending up puffs of
dust. She preferred going fast and getting things over with, but his
pace forced her to slow down.

"I have a test for you," he said.

At the word *test,* her pulse quickened.

"What would you do if a bear was chasing you?"

"Run," she blurted out in a tone that meant *duh?*

"Nope."

"What?" she said. "Let it eat me?" She laughed.

"Running is the worst thing you can do," he said. "If you run,
you give the bear reason to chase you. You should never turn
your back on a bear. Instead, you should face it, and you should
speak to it."

"I don't believe you," she said.

"Be my guest," he said.

She laughed. "What are you supposed to say? *Excuse me, Mr.
Bear, but I'm not a very tasty morsel.*"

"Sort of," he said, "though I'd be more direct. *I'm backing
away, Bear. I mean you no harm.* And then you keep backing away
slowly because the bear doesn't really want to hurt you."

"OK," she said.

"Another thing," he said, "if you're in bear country, you should
sing."

"Should we be singing? *The ants go marching one by one, hur-
rah.*" It was the first song that sprang to mind.

"You have a good voice, runner girl," he said.

"You do, too," she said. "Are we?"

"What?"

"In bear country," she asked.

"Yeah," he said.

"Yikes," she said. Maybe the sounds she'd heard last night had been a bear.

"But don't worry," he said, "we're talking, and that's just as good as singing. The point is that you want to give a bear advance warning."

"To eat you?"

"Ha ha," he said. "To hide. Bears just want to be left alone."

She sang "Girls Just Want to Have Fun," replacing "girls" with "bears." "Oh Daddy dearest, you know you still make me groan. But bears just like to be alone, yeah, bears just want to be alone."

"I like it when you call me Daddy dearest," he said. "Now you ask me a question."

"Umm," she said, unsure of what sort of question she was supposed to ask. Her feelings kept shifting, like leaves being whirled by the wind; sometimes she felt like herself, confident and articulate, but then something like self-consciousness would wash over her. Though she wanted to be spontaneous, she was always second-guessing herself. "How old are you?"

"Oh." He sounded surprised. "I guess you don't know, do you? How old do you think I am?"

"Twenty-five?"

"Close. Twenty-seven."

He was even older than she thought. What was a twenty-seven-year-old doing hanging around with a twenty-year-old? It sounded like a question her mother would ask. "Your turn," she said, expecting a subject that would show how little she knew.

"What's your favorite color?"

She breathed more easily.

"Pink. What's yours?"

"Red. Favorite animal?"

"Cat," she said.

"I could have predicted that," he said.

"Why?" she asked.

"You have a catlike personality," he said.

"How so?"

"You're standoffish in a very alluring way. You know how cats are. You have to prove yourself to them before they let you pet them."

"I don't think I'm like that," she said, not because she was hurt by this description, but because she didn't think it was true. She knew girls like that, and she wasn't one of them. She didn't play games, which many people mistook for playing games.

"I'm joking," he said.

He had a teasing way of talking to her that she recognized as a form of male affection. Sometimes Eli teased her like this.

"Anyway, what's your favorite animal?"

"Raccoon."

"Really? Why?"

"Because everyone loves to hate them, but they're really quite intelligent. And those paws? They have fingers like humans."

"I do like the way they trundle," she said. "They sort of prance around on their toes with their backs arched. Like little masked bandits."

"Totally," he said.

They stopped and drank lemonade from a recycled one-liter Coke bottle as they leaned against a rock. This way, as Jed explained, they could take the weight off their backs without actually removing their packs. Then they continued up the trail.

"Most treasured object," he said.

"The photos of my father." As soon as the words were out of her mouth, she wanted to snatch them back.

"What's his story?"

"He was a pirate," she said.

"Seriously?

"He also spent years tracking Bigfoot,"

"I see," Jed said. "OK, next question."

"What's your most treasured object?"

"You can't keep copying me."

"But it's a great question."

"But I want to know what you want to know."

What did she want to know? She wanted to know if he liked her, and if so, how much. She took one small step and then another. She looked down at the zigzagging trail they'd climbed. The lake was still close enough that she could hike back if they ran out of things to talk about. Or what if Jed decided she was boring and turned back?

"What are you afraid of?"

"Oh, that's easy," he said. "Small enclosed spaces. Like elevators. And caves."

"Wait, is that why you didn't want to pitch the tent last night?"

"You're smart, runner girl," he said. "I actually didn't bring a tent."

"Oh. But what if it rains?"

"I looked at the forecast. And I have a tarp. We can always rig up a shelter if we need to."

She rubbed a pebble in her pocket. She applied Carmex from a little pot. Her lips burned. "Is that why you don't work in an office?"

"What?"

"Because of your claustrophobia."

"No."

"I'm being serious."

"Why would I want to work in an office?"

"You're twenty-seven . . ."

"And . . ."

"I don't know."

"I could work in an open office," he said. "Cubicles are actually fine, too."

She had no idea what they were talking about.

"I don't want to work in an office," he said.

"OK," she said, searching for something to say next. "You want to be a pirate."

It was quiet for a moment, except for the sound of them walking and the saw of the cicadas. Jed laughed. "Or I want to be a Sasquatch hunter."

"Bigfoot."

"Same diff," he said.

"Same creature. Totally different perspective," she said. "How you name it changes how you track it."

Stopping, he turned and smiled at her. Her pink bandanna was wound around his forehead. He must have put it on while they were walking. She'd completely forgotten to get it back from him last night.

"That reminds me," he said. "All bears aren't created equal."

"What do you mean?"

"You shouldn't run from any bear," he said. "Right?"

"Right."

"But if the bear doesn't back off . . ."

"Yeah."

". . . what you do next depends on its species. If it's a grizzly who's charging you, you should lie down on your belly and play dead. With your arms like this." He held them above his head in a diamond shape. "You want to stay calm and guard your soft parts."

"Right." She took out the Carmex again and slicked more on.

"If it's a black bear, however, then you have to fight back."

"Why?" she asked.

"Because black bears don't typically charge humans. So when

they do, it's because something's wrong with them."

He stopped again, turned, and twirled his index finger around his ear. It was the universal gesture of craziness, dating all the way back to first grade. She watched him doing it and realized she had no idea why it meant what it did.

"You have to fight back like your life depends on it."

"How?"

"How?"

"Yeah, how?"

"Kick 'em. Bop 'em on the nose."

He turned and started taking small steps up the dusty trail again. She should have asked the most basic follow-up question: What if you couldn't tell the difference? What if you played dead when you should have fought back?

Later that afternoon, when they'd finally reached Alpine Lake, a palmful of melted snow cradled in the hand of the mountains, they shrugged off their packs at the first campsite, ate some gorp (though Kristin avoided the M&Ms), and drank a little water. They hadn't stopped for lunch, and Kristin was enjoying the sensation of her hunger and her shorts sliding over her hips and just catching on the lip of the bone. It made little sense, but feeling hungry fueled her desire to not eat. They continued along the perimeter of the lake, looking for the best campsite, and then looped back to the beginning to grab their packs. Kristin liked the spot next to the stream that fed the lake, but Jed said the mosquitoes would be murderous, so instead they chose a site on a rocky outcropping.

"It's already got a leaning log," Jed said, pointing to the piece of wood about five feet away from the fire ring. They could put their pads there. It would all be very civilized, he said. He pointed to another spot—an almost level patch of hard packed earth. "And we can lay our bags out there."

Standing on the edge of the lake, Kristin could see all the way to the bottom. A silvery brown fish darted out of the shadows and into the sun.

"Triple-dog-dare you to jump in," Jed said.

"Easy peasy," she said with mock bravado. She was wondering where she would change into her swimming suit since they didn't have a tent. Was Jed even going to put on a suit? It reminded her of a time the girls' team had ended up at the reservoir on a hot day, and the guys' team was already there, and judging from the piles of clothes on the shore, they were skinny- dipping. Most of the girls immediately stripped off their clothes and dove in, but Kristin's self-consciousness made her pause, and it was a moment too long because suddenly everyone except for dorky Chloe was splashing around in the water, and they were watching her, or at least she felt this way, and no decision was a good one since anything she did would expose her embarrassment to them. She didn't want them to see her struggling to wiggle out of her running bra, and she didn't want them to see her running into the water fully dressed. Chloe sighed loudly, and Kristin said, "It really sucks sometimes," and something passed between them that made them both burst into laughter.

Now Kristin asked Jed, "Are you coming in?"

"After you, runner girl."

What was the big deal? she thought as she sat and unlaced her boots. She undressed with her back to him. Butts weren't a big deal. Certain bikinis revealed everything but the crack. And even without some ass floss, it's not as though Jed would see anything. It was all discreetly tucked up inside. Protected. Not like chimpanzees' red asses. Anyway, it wasn't her body, per se, that she was so afraid of him seeing, but rather her relationship to her body, which he would see emblazoned across her face. And not just her feelings about her body, but also her feelings about someone else observing her body. The embarrassment. Her desire not to be seen and the thrill of being noticed and the hypocrisy of experiencing both states at the same time. It was like being secretly proud to be catcalled while loudly complaining about how demeaning it was. It was so lame, sexist, offensive, blah, blah, blah. Gingerly picking her way back to the edge of the lake, she paused—just for a moment—before diving in. When she hit the water, her mind immediately emptied. She came to the surface gasping for breath. It was so cold. Her lungs shriveled.

"Are you OK?" Jed asked, just a black silhouette on the edge.

But she couldn't talk. She was treading water, her legs doing frog kicks, her arms swishing back and forth. She thought if she moved fast enough she would get used to the water, but she felt flayed, the skin from her scalp to her toes peeled back. Her heart was going cuckoo, and she couldn't take a full breath. Her neck ached. Somehow her limbs moved, and she flopped for shore, clawed at the rocks, and scampered out, scraping her thigh, the front of her shin. Blood beaded along the edge of the wound, but she felt nothing. She was shaking uncontrollably. She took a big open-mouthed breath, hoping to calm her body, but as soon as her jaw closed, her teeth were clattering again. Despite her conscious attempt to quiet it, her body wouldn't stop moving.

"Get in this, you fool." Jed was holding her sleeping bag, and he threw it down in a sunny spot before coming over, grabbing her under the armpits and maneuvering her in. "You're too skinny for polar bear swimming." He was still wearing his clothes.

Once she was in the bag, she felt her whole body contract, like a turtle pulling its head and legs into its shell. If she could just make herself a little smaller. Jed crouched next to her and put a wool cap on her wet head. "Aren't you," she said through chattering teeth, "going in?"

"After watching you?" he said. "No way."

She'd been in the water for sixty seconds. "Maybe you were pushing ninety," Jed said. "Nowhere did I say it was a contest to see who could last the longest." He was stretched out on the rock next to her. "If you don't stop shivering soon, I'm going to climb into the bag with you."

She wouldn't mind that, she thought, and then she realized that she was naked, and her feelings of self-consciousness had evaporated the moment she hit the water. He flung an arm over her shoulder and pressed the full length of his body against her sleeping-bagged form. His breath, on her neck, smelled like baking bread.

The rocks beneath her eventually released their heat, and her face tingled deliciously in the sun, and her whole body was softening, melting, letting go in the wonderfully hot sleeping bag, and she was drifting away. The last thing she remembered was Jed saying it would be dangerous for her to sleep if she were still cold. Touching two fingers to her wrist, pressing his palm flat against her heart, then her belly, he declared that her core had warmed up enough, and she was out of the danger zone.

"I was going to die?" she asked drowsily.

His lips brushed hers. Sleep was pulling her away and she tried to resist. "No, but you were pretty cold."

When she woke, the sun had slid three quarters of the way behind the toothy peaks, and Jed was sitting next to a fire. "Good morning, beautiful," he said for the second time that day. She wiggled her fingers and toes, patted her face, touched her hair.

She tried to picture how she looked, but it was impossible. "Ready for some grub?"

It had been a strange evening. Good and then not good and then good again. And then really not good. They'd eaten freeze-dried shrimp cocktails for dinner followed by beef stew. Had butterscotch pudding topped with granola for dessert. Jed kept producing tin pouches from a stuff sack. It was amazing how yummy food tasted out on the trail. She joked that she was hard at work developing a taste for whiskey, taking small deliberate sips from her Sierra cup. While she slept, Jed had hiked up to a patch of snow on the slopes above them and scooped up a lid full of ice that she kept sprinkling over the surface of her drink. Jed poured the whiskey from a plastic Sprite bottle. "Another?" Jed asked, trickling brown liquid into her cup. As she drank more, she felt herself growing loose and chatty, and everything was funny, even the coffee pot of boiling water sliding into the fire. If they were going to make hot cocoa, they had to figure out how to fish it out with sticks. She shrieked with laughter, and the sound lingered in the absolute silence of the lake.

"The quiet is so profound," she said in a loud whisper.

"It's sacred," he said later, sliding a hand under her shirt and cupping her breast. "It doesn't get any more sacred than this." He hummed. Steam rose from the pan of cocoa that sat in the dirt between them. They were going to share it since their tin cups were still filled with whiskey.

With a start, she realized she wasn't wearing a bra. Of course, she knew she hadn't put it on when she finally climbed out of the sleeping bag, scrambling to throw on some clothes as quickly as possible, both because she was finally warm and she wanted to stay that way, and because it remained embarrassing for Jed to feast his eyes upon her naked body. He scooted closer to her, and some fine dirt lifted and settled on the surface of the cocoa.

"You know what you could do?" he said.

His hand remained on her breast. She liked it; she wasn't going to think about it. His thumb was making slow circles around her nipple, making her quiver.

He repeated his question.

"What?" She giggled in a way that would have embarrassed her at another moment.

"You could pretend to be a bear."

This wasn't what she was expecting him to propose.

"You could creep out into the darkness."

"No way," she laughed lightly.

"You could make bear noises."

"Like what?" she said.

"Rustling noises," he said, his thumb still making hypnotic little circles.

"Rustling noises?" It was hard to focus while he was doing that to her. She wanted to crawl onto his lap. "Bear noises," she said in a deeper voice as she scooted closer to him. "I'm a bear."

"Not like that," he said, "Seriously. You don't talk. You just creep toward the campfire."

"But I thought bears were afraid of fires."

"No. That's bullshit. If there's a fire, there's the possibility of a hot dog."

This was so weird. She wasn't sure what they were talking about.

"So, you're coming closer and closer to the fire. And I hear you." As he said this, he pinched her nipple, hard!—and she sputtered in surprise. The sound reminded her of the noises little kids make when they're pretending to drive an imaginary vehicle—a tank, a space ship, a fighter jet.

"Oh," he said, his voice low and gravelly. "That was good. That was so good. Do it again."

While she was doing it again, louder now, she spit on him. "Sorry."

"Why?"

"For spitting on you."

"No that's good, that's perfect," he said. "When bears are aroused, they've got saliva swinging from their chops. They're frothing. Do it again. You're getting closer and closer to the fire. . . ."

"Are you a bear, too?" she couldn't help but ask.

"No," he sighed. "I'm a human. You're going to attack me."

"What?" She scooted away from him, and his hand slid out from underneath her shirt. She took a bigger mouthful of her whiskey then she meant to. The more she drank, the more she liked the way it tasted. Then she picked up the hot cocoa. The pan was almost too hot to hold. Putting it down, she pulled her sleeves over her hands and picked it up again. The liquid scalded her tongue. She offered Jed some, but he shook his head and jammed his hands in his armpits. All of the friendliness was gone from his eyes. He set his jaw and swallowed audibly. Her hand went to her neck, and she gently touched the place where she thought her own Adam's apple sat. The cocoa tasted metallic, like an old scratched-up spoon. "I'm sorry," she said, unsure of what she was apologizing for, except perhaps that she was more clueless than she should have been.

He ignored her. She repeated his name again, but he wouldn't turn his face away from the fire.

"So I'm the bear," she tried, "and you're the human, and I'm going to attack you."

Still nothing.

"I'm getting closer and closer." She roared unconvincingly

and swiped his arm. Did bears even roar? Or did they grunt? She pawed at him again, but she couldn't get him to look at her. It felt like that joke where everyone agrees to ignore one person, to pretend like she's invisible, and sooner or later, the object of the joke really does start to feel like she's disappeared.

"What are you going to do?"

Silence.

"Jed?"

She threw a stick at him, not a terribly mature thing to do, but how was she supposed to act under the circumstances? He didn't react. When she stood, her legs were stiff, and she wobbled, either from sitting for so long or drinking too much whiskey. Away from the fire, the world was fading, everything becoming less and less recognizable. She had to pee. When she returned, she hoped everything might be normal again. A pale sliver of a moon hung low in the sky before vanishing behind a bank of clouds. She walked farther and farther from their camp, turning every minute or so to make sure the fire was still visible behind her. As long as she could see the light, she could make her way back, even though she wished she had somewhere else to go.

She thought of her mom. Later tonight—though dark, it was still early—she'd be wearing her old red bathrobe that Kristin always mocked, a bowl of buttered popcorn in her lap, watching *Saturday Night Live*. If Kristin were there, she'd be watching too, propped up on the side of the bed where she'd always sat for as long as she could remember. Their only TV was in here, and when Kristin was younger and liked cartoons, she often asked why they couldn't buy another TV and put it in a different room. She wanted to be able to watch whatever she wanted whenever she wanted (especially early Saturdays, the one morning her mom slept late), but her mom said if they had a TV in the family room Kristin would watch too much TV and stay up too late, and both would stunt her growth. Kristin had grown up with few rules, except that her mom wanted her to be a kid and enjoy her childhood—which meant she couldn't get her ear pierced until she was thirteen or wear makeup until she was sixteen. Now that she was living on the other side of the country from her mom, Kristin could mostly do whatever she pleased. In fact, her mom had made a point of telling Kristin that she was an adult now, and yet when Kristin went to her for advice, her mom's response often was *You tell me*, which did not feel like one adult talking to another, but a mom still being a mom.

What should she do? Even if she could negotiate the switchbacks in the dark and make it safely down to Redfish Lake, she'd be stuck alone at the transfer station until the boat arrived to drop off hikers at nine the next morning. Or she'd have to hike six more miles along the trail that hugged the shore of the lake. Twelve miles alone. And what if she encountered an actual bear?

Behind her, the fire shrank until it was no bigger than the shimmering tip of a sparkler, as though just moments from sputtering out.

"Listen," he called out as Kristin was tramping back to their campsite. "I know I'm in your home, but I mean you no harm."

"Jed," she said, swallowing back her panic. "Can we please stop playing this game?"

"I'm going to back away slowly." He stood.

She wasn't sure he could actually see her; she was still far from the fire. She wished she had brought a flashlight because she was having trouble picking her way over the uneven ground; fallen trees that she couldn't see until she was practically bumping into them crisscrossed her path. As she was climbing over one, her running tights had gotten snagged on a branch, and she'd had to rip them to free herself. The downed trees had not been a problem earlier, but now they were everywhere, even though she believed she was taking the same route back.

"I am backing away." He stood just at the edge of the circle of light, his arms hanging by his sides. "You can have whatever you want. Butterscotch pudding. The dregs of the beef stew. Jerky. Whiskey, except I don't think bears drink. You're all teetotalers, aren't you?" He laughed. "Or you were mostly a teetotaler until you met me. Definitely not a whiskey drinker. The gorp is in the side pocket of my pack. I noticed that you don't eat the M&Ms. That's good. I've heard chocolate isn't so good for bears. Same goes for dogs. It can poison them. This is your country, and it's a beautiful country, isn't it? Some say it's God's country, not that I'm a believer, except for the fact that we're more than our physical bodies. We don't just stop. If the present circumstances take a tragic turn, if my voice isn't enough to set you back on the right path, if you . . ." He laughed. ". . . eat me." He laughed again. "Well, then, maybe when my energy finds a new form, it'll be a bear's. I'd like that—shambling through these mountains, eating rainbow trout and huckleberries, helping myself to bees' honey when I'm lucky enough to find it, avoiding humans . . ."

Kristin shook her head—once, twice, then again and again—trying to make sense of what she was hearing. Earlier after they'd shrugged off their heavy packs, they'd celebrated the fact that they had the lake all to themselves with high fives. It was all theirs. Only theirs. It was so cool. Here was a place where you could escape everything and everyone. "In wilderness is the preservation of the world," Jed declared, twisting his baseball cap so that it sat backward on his head and smiling. The dimple on his left cheek appeared. He'd chosen her, and he was so cute. And not just cute, but also something she couldn't quite name. Grown up? Manly? The blond stubble on his jaw made a sexy raspy sound as he rubbed his face. She liked his forearms, too, furred in golden-brown hair, his veins twisting their way up to where they disappeared in the rolled-up cuffs of his plaid shirt. Taking a step toward her, turning her baseball cap so that it matched his, he leaned over and kissed her until her body ached with pleasure.

It was impossible to reconcile her memory of the afternoon with what was happening right then.

"The question is . . ." He paused, taking a sip from something that he slipped back into his pocket. Did he have a flask? "The question is whether you're a black bear or a grizzly."

"I am not doing this," she said.

"What's that?" He swayed as though he were having trouble standing.

"I am not doing this," she warned him more insistently. "Can we please stop?"

"The question is," he said, "the question is whether you're a black bear or a grizzly. To the best of my knowledge there aren't many grizzlies in these parts. Maybe none at all. I think you need to go a little farther north if you want to find them. That means you're probably a black bear. Probably harmless. Probably nothing to worry about."

Every time he said *probably*, he enunciated every syllable. *Prob bub lee.*

"Probably not crazy. Though you know what they say, if a black bear doesn't back off quick, there's probably something wrong with it. A screw loose, so to speak. Missing marbles. Then you need to worry. Then you need to get ready to fight for your life."

She started to run toward the fire. What else could she do? She couldn't just wander off. It was getting cold, and she wasn't even wearing a jacket—just her fleece and a pair of tights. It was probably the wrong thing to do. Hadn't he just warned her that she should back off? That if she didn't, something was wrong with her? But she wasn't a bear. The thought was so ludicrous, she let out a mean little laugh. As she ran, she felt like a creature lumbering toward the camp, not like a runner fleet and fast of foot. She tripped once and barely caught her balance. A branch she didn't see whipped across her cheek, just missing her eye, leaving behind a scratch that throbbed angrily. Jed said something that she couldn't understand. It sounded like gibberish.

And then the distance was closing, between man and bear, between Jed and Kristin, or Kristin and Jed, between one kind of wildness and another, between what Kristin feared would happen and what would actually come to pass, and Jed screamed and threw himself on the ground, his arms over his head in the diamond-shape he'd described earlier in the day, and Kristin reared up and screamed, "You're crazy. I'm not a bear." Her heart was beating wildly, and for a moment the urge to do something violent came over her. She wanted to kick Jed, not gently or play-fully, but hard hard hard in the soft tender spot just beneath his ribcage where it would do the most damage. She wanted to hurt him.

He was laughing.

He was laughing?

"Kristin, honey, I was just fooling around." He turned his head, his cheek stamped with dust. "You should see your face. You look like you want to kill me. But it was just a joke. Don't be mad. I was just joking. We've both had a lot to drink." He pushed himself up until he was kneeling and offered her his hand, but she wouldn't take it. He winced as he walked toward her on his knees, the distance between them disappearing until he was close enough to throw his arm around her waist and squeeze her. She almost lost her balance, sitting back heavily on the log. "You couldn't see that I was joking? I'm so sorry, honey."

He'd never called her honey before. Why she should notice this, she didn't know.

"I was joking." He laughed. "Come on. I didn't really think you were a bear." His laughter slapped her. "I can't believe you're so gullible. I'm so sorry, honey, I didn't mean to scare you."

She didn't believe him. The fire abruptly flared, and the flames put on a little show. Her feet and calves, closest to the heat, started to feel warm and then hot, and she pulled them closer to her body. She didn't believe him. She felt, as she had earlier in the summer when he claimed that he'd been at her house, throwing stones at her windows, and she'd slept through his efforts to rouse her, that he enjoyed watching her stumble. Maybe he wasn't totally lying now. But she didn't think she'd misinterpreted everything. She'd heard something threatening beneath all of the crazy things he'd been saying.

"Say something," he said. "Please don't ignore me."

She wanted to go home. She didn't know how she was going to survive the hours until she was back there, sitting at the kitchen counter while her mother complained about this or that, state politics or the other partners at her law firm. All sexist a-holes, she liked to say. She was the one who'd taught Kristin to curse without using profanity. It drove the girls on her team crazy because they thought she was trying to be sanctimonious, but it was just a habit she'd picked up without even thinking about it, totally harmless, like folding her socks instead of rolling them, something else her mother did. When this night was over, she hoped she could scrub away everything Jed had ever said or done.

"Come on, Kristin." Jed pulled her closer. "We've both had a lot to drink. You never know if you're going to be a mean drunk or a weepy one. Some nights my dad would tell the best stories you'd ever heard, and other nights the safest place was hiding in the back corner of the closet. You just never could tell." Before, she would have been thrilled that he was confiding in her. She would have coaxed out the details, and any hesitation on his part would have just been a challenge. But right then she felt hard-hearted: she didn't care. It wasn't her problem.

He took something out his pocket. A silver flask. Unscrewed it. He threw one arm into the air as though conducting an orchestra or trying to catch himself from falling, and the fire blazed before dying down.

"A joke isn't funny if you're the only one having fun," she said at last.

"Runner girl, so smart." He pressed his lips against the crown of her head. A sudden breeze coaxed a shushing sound from the trees. A squirrel made a squeak like a baby's toy. "You're right. I'm really sorry. It wasn't funny."

And because he sounded sincere, Kristin stopped holding her breath for the first time since the whole crazy thing had started. What had just happened? She couldn't make head or tail of it.

After the stars gradually emerged from the inky blue fabric of the sky, and the sharp edges of the granite knifelike peaks dulled in the gloaming, after Jed had stirred the fire one last time, breaking up any embers that might magically flare in the middle of the night, after they had used the last of their hot water to rinse out their cooking pots, both of them saying almost simultaneously that they would give them a real wash in the morning, and then *Coke Coke* and genuine laughter that released some of the fear still bottled up inside Kristin, after they had moved their pads from the log to a flat spot farther from the lake, and a mayfly, one of thousands that was barely visible in the daylight and was completely unseeable now, landed on the glassy surface and faster than a blink was snapped up by a tiny fish, after Kristin had laid out both of their sleeping bags and turned her stuff sack into a pillow by filling it with extra clothes while Jed wandered off in search of a tree where he could hang their food, after Jed had taken a whiz and Kristin had crouched over a log so that she could pee one final time without accidentally soaking her shoes, after Kristin brushed her teeth, though not until after she asked Jed whether it was OK to spit into the bushes, whether toothpaste spit was biodegradable, etc., after all the bears they could not see had bedded down in the mountains that stretched for hundreds of miles around them and Kristin had made a conscious decision to stow her flashlight in one of her hiking boots, which she placed to the left of her sleeping bag close to her feet just in case she had to get up in the middle of the night, after she'd decided to put on clean wool socks so she wouldn't have to deal with a cold pair in the morning ("Good idea," Jed said), after a star streaked across the sky, and Jed searched fruitlessly for his wool hat before re-membering that he'd already given it to Kristin, after they de-cided that she should keep it, even after she took it off and tossed it back to him, hitting him in the face, making him flinch in sur-prise (because he hadn't seen it coming in the dark), after two small creatures—probably black-tailed squirrels like the one they might have hit the day before—galloped through their camp, star-tling both of them, because against the quiet they did, in fact, sound like galloping horses, and they laughed again and more of Kristin's uneasiness leaked away, after all of this, and dozens of other things, they both crawled into their sleeping bags, finally down for the night.

"Do you want to have sex?" Jed said.

Kristin snorted in surprise. "I'm sorry." And then she got quiet. Much of the night had felt like a dream, with a dream's mysterious logic and menace, and she'd been frantically looking for a way back into the world she knew, and though now she was out—Jed had said it had all been a joke, he'd apologized, and everything felt almost normal again—she was afraid of the door opening again.

She heard him sigh, a sound so human and tender that she softened a bit.

"We could just fool around," he said.

"OK," she agreed.

He was lying on top of her in her sleeping bag. It felt good to be pressed up against him, his knee driving apart her legs, putting delicious pressure there. She could feel his hard-on against her leg, and this felt curiously good, too. They were kissing, and he was nuzzling her neck, her ear, pulling the lobe between his teeth and biting gently. Her stomach lurched, all of her energy drawing together. She didn't know she liked this. It was a revelation that her ear had so many nerves, her pleasure barely containable when he brushed his lips across the seashell swirl of the cartilage and whispered. It was like the sound of water trickling in some unexpected place—a creek in a dried-up landscape, a water fountain in an echoey hallway, hot water into a cooling bath. Then he was guiding her hand into his long johns, fumbling, trying to maneuver under the elastic waistband—she could help, slip the tips of her fingers between his skin and the fabric, she could help if she wanted to, but she wasn't sure she did.

"Honey," he whispered. "You've got me so excited."

"What about the satellites?" she joked while he shifted uncomfortably on top of her so that it felt like she was bearing all of his weight. "I'm not sure . . ."

"But you've got me so hard, Kristin."

Under the best of circumstances, her mummy bag was cozy, but with Jed writhing around, trying to wiggle out of his long underwear, it became sweaty and claustrophobic.

He kept whispering what she had done to him, was doing to him, punctuating the start or end of each accusation with honey: "Honey, you're gonna give me blue balls," he said, his voice rumbling. Her freshman boyfriend had used that term once, which had prompted her to stop doing whatever was causing him to suffer and ask him to define *blue balls* and he admitted that he didn't actually know, he'd just heard other guys using the term usually in combination with *cock tease* and *ball buster.* His balls weren't actually blue; they checked before he promised never ever to use those words again.

"You're squishing me," she said as his penis came out. Her shirt was twisted and riding up, exposing her midriff, where his penis was now pressed, hot and clammy.

"Do you want to be on top?" he said. "That would be hot."

"I don't want to have sex, Jed," she said because she really didn't.

"C'mon," he said. "Please."

He started kissing her neck again, and his hand found the top of her running tights, and he was trying to pull them down, but she wouldn't lift her hips as he tugged on one side and then the other.

"I don't want to do this," she repeated louder now and tried to shove him away.

But he wasn't listening to her. He was working the sleeping bag zipper with one hand, the space between her legs with the other, his lips were moving up her neck, along her jaw, his teeth gently pulling at her ear, then her bottom lip. He sucked on her neck, and her body responded, shivering, her stomach flipping the way it did on carnival rides—just as the Ferris wheel crested, that moment of magical suspension. When his lips weren't on her face, they were whispering things, things she couldn't understand because she was sinking farther underwater, farther into her own fuzzy thoughts.

One last-ditch effort: "I'm a bear," she said. "I'm a grizzly, and if you persist, I will kill you." She was both joking and dead serious. Sometimes jokes, especially the most cutting ones, were the best way to get through to guys, jokiness their lingua franca, the thing that brought them back into their senses. It wasn't her language, but if she had to speak it, she would.

He stopped as though he'd just been shot with a stun gun and seemed to peer down at her, searching her eyes for something she hadn't given him, and then he stopped looking at her and resumed doing what he intended to do.

Maybe later he would say that he hadn't heard her, or that after saying no two or three times, nicely, less nicely, always seriously, even when it was disguised as a joke, she'd stopped saying anything, and he thought she'd changed her mind because she seemed to be enjoying it (her body was responding, wasn't it?) but mostly she'd given up, was playing dead. So she'd had to leave her head in the jaws of the beast. Weren't you supposed to do whatever was necessary to survive?

PART III

//

INTO THE WOODS

EACH IS GOOD

IF YOU'VE NEVER STOOD AT THE END OF A CROSS COUNTRY RACE, YOU really should. All those women with Superman thighs and arms hardly bigger than a broom handle coming out of the woods and down the final straightaway. Up until this point, they've been running and now the racing really starts: floating, kicking, stumbling, hurtling, speeding, tightening up, collapsing, rising, weaving, limping, panting, grimacing, determined, pissed off, arms crossing their bodies, arms bunching up or driving forward, hands clenched in determined fists or loose and floppy. "Look at their faces," someone says. "Who looks the strongest?" But their expressions are inscrutable, their mouths open like daydreaming toddlers, their eyes as blank as zombies. Who knows what they're thinking, except *End*. It's "mass carnage" when they "empty their tanks." It's organized chaos. It's disorganized chaos. This is where each of them has to run her race, beating everyone around her, where twenty-ninth place is significantly better than thirty-first, where the spread matters, where an eighth-place finisher can lead her team to a national championship if her girls are close behind.

They throw themselves toward the finish line. They thrust out their bony chests, unfurling their arms to keep them from falling too soon. If they could leap out of their bodies, they would.

If they're good, they give it everything, and each one of them is good, even if she isn't the fastest.

REPEATS

Danielle

IT'S THURSDAY NIGHT, RIGHT BEFORE EIGHT, THE QUIET HOUR, EV-
eryone cubicled in the library or cozied up in their rooms, buzzy
with after-dinner coffee, laser-sharp and spongy at the same time.
The metal bleachers where Danielle sits are unpleasantly cold
against the backs of her thighs. She is waiting for Kristin. They
still have time, she thinks, even though all the time in the world
doesn't guarantee anything. It's late October, and they have two
more meets and then it's their *Come to Jesus* moment, as Assistant
Coach keeps reminding her. She doesn't even know what that
means, except that if they don't qualify then Danielle will never
stand on the starting line of a cross country course again, prepar-
ing to throw a few elbows to clear the way for her girls. Her team.
A lump rises in her throat.

She glances at her watch. Assistant Coach hatched this plan
two days ago at their coffee date. She and Kristin would meet
after dinner and do some casual intervals—nothing too hard,

they agreed, 400s at pace. A couple of 800s at the end. The work-out would feel easy since the whole point of repeats is to do them faster than you would normally run in a race. If you're shooting for a six-minute pace, you do repeats at a five-minute pace. *Faster, harder, stronger.* That's the way to build speed. But tonight they'll keep it easy. Kristin needs to remember what she's capable of doing.

Danielle, who prides herself on reading people, cannot figure out what's wrong with Kristin. Worse, she can't get Kristin to talk to her. She doesn't know where Kristin went, and she doesn't know why Kristin's room looks like she never moved in, and she doesn't know whether it's true that Kristin punched Chloe during Little IIIs, which is the rumor going around. This is what she knows: that they placed third last weekend without Kristin. Chloe was Chloe, and Liv ran well, but seventeen runners from other teams squeezed between Chloe and Liv and Patricia. Too many.

She checks her watch again, takes a sip of water because she skipped dinner and her stomach is complaining. The track is three blocks from campus in a quasi-residential neighborhood. Flores from the Spanish department lives in the shabby Victorian across the street. He's rumored to smoke pot with his students, says a little weed helps everyone roll their Rs. Danielle can't imag-ine her parents ever smoking pot, not even back when they were in college. Flores has a teenage son, a mini version of him except without the little potbelly or gray hair, who shows up at Tap, chugs beer, and then goes crazy on the dance floor, moving in a way that looks only a little more controlled than convulsions. She wonders whether Flores even knows that his son goes to college parties. She thinks (while thinking she shouldn't think this way) that if Flores didn't smoke pot, he would probably be a more at-tentive parent. Then she thinks that she is being judgmental. There's a lot her parents don't know about her, which is not their fault. She's just very good at hiding things.

They don't know, for example, that she was a bitten by a bat three times the summer after her freshman year. She kept the last incident a secret, even though she was more frightened the third time, more in need of the balm of their parental concern, the fiction that they could fix everything. But if they found out, she thought, then they would know that something was really wrong with her. No one gets bitten by bats three times in a single month.

"Da Da Dani." A figure trots through the gates.

"Kristi," Danielle calls out, relieved to hear the lightness in her voice.

These are their Barbie names, a joke from last year. Shorten your name, add a y, or an i. Neither of them has a Barbie body, but Kristin, Danielle thinks, has Barbie's looks, plus boobs to make her waist look tiny by comparison. The fact that she makes no effort to be beautiful only makes her more alluring. Now she stops in front of Danielle. Her racing flats on her hands, she seems to be a million times better than the other day, Danielle thinks, though maybe a little tired. When she smiles, her face lights up.

"Shall we get this show on the road?" Danielle asks.

"What are we thinking?" Kristin says.

"A little warm-up, maybe a mile, and then some easy fours? Like 90 to 95."

"Stupidly slow," Kristin says, her voice tinged with something. Disappointment? Irritation? Does she think they've lost faith in her?

"No, intentionally slow," Danielle says. The way you frame things matters. She needs to get Kristin to be strategic. "You know, like choosing not to set your alarm and letting yourself sleep in instead of pushing snooze a gazillion times. We'll take the first ones easy, and if we're feeling fresh, we can crank it up at the end."

"Aye, aye, Captain," Kristin says before lining up her impossibly clean flats next to Danielle's and stripping down to shorts and a T-shirt.

They walk a few steps, then a few more. This is always the sticky part, crossing the invisible line between walking and running. They have to rev their engines, even if they're just shifting into first gear. And then Kristin's off, which Danielle is happy to see. She takes the inside lane, and Danielle glides up next to her, perfectly in synch. The warm-up before intervals is always harder than it should be—all that anticipatory dread and the endorphins haven't yet kicked in. Assistant Coach says the first ten minutes are hell, but if you can get through them, then you can run for hours. For Danielle, it's closer to fifteen. Tonight, however, nothing should be hard, except that it's always hard. That's part of the pleasure: doing it, even if you aren't the best. If it was easy, then it wouldn't be worth doing.

They finish one lap, start the next. Except for the steady sound of their breathing and pounding feet, they're both quiet. The sky is darkening and the air pricks deliciously. The lights above the track shine bright, making their workout feel like a performance. Danielle wonders whether Assistant Coach arranged to have them turned on. They start the third lap of their mile warm-up, then the fourth. The knot in Danielle's left calf softens, though her right tendon still feels as brittle as an old rubber band. This is the thing that novice runners fail to appreciate: something is always hurting. If Danielle let discomfort—or, worse, real pain—stop her, then she would never run a step. The trick is knowing when you have crossed an invisible line between uncomfortable and serious, between something-to-be-tolerated and something-which-requires-professional-care and worse: rest. About a quarter of the time, it feels like she is training through serious pain. Her tricky knee. A cold that hangs on for weeks. Harriet says you're in peak condition when you're on the edge of falling apart. That's what happened to Chloe last year. She kept running when she should have stopped.

"Ready?" Danielle asks.

"Yep," Kristin says.

Fifty meters from the starting line, Kristin starts to accelerate, gradually at first, then with some heat. Danielle is right on her shoulder, just half a step behind. Kristin will lead. That's what she and Assistant Coach decided. And besides, if Kristin were herself, if she wasn't choking, or almost choking, she'd just naturally assume it. They hit the 100 mark at a good clip, maybe even where they need to be. Danielle doesn't have an internal clock as precise as Kristin's. At the 200 mark, she always checks her watch and makes adjustments. They float around the curve, glide down the backstretch, smooth. The front knee rises, the calf and foot swinging forward. Drive with the back leg. Roll and push off. Switch. Left. Right. Left. Right. Her legs swing out slightly in arcs, making her stride less efficient than it should be. Coach is always telling her to drive straight; once he made her run back and forth on a straight line, it seemed like a hundred times, trying to drill away her slight waddle. Maybe it helped a tiny bit, but her biomechanics are still basically what they are. She's tall and a little knock-kneed, and these biological facts require her to work that much harder. When they come by the halfway mark at 200 meters, she glances down at her watch. Forty-five seconds.

"Right . . . on . . . ," she says with some effort because the pace is still fast, even though they could run faster.

In response Kristin tilts forward, rolling up on her toes just a touch higher, pushing a smidge harder, a mite faster. The second half always requires more effort than the first as the body wearies. Maintaining pace demands an explosion forward but appears, to a spectator, like more of the same. Danielle rockets with Kristin, her legs turning over and over, telling herself that she needs to keep pushing and keep pushing if she wants to keep pace and driving her arms harder because the legs will follow. With just 100 meters to go, there's no reason not to give it everything because the end is so close, and Kristin is gliding toward the finish line, like a wave breaking across the sand, and Danielle's right there, and soon, very soon, they'll be able to return to their natural state of rest—just for a moment or two, bent over, hands briefly on knees, taking a few deep breaths—not that it was tits out, but no matter what, it's hard. Hard and exhilarating. And now they're there. They've run their lap in 81; the second half in just 36 seconds. Negative splits that have teetered too far in one direction. Danielle huffs in one lungful of air and then another. Claps Kristin on the back. They stand for five or ten seconds and then Kristin shuffles away, moving into their recovery lap before they tackle another interval.

"Where were we?" Kristin asks after a stride or two.

Danielle's surprised. This is unlike Kristin, whose sense of pace is legendary. "Nine seconds under," Danielle tells her.

Kristin shakes her head. "That's so weird. I thought it was slow."

"Really?" Danielle asks. "You killed it. Let's ease up on the next one."

"Yep," Kristin says. Their shuffle quickens to a jog. A recovery lap can take twice as long as a repeat and yet flash by. By the time they're heading down the final straightaway, Danielle can feel Kristin's energy bursting out of her. She burns like a giant bonfire. It makes Danielle feel a little sick.

The next three 400s are all too fast. Way too fast. After each one,

Kristin claims she thought it was slow. On the one hand, Danielle's happy that Kristin is running so well, that she's ticking through the workout like a series of easy striders across a grassy field at the end of a long, slow run. On the other, she's more certain that whatever is wrong with Kristin is serious. Kristin blazes into their final repeat—an 800—like she's racing. Danielle just manages to stay with her during the first lap, but in the second and final one, Kristin shoots forward, accelerating steadily, pulling away from Danielle until Kristin is more than 50 meters ahead of her. It's absolutely insane. By Danielle's estimate, Kristin has knocked off the second lap as fast as most of the sprinters run the 400.

"What is wrong with you?" Danielle demands when she finally catches her breath. She knows she sounds irritated, but she's too tired and confused to mask it. Her legs are going to be leaden tomorrow. The whole point was to run at a slow and comfortable pace. Not to kill each other. They're walking now. They get half a lap, or maybe a whole one, before they start their two-mile cooldown.

"I don't know." Kristin barely sounds winded

"Your pace is off," Danielle continues. Her dorm room beckons, with microwave popcorn for dinner and definitely a couple glasses of the merlot from her dad after what Kristin has put her through. "Way off."

"I'm sorry," Kristin says, walking faster and pulling ahead again.

"You couldn't tell?" Danielle's upset because she's hungry and tired, and she feels like she's been tricked in some way—she came out here to lift Kristin up, not to let Kristin beat her down. Now she's worried she's going to be dead on Saturday, and she's worried about worrying, and she senses herself spiraling to a place she doesn't want to go. She can appreciate how Chloe felt that day Kirstin wouldn't stop running.

Kristin says something that Danielle doesn't catch. "What?" Danielle asks.

"I can't feel anything," Kristin says.

Suddenly the lights go off and the track plunges into darkness, and Kristin is a cutout of darker darkness in front of Danielle, as flat as a paper doll. Though she doesn't want to, Danielle jogs forward. "What do you mean?"

"I just keep thinking about running away," Kristin says in a robotic way, and Danielle's mood starts to sink.

She hurries forward as though proximity will help her decipher what's going on. "Why?" Danielle asks. "Running away from what?"

"I'm fast," Kristin continues, still facing away from Danielle as though she doesn't care about being heard. "If I'd known it was going to happen, I could have run away. I could have just headed back down the mountain before it got so dark. Instead, I waited and I got lost."

"I don't understand," she says. "What are you talking about?" She thinks of when she tried to run away from a bat. The first time, she didn't know she had anything to fear. But the second time, she was overcome by the terror of trying to outrun something that shouldn't be pursuing you but will catch you even if you are running the best race of your life.

"There was this guy who I liked," Kristin whimpers.

"Jed? The coffee-shop guy? What happened?" Danielle grabs Kristin's hand. It's cold. Despite the work she's done, despite everything and nothing, Danielle's mind leaps to the worst, and she pictures something she doesn't want to see.

The story unspools slowly. Every minute or two, Kristin stops and cries for a few minutes, and Danielle says she's sorry. He was older than she was. Shockingly handsome, outdoorsy, adventurous. He took her to places in Boise that she didn't even know existed. They hung out a lot, and she thought she really liked him.

"And I think he was really into me," Kristin says as though surprised by this possibility. Danielle almost can't believe that Kristin is so oblivious, except that she has tons of evidence from the past two years. Everyone's a little in love with Kristin, and she has no idea.

"Once we were making out on top of a hill in a park, and he said he liked me too much to fuck me there."

"He said that?" Danielle blurts out. "That's kind of gross."

"Is it?" Kristin says, lapsing back into the same cold voice that sounds nothing like her. "I don't know. It seemed kind of thrilling at the time. I mean," she laughs a little, "no one has ever said that to me."

A wave of nausea makes Danielle realize how tired she is. Cold and tired and almost broken. There's nothing cool about a guy saying he wants to fuck you, she's tempted to point out. They say it all the time. Maybe if you're a girl, it's OK, or edgy, or whatever. But from a guy, it's lame and predictable. Her damp shirt sticks to her torso. She wants to go back to the bleachers and get a sweatshirt. But she doesn't because Kristin has started talking again about a backpacking trip in some place called the Sawtooths. She listens more closely, trying to hear what Kristin is really saying. She hears the words *lake* and *hypothermia*.

"He wanted me to pretend to be a bear," Kristin says. She's crying again. "And then he started pretending like I was a bear, like I was actually going to hurt him. But I wasn't a bear."

Danielle doesn't know what to think.

"Then he said it was all a joke," Kristin continues. "Maybe he was right. I'd drunk a lot. I just can't believe I was so stupid. We were miles from anywhere."

The outline of Kristin's face is visible, but not the details of her expression. "Kristin," Danielle asks very quietly. "What happened? Did he . . ." She searches for the right word. "Did he attack you?" Her heart bursts with energy with nowhere to go.

"No," she spits out. "No, he didn't rape me."

"Are you sure?"

"Yes!" she insists.

"Then what happened?"

"I didn't want to have sex," she says. "Everything had been so weird. I just didn't want to, and he did."

"Did you end up . . ." Danielle doesn't have to finish her sentence.

Kristin nods.

"I'm sorry," Danielle says. "That really sucks. Had you guys had sex before then?" She can't say why this is relevant.

"No," Kristin says.

"I'm so sorry, Kristin." Danielle lets go of Kristin's hand because her own is getting sweaty. They have moved back to safer territory, and something closes inside her, the click imperceptible. Who hasn't wound up giving in and having sex? Most of her friends have. She has. It's a girl's job to say no, and it's a guy's job to beg and wheedle until eventually the girl caves in. It's fucked up, but that's the dance.

Kristin hugs herself. "I was fine until he wrote to me."

"He wrote to you?"

"I thought he might apologize, but he's crazy."

"What did he say?"

"Nothing," she says. "Nothing that made any sense."

"I'm sorry," Danielle says again. What was it that Harriet said to her? We're not defined by what happens to us? Or was that Assistant Coach? Her mind is getting foggy. "You're going to be OK," she says, putting her arm around Kristin's shoulder and steering them both back toward the bleachers. It's too dark for

Danielle to read the numbers on her watch, and she doesn't want to push the light for fear that Kristin will think she's in a hurry. She's not. They have plenty of time. All that matters is that Kristin starts to feel better.

"I hope so," Kristin says.

"I really think you will be," Danielle says again, giving her arm a squeeze. All of this sounds so familiar. How many times has she said the same to herself? "You're strong."

"I know."

"You said it yourself," Danielle continues. "You could have outrun him."

Kristin hiccoughs. "The irony."

"He sounds like such a creep," Danielle says, "but you're going to be OK. Look how fast you've been running."

"I thought if I was the best, I'd be OK," Kristin says.

"You're the best," Danielle says. "You are."

"But I missed the meet."

"Don't worry about it," Danielle says. "There's still time. And you're going to be fine."

"I am," Kristin says.

"Say it like you believe it," Danielle demands. "*I am fine.* And not just fine. *I am fast and strong and beautiful. I am so strong.*"

"I am fine," Kristin says in a slightly shaky voice. "I am fast and strong and . . . I'm not going to say beautiful."

"Kristi!" Danielle gives Kristin playful punch on the arm. She can't help herself. Harriet has rubbed off on her. "Oh my god, you are so annoying."

Kristin is quiet for a moment. "I'm OK."

"You are," Danielle says. "You really are. If you'd known what was going to happen, you could have run away."

"I could have run away," she says. "I am so much faster than Jed."

"And you've been running so well all season."

"I have," she says.

At the bleachers, though Danielle is shivering, she hands Kristin her sweats, bundles up the rest of their clothes, and stuffs them into her backpack. Beyond the gates to the track, the neighborhood houses are brightly lit, and the moon has climbed halfway up the sky. Somewhere a sprinkler is making a sound of paper being ripped into strips. Why would someone be watering so late in the fall? They just need to keep moving forward—past the house where Flores lives with his crazy teenage son and into the neighborhood where professors are watching TV or giving their children baths or writing the next day's lectures and then back on campus where Danielle will take Kristin to the café in the campus center and buy her a hot cocoa and a slice of pizza, diets and healthy eating be damned. They have time. Everything will be OK. Danielle will make sure of it. Kristin just needs to see that it's not as bad as she thinks. Or, failing that, Kristin needs to channel her fury, as she did tonight, and imagine she's running away, putting distance between her and the guy who wasn't listening when she said she didn't want to have sex. Almost every girl on the team could tap into a memory like that.

SAWYER INVITATIONAL

October 24

DANIELLE WHISPERED SOMETHING TO KRISTIN RIGHT BEFORE OUR next race at Sawyer. We were happy she was back, happy and relieved, but also irritated, because she wouldn't tell us where she'd gone.

Kristin pulled away from the pack almost immediately and never gave anyone a chance to get close. It was a brutal start on an uphill that lasted most of a mile. The course belonged to our rival. In every way, we felt superior to Sawyer, except that their school colors were better than ours, they weren't saddled with a mascot who extolled indecisiveness and ambiguity, and they had topped Frost for several years in a row in the *U.S. News and World Report* ranking of the best liberal arts colleges in the country. It was painful to come in second.

We loved to hate Sawyer (mascot the Beavers). Ours was a rivalry that had started a hundred years earlier when their president snuck away under the cover of darkness from their campus way off in a slightly more rural part of western Massachusetts to become president of our college. Rumor had it that he brought half of Sawyer's students with him, their knapsacks filled with stolen library books. The Beaves unsuccessfully tried to lure him back by telling him they would forgive all of the library fines.

We also truly hated the Beaves, our hatred fed by real and serious envy. For years their school in the middle of bumfuck nowhere had fielded cross country teams of incredible depth and heart, and they'd sent groups of girls to Nationals repeatedly, and won the championship three years in a row. Season after season, someone on their team insisted on running barefoot. Cross country. Track. The steeplechase. It was disgustingly wholesome. For fun, they tipped cows, made their own granola, knit sweaters while listening to *Prairie Home Companion,* ate pancakes whipped up with their own sourdough starter, drummed and danced in the rain, and played charades. At meets, we met the female Beaves' unshaven armpits, their boobs that needed more restrictive bras, the homemade bran muffins that they wolfed down after they had creamed us yet again. And their chants. Oh God, their chants.

> *Beaver one, and beaver all*
> *Let's all do the beaver crawl*

> *Beaver two, and beaver three*
> *We'll win today or fell a tree*

> *Beaver four, and beaver five*
> *Thump your tails and make them cry*

> *Beavers, beavers build your dam*
> *And strand your foe in Ketchikan*

Go Beavers!

They did not watch the news or listen to the radio. They did not seem to know that we were living in the shadow of what happened to Anita Hill during Clarence Thomas's confirmation hearings. As Harriet put it, "The good old boys made a deal with the devil and decided that a sexist Black justice was better than no Black justice at all." Now whenever we saw him sitting at the bench draped in a robe like the ones our professors donned for convocation and commencement, we'd have to imagine him eyeing a can of Coke on his desk and asking poor Anita Hill, "Who put pubic hair on my Coke?" We discussed this detail at length. Sloane absolutely insisted that a guy would never in a million years notice a single pubic hair anywhere. It just wasn't in their DNA. If it were a bush's worth of pubic hair, Sloane said, that would be a different matter. Sloane was captain of the men's team, a delightful wise-ass. "Then I believe the utterance would have been, 'Who put a vajungle on my Coke?'" Harriet smacked Sloane in the arm, even though she was laughing.

After the meet, Coach congratulated us. We had come very close to living up to our potential, Coach said. Very well done. We had drummed the Beaves. This was lavish praise coming from him. Next time he'd expect more, he said, as though offering real encouragement. He pounded his fist in his open palm before stuffing both hands deep into the pockets of his tracksuit. Even when he was happy, he looked upset. Assistant Coach grinned sheepishly, the hood of his windbreaker pulled tight and protecting him from the wind and rain that buffeted our bare legs and arms.

Chloe took off on the cool-down while the rest of us were still wrestling with our rain pants. She looked as happy as Dorothy

Hamill after taking a spill on the ice. Danielle announced that she and Kristin needed to talk, and they headed off in the opposite direction. Coach waved Liv over, and the two of them walked toward the apple orchard on one side of the course. She'd had a very good race, sticking with Chloe and nearly outkicking her in the last fifty meters. We watched as Coach kept pointing at Liv's shoes. Then he started running.

"*Mon doo doo,*" Patricia said.

"That's a shocker," Harriet agreed.

He kept running for a dozen strides or so before slowing to his distinctive amble. Coach never ran. It was the part of his story that seemed unbearably tragic to us. Once an incredibly talented runner, he'd given it up completely. When he'd been forced to stop competing, what was the point? We thought we'd love running for the rest of our lives. Losing it would be like losing the sun, like living in perpetual night. "You will see," he'd once told us, "there's no reason to do it for fun since it was never fun to begin with. That's not why you run."

BOOK OF LOVE

Danielle

DANIELLE NEEDS TO BLOW OFF STEAM. THOUGH THEY WON THE SAW-
yer Invitational, she feels unsettled.

She comes through the door of her common room, tattooed
in dried mud and mucus, freaking out about the team's prospects
while trying to maintain a positive outlook, and the Darlings are
there to greet her. "Let's have a party," they cry.

Danielle is so grateful for these friends. "Let's do," she cries
back. "Let's get wasted."

They are a well-oiled machine. One of the Darlings is in
charge of mood and music. A second Darling makes a run to Stop
& Shop for nibbles. Baked brie, with dried cranberries sprinkled
over the top, is their latest obsession. The third Darling returns
from her shift at the cafeteria with a wine bucket filled with ice, a
case of small cans of spicy tomato juice, an industrial-sized bottle
of vanilla extract, a bag of walnuts, and chocolate chips. Her
kleptomania is a running joke because humor is the only way of

dealing with the fact that she is a thief. Danielle goes to the package store for the booze.

"Mirror in the Bathroom" is playing when she returns. Two of the Darlings are doing something that looks like a cross between dancing and an aerobics routine. The other is lighting candles, her hand cupped around the glow of the lit match as she moves around the room. The smell of this—of the burnt matches and wax and baking cookies—gives Danielle déjà vu, and for a moment she feels confused: Has the night already happened, or is it just beginning? She shakes her head, her hair still damp from the shower. She blinks back tears. "You girls are the best," she calls out. "Everything's perfect."

"Not quite," a Darling says, taking the box of drinks from Danielle, and before Danielle quite knows how, she has a glass of prosecco in one hand and a fizzing sparkler in the other. "Where did this come from?" she yips. They're all holding sparklers.

"To the Darlings," the Darlings say.

The first sip of prosecco feels like crumpled-up aluminum foil in Danielle's mouth. The next one tickles pleasantly. The pre-party, when it's just the four of them, is almost better than the party itself, just like the smell of steak is usually better than the act of chewing it. Most things are like that, with the exception of having sex with Spanky, her latest crush. "Write your name," one of her roommates instructs her. "Make a D in the air."

"We're going to set off the fire alarm," Danielle says, feeling dizzy. Already, her anxiety is receding. If only she can get it to stay there.

But no, the alarms are already disabled and have been since the beginning of the school year, since there is always smoke of one kind or another in their common room. With her sparkler,

Danielle draws a straight line, then half a circle. The air seems to hold the light, even after it's gone. Her glass is full again. She should pace herself since she's hardly eaten anything since breakfast, just the McIntosh from their bag lunches. And yet the moment she has this thought, she knows she won't. She laughs. A carrot is the perfect vehicle for transporting hummus into her mouth. So is her finger. The glow of the candles blurs the room. She gets up to dance when "Boy" comes on. They're all mouthing the lyrics.

I want to be where the boys are, but I'm not allowed.

Ridiculous.

The carpet is undulating, and she's riding it like a surfboard until she slips off.

And then they're all sitting around on the floor, popping open the tiny cans of tomato juice and pouring them into the glass vase. Of course, they have glass vases, which double as vessels for mixing drinks. Harriet is there, without Karen—thank goodness. She wants Harriet all to herself. Harriet looks fetching in overalls and red lipstick. A little jig of kisses, left, right, left, which Danielle amazingly doesn't mess up. Harriet cheeks are soft and smell of geraniums. Tears of gratitude leak from Danielle's eyes.

"Where's Kristin?" Harriet asks.

Danielle shakes her head. "She's fine," Danielle says. "You know how Kristin is. She hates parties."

"I'm more than a little worried," Harriet says.

Before she can answer, Chloe materializes at her side. Who invited her?

"Is Joe here?" Chloe asks.

"Who's Joe?" Harriet asks.

"Chloe has a crush on Joe," Danielle says, melting into the carpet. Poor Chloe and her unattainable crushes. "I'm sorry you didn't win today," she says to Chloe.

"Are you?" Chloe demands.

Of course she is. Danielle is sorry about everything.

One of the Darlings is measuring teaspoons of vanilla into shot glasses of vodka.

"What are you doing?" Harriet asks.

"It's a variation on the pickle back," the Darling says.

"Pickle what?" Harriet asks.

The door pounds. Fear surges through Danielle as surely as the adrenaline that floods her body before the gun goes off. She must look ill, because Harriet grabs her hand and squeezes. One. Two. Three times. You're fine, Harriet mouths. She has nowhere to run, which is the worst part of it. Her only choice is to stand there and go nowhere and do nothing. It feels like forever, but before she knows it, she has a new drink in her hand. A Bloody Mary. Harriet says, No tears. Or maybe cheers. There are baby carrots at the bottom of it. The guys from downstairs burst into their common room.

The baseball boys! In their baseball caps! They like to party with them because baseball is such a head game—all that time sitting in the dugout, waiting to come up to bat, or standing in the outfield, wondering whether someone's going to hit a ball. It's possible baseball is a bigger mind-fuck than cross country.

"Joe!" Chloe cries, but Joe lives off campus in a specialty house for kids who are devoted to cooking their own food and smoking. Danielle doesn't know how she knows this.

"Why don't you just call him?" Danielle shouts over the din as she scans the room for Spanky, but the only ponytails are being worn by women.

"It's too late," Chloe says. She gathers her hair and drops it. Gathers and drops. Gathers and drops. Danielle can smell the lavender shampoo she uses.

"Stop fiddling." Danielle looks at her watch. "It's only 10:07."

She remembers that Spanky's parents are in town. He invited her to go out to dinner with them, but she said she would probably be too tired. "If you change your mind," he said hopefully, and she said, "I'm like a head of wilted lettuce after meets." Even though she hates PDA, she gave him a quick but meaningful kiss in the campus center to cheer him up.

"I can't call him," Chloe says. "I can only prank-call him."

Danielle and Harriet look at each other and laugh.

"Do you want us to call him?" Harriet screams.

"No!"

"We could tell him we're having a party," Danielle says, her voice hoarse from half-shouting.

"Do you guys know him?" Chloe asks.

"Not really. But we could tell him that you like him, and we're having a party."

"That would be so embarrassing," Chloe says.

Somehow Harriet finds the phone stashed under a table. It has a very long cord. "Hi, Joe," she says. "It's your lucky day."

Chloe looks peeved. "You don't even know his number."

"Where's the directory?" Danielle asks.

"This is so embarrassing," Chloe says.

"Joe? Hey, this is Danielle. You don't know me, but I'm Chloe's teammate, and she thinks you're hot."

Chloe clamps her hands against her bright red face. "Hang up."

"I'm just joking. But I'll call him if you want me to." The issue suddenly feels very serious. Now that Danielle understands why Kristin must usurp Chloe's position, Chloe needs something else. A boyfriend would balance everything out. "Do you want me to?"

"I don't know."

"Chloe, just make up your mind," Danielle says. "It's not a big deal. It's not like I'm asking him to ask you to marry him."

"Why doesn't he?"

Danielle laughs. "Are you insane? You want to marry him?"

"Marriage is the site of women's oppression," Harriet says sternly.

And then Danielle's in the bathroom because Harriet needs to pee. They lock the door, and the noise of the party fades. There's a certain way that Danielle looks when she's drunk, a softer version of herself. Tendrils of hair are loose around her face, and her eyes are sad. She smiles, but she still looks weary. *Lovelorn* comes to mind, though she's not even sure what the word means, just that it sounds romantic. But it's too late for her to believe in romance. Harriet would say that's a good thing, but Danielle doesn't think so.

"What?" Harriet says as she unfastens her overall straps, folds the bib down, unbuttons the sides, pushes the whole contraption over her hips to her ankles. Overalls are not very feminist, Danielle thinks. They're more effort than pantyhose. Harriet pees like a racehorse, ferociously loud and splashy.

"I don't know," Danielle says.

"You don't know what?" Harriet asks.

"Everything," she says. She can't find her lipstick anywhere until she realizes she's rooting around in the wrong drawer.

"A little *je ne sais quoi* is good for you," Harriet says. "You need to learn to embrace uncertainty. What do you think life is going to be like once we graduate?"

"Shit," Danielle says as she smacks her lips and then touches her pinky finger to her tongue and smudges her eye makeup. "I'm going to go out faster in next week's race."

Harriet laughs. "Everything is not about running."

"For now it is," she continues, thinking if she says it, maybe Harriet will say it, too. She holds her breath.

"You're insane." Harriet is still unspooling toilet paper and letting it pile up in her lap. "You're like the mommy Energizer
bunny."

Danielle's love for Harriet is immense. "I am so drunk," she
thinks out loud.

"If you know it, then you're not as drunk as you think," Harriet says.

"Except if you don't remember it the next day. If you don't
remember, then it didn't happen." She's tempted to add: If you
never try, you'll never fail.

Harriet laughs. "Whatever gets you through the day, *mon
amie*. But please be careful." She stands, repeating the process of
taking off her overalls in reverse.

"I will," Danielle says. "I promise."

And then she has an arm around Chloe and an arm around Joe,
and she is shouting, "You guys are so cute together. You should
definitely go out." Joe is wearing a tweed newsie and brown cor-
duroys. His eyes are emerald-green, sensitive, and his leather
shoes' rounded toes remind Danielle of her dad. He's definitely a
catch. "Did you know that Chloe has a tattoo?" She has never
seen Chloe blush before. "Chloe, you should show Joe your butterfly tattoo."

Someone hands her a Budweiser. She doesn't normally drink
beer, but she's hot and thirsty and her throat is hoarse from
shouting over the music. It's so cold. It's nice to press the can
against her lips and temple. "Beer tastes like college," she talk-
screams to the guy who stands next to her. "All the happy memories." It slides down her throat, and she barely tastes it at all.

She switches to apple cider and rum, her superego feebly pro-
testing that it is never a good idea for her to drink hard alcohol.

She has no idea where the rum came from, but all the other bottles on the table are empty. And if she drinks Coke now, she'll never go to sleep. She's telling someone that she has to go for a run in the morning, even the day after a meet. It's especially important the day after. You know, you need to move your legs and drain the lactic acid. She's nodding emphatically. Recovery is every bit as important as building.

Who are all these people? she wonders. Where's Harriet?

And then one of the Darlings leans down, grabs her hands, and pulls her up from the couch. They swing back and forth for a moment, heel to toe, heel to toe, until Danielle almost falls backward. "I've been looking for you everywhere," the Darling says, "You disappeared. You left me." She opens her hand. In her palm is Danielle's missing diamond stud.

"Where did you find that?" Danielle asks with glee. "I didn't even know I lost it."

Thigh to thigh, they're all getting down. *Boys, uh huh. Boys, uh huh.* It's so juicy. Something smells like it's burning, but it's just that someone knocked over a candle.

The cookies!

Danielle's fingers are gooey with wax and chocolate. She licks them off one by one. Someone whispers, "That's sexy."

He's very close to her, practically touching her face. It's funny how they sneak up like that, how you don't know what's going to happen until it's happening. And then sometimes you just have to forget.

"Do you want one?" she asks.

"If you feed me," he says.

And then she's the dancing queen, though her legs are so tired that she's having a little trouble standing, but she's getting by. Girls just want to have fun, even Frosties. The Darlings are dancing close, they're lip-synching in each other's faces, they're pointing and being emphatic. This is their moment. THIS IS THEIR MOMENT. Even Chloe is trying to dance. She's stuttering around Joe like wind-up toy, and he's moving like honey oozing off a spoon, and Danielle thinks Chloe doesn't stand a chance. Poor Chloe. Something somewhere smells like it's burning again, but it's just another tipped-over candle, spilling wax onto the top of the microwave.

And then she's outside and someone is telling her to look up, there's Pegasus, the winged horse. She shivers and pulls her sweater around her, but it's not there anymore. She can barely see the stars through her own haze. "That's yours," someone is saying. Not Spanky. She wishes she could find him, but he's not there. "Your mascot. Fast and fleet of foot. You ladies rock." The sky looks black and endless. She starts to sway but someone grabs her arm and steadies her.

"Thank you," she says.

And then somehow she is slumped against the dorm; the bricks hold the tiniest bit of heat from the day, and someone is embracing her, which makes her a little bit cozier, too, and she is talking all about Kristin—how she went out this guy over the summer. She went camping with him. Danielle snorts and then she starts to cough. Sorry, she says, pressing her palm against her mouth. She was in the mountains with him.

She recalls the second bat. She thinks about how dumb it was to go running in the exact same place. What was she thinking?

It's like the dumbest thing ever, she says. Why would she do that?

And she's telling Kristin's story to someone; she's telling her story, which has a happy ending because it's not a big deal. It's not great, but it's also, like, not the biggest deal in the world. You just have to get over it. We all have to get over things, you know. When shitty things happen, which they do, all the time—it's not like I don't know that—I have seen the shit, the shitty shit, she says, when shitty things happen, you just have to put them behind you.

And then Harriet's there, extricating her from a warm embrace, saying to someone, "Dude, she's wasted," and then in a different voice, "There you are *mon cherie,* you disappeared. Let's get you inside."

And now she's back in the bathroom, and Harriet hands her one glass of water and then another and another until she is going to burst open. *Drink up, Dani, Dani.* She finds a toothbrush in her hand, and Harriet helps her kneel down in front of the toilet.

"I'll be right outside," Harriet says because one of Harriet's few flaws is that she can't stomach the sight of other people getting sick.

Danielle sticks the handle end of the toothbrush down her throat—it doesn't take much, just a couple of swipes. She's done it enough times that it's automatic, like pushing a little harder when her legs start to tighten or trying to get control of her breathing by inhaling through her nose and exhaling through her mouth. Harriet reluctantly taught Danielle how to make herself vomit at the end of freshman year because she sometimes drank herself into darkness, and if she could just remember this one thing. "Promise," Harriet had said. *Vomit,* such a Harriet word.

After wiping off the toilet seat, she flushes twice. Rinses her mouth and cheeks, sprays air freshener to mask the smell, though no one will be deceived. There's no guarantee that she won't have a hangover tomorrow, but maybe it won't be too bad. Her reflection in the mirror is blurred, and she knuckles her eyes, trying to see herself more clearly. "You're OK," she says to the girl in the mirror. Is that her? She shakes her heads, tucks her bangs behind her ears. "You're going to be OK, sweetie," she says, trying out compassion. "You really will be."

Out in the common room, the music is still thumping. It sounds like rap, which means the baseball boys have seized control of the stereo. She wonders whether Spanky is finally there. She thinks about trying to find him, but she's not sure she can. Maybe later. Maybe she will rally. She could have another drink. Maybe that will help her get back into her groove. "You are so strong," she says to the girl in the mirror, who looks back at her, unconvinced.

AFFIRMATIONS

We said, "That was rough."

We said, "The second mile was brutal."

We said, "I ran a PR."

We said, "The doctor thinks I have a stress fracture in my hip, but as long as I ice it, I should be able to get through the rest of the season."

We said, "I should work on my kick."

We said, "Next week's a fifty-miler."

We said, "Coach told me to lose five pounds."

We said, "I peed my pants in the first mile."

We said, "When someone goes by me, I need to get angry, I need to fight back."

We said, "I felt like throwing up."

We said, "I threw up."

We said, "I need to lose ten pounds."

These were not affirmations, not in the technical sense, not like, *You can do it!* And *You're great!* And *You're beautiful on the in-*

side, too. We understood the difference between the affirmative and the declarative; we understood the slippery slope of description, how a slope became even more slippery when certain words (treacherous, scary, suicidal, nonconsensual, alcoholic, brutal) were applied to it. As runners, we'd practically been born with the ability to accept the imperative. Even to embrace it. Commands were so natural it was hardly necessary for anyone else to issue them. Even when someone as seemingly well-adjusted as Danielle came upon the lists she'd made during college, lists that appeared on the title page of books she loved (anything by Jane Austen) and in the middle of notebooks from courses like Consciousness and the Brain and Close Relationships, she'd be amazed by the number of times *STAY FOCUSED* or *EAT LESS SUGAR* appeared among more worthy tasks like *RESEARCH GRAD SCHOOLS* and *APPLY FOR INTERNSHIPS.*

We thought (at least once a month after a rough night): "Stop drinking."

We thought (about once a week immediately after finishing a workout, a repeat, a race), "Don't be a crybaby."

Chloe told herself, "You can beat Kristin." Even though she felt bad about her stupid prank, she still wanted to win.

Danielle told herself, "You're going to be OK."

Then: "Just forgive yourself."

Liv told herself, "Don't worry."

Patricia told herself, "Be in the present. Stop counting down the days." Then she always added, "Fuck that. Don't be in the present. Do whatever it takes to survive."

Kristin told herself, "You're going to be OK." She did not tell herself, "Just forgive yourself."

Harriet told herself, "Be grateful for what you have." Everyone would have been surprised by how earnest Harriet's interior monologue could sometimes sound.

THE TRAVELING SPONGE

HERE'S WHAT WE DID: TELL EACH OTHER STUFF, TRADING ONE INTImacy for another, the more personal, the better.

We didn't know everything, though. We didn't know that something bad had happened to Danielle at the end of freshman year, and we didn't know that Patricia wanted to leave Frost, and we couldn't fathom the depths of Chloe's insecurity, especially after Zoo Boy tried to kiss her on the cheek at the end of the Darlings' party and wound up slobbering on her ear because Chloe abruptly turned her head. We didn't know that Harriet taught Danielle to throw up, even though she never did it herself, and could never have imagined Liv punching herself in the stomach when she thought she might be pregnant, though we did know that she could have been pregnant, because of the incident with the sponge.

It was the perfect story to tell, especially once she'd gotten her period: just humiliating enough to be funny, just intimate enough to seem important, harrowing but with a happy ending. Liv told Harriet, hoping to amuse her. Harriet had made some gestures at friendship, and Liv wanted to reciprocate. Afterward, Harriet told Liv about losing her virginity, only she didn't say that; Harriet being Harriet, called it her first fuck and said it had been a real disappointment. "I thought it would be like—I don't know—like skydiving," Harriet said, "I mean everyone makes such a big deal out of it. But it was more like being turned inside-out."

"What's it like sleeping with girls?" Liv asked, which was what she really wanted to know. "Is it like skydiving?"

Harriet didn't answer.

"Aren't you and Karen . . . ?"

Harriet still didn't answer.

Was Harriet actually being secretive? Liv couldn't believe it.

Then, Harriet told Danielle about what had happened to Liv because Harriet and Danielle liked to gossip, even though neither of them would cop to this publicly, and Harriet thought Danielle would find it interesting that the ER doc told Liv that there was nothing to be embarrassed about—a sponge was one of the more mundane objects he'd extracted from a vagina.

"Doesn't it make you wonder about what else women get stuck in their vajayjays."

Danielle stuck out her tongue. Then she said, "I once stuck in another tampon without taking out the first one."

"Oh my god," Harriet said. "Were you drunk?"

"No," Danielle said. "I was just tired."

"Tired?" Harriet asked.

"End of freshman year," Danielle said. "You remember."

Harriet laughed. "Right. That was the time you passed out at dinner."

"Did I?" Danielle said.

"Yeah, you took a bite of Grape-Nuts, put your head down on

the table, and just totally konked out. I had to walk you back to your room and put you to bed."

"What would I do without you?" Danielle asked.

Harriet punched her on the arm. Danielle's arm had a perma-bruise because of their friendship.

And then Danielle told Patricia on a long Sunday burner when they'd found themselves separated from the rest of the team. Maybe they'd taken a wrong turn? It didn't matter. Danielle didn't know Patricia very well, and she was enjoying their conversation, which had wandered from the bratwurst parties at the German house to a novel that took place in the pueblo where Patricia lived that she thought Danielle should read if she wanted to understand anything about indigenous history. "It's a big country," Patricia said several times. "The mountains kiss the plains, and the rivers water both, and the yucca, which you might associate with the desert, climb the slopes of the Jemez, mingling with the scrub pine until they seem to disappear. The boundaries between things are not nearly as distinct as we tell ourselves." Patricia was a bit of a mystery. Last year, she wore a silver bird on a black cord. The raven was her totem animal, she had told someone, and though Danielle had been curious why, she'd never asked Patricia about it, not wanting to make her feel self-conscious. If you were different, you didn't need others to comment on how different you were. Though, of course, Danielle was already betraying her bias by categorizing Patricia in such a way.

Somehow the subject of the lost sponge came up as they were running by one of the big dairy farms, the sad, heavy smell of cows standing nose to butt prompting Danielle to blurt out that Liv had almost ruined her life by getting pregnant, and Patricia, who perhaps hadn't heard her, had said, "I love the smell of cows.

They're so ripe and fertile." And then she started talking about the time that she'd watched a cow give birth, her neighbor Yvette going elbow-deep to pull the struggling calf out of the mama cow's birth canal with a loud slurp and a torrent of fluid. "That's gross," Danielle said, and Patricia shook her head because Jesus! Gross?

"It's miracle," she muttered.

"What?" Danielle asked.

"Nothing," Patricia said.

"I'm sorry, I didn't hear you," Danielle continued. "What did you say?"

And so on and so on.

Long runs could be like that, a stream-of-consciousness conversation, like dreaming with another person, or having a nightmare. Something happened to the brain when you were doing something highly rhythmic and repetitive with your body. It got a little loosey-goosey. It was like being drunk without drinking. That's what people who didn't run (PWDRs) would never understand. It wasn't only painful. It could be an ecstatic experience, too.

And so we knew about Liv, and we knew about Danielle, how she drank too much at times, and she was always joking about it, saying when she didn't wake up she'd know it was finally time to cut back, and weirdly enough the fact that she could crack such jokes made her drinking seem benign. There was also the fact that her dad gave her cases of wine. We knew Harriet was recovering from an eating disorder, and it was doubly hard because she was so deeply ashamed of falling victim to a way of seeing herself and exercising control that was the antithesis of everything she believed in as a feminist. That she made a big show of eschewing cafeteria dessert wasn't cool. We knew next to nothing about Patricia because she was private, though if you asked Patricia she'd say that every time she'd tried to tell us something about herself, we fucked up so badly, showing how clueless we were, that she just couldn't. She couldn't. Worse, we didn't even notice. And we knew that Chloe had lost her virginity in a drunken hookup situation freshman year, and she was embarrassed by the fact that the guy was so short and frankly unattractive, not that she ever said that, but it was easy to read between the lines when she kept insisting that she didn't remember a thing from that evening, not a thing. "I must have blacked out," she insisted. "And the next thing I knew I was putting on my bra, and he said, 'Oh, so that's how you do it.'"

Days later, she and the dude had to meet for lunch because that's what Frosties did—process their hookups, especially if they were drunken hookups. Chloe couldn't quite believe that this was the guy who'd taken her virginity as she watched him chow down on a burger, chewing with his mouth open so she could see the mashup of bun, beef, and lettuce. (When Harriet heard the story, she would say that Chloe needed to reframe the experience, stop seeing it through the lens of the patriarchy. If Chloe did this, she would discover that her vagina had enveloped his penis, surrounded it, *contracting like a fist shutting tight, releasing with a force that pushed hard on the tender thing.* This was one of Harriet's favorite bits from Dworkin's *Intercourse. Tender thing.* "Not sword, not cock, not the mighty phallus, but *tender thing*," Harriet said a bit too gleefully. "Picture how it shrivels up afterward, like a balloon that's losing its air." Picture that? Chloe still didn't have a mental picture of what an erect penis even looked like.)

And we knew that something had happened to Kristin that summer with a guy who was a regular at the coffee shop where she ground espresso and frothed milk. We knew she'd had a *bad* sexual encounter with him. Somehow Danielle knew, and she had gotten drunk and told some dude, and Harriet had overheard the whole thing.

She had a bad sexual encounter, but who hadn't had a bad sexual encounter? we said. That was just part of life.

Right?

WALK AND TALK

Kristin

ELI SWINGS BY HER ROOM AT 6:30, NOT THEIR USUAL TIME, BUT ELI has an editorial meeting later that night.

"I see you're still going for a minimalist vibe," he says as she opens the door, because her room is still mostly empty, like a brand-new notebook.

"I put up my favorite poster," she says, pointing to the photograph of Mary Decker and Zola Budd, moments before their feet tangle and Decker goes crashing to the ground. Budd is bounding forward in bare feet; Decker's face is a mask of calm. She admires both of them. So much can change in a single moment.

"Very uplifting," Eli comments.

"Ha ha," she says.

"I mean if I were the star of the cross country team," he continues, "I'd want to put up a picture to remind me that any moment someone could trip me."

"Or that I could trip someone else." She starts to feel bad

about everything she's done and then she remembers that she's not herself, she's alien. What was it that Danielle told her to do? Channel her anger into winning races. She's an angry alien. And the girl who dove into the lake without first dipping in her toe? What a fricking idiot.

"I'm glad you're not on the lam anymore," Eli says.

"Is that what I was?" she asks.

"An outlaw," he says and then adds, "with room service."

"You call that room service?" she asks. "Where was the Champagne? The chocolate- covered strawberries?"

She laughs because that's what Eli expects.

Outside it's dark and crisp. It would be a beautiful evening, except that Kristin isn't really there. Everyone else is making their way somewhere, from the cafeteria to the library, or from their dorm rooms to a cappella practice or study groups. A group of noisy freshmen throws a Nerf football back and forth on the main quad, cheering every time they manage to pull the object out of the darkness.

"Where do they get the energy for that?" Eli says. "Kids these days."

"Kids," she echoes.

"Hey, Eli," a group of girls calls out.

"Hey," he says. Then in a friendlier voice with a funny fake British accent: "Good evening. Where are you fine ladies off to?"

There is laughter.

"What's so funny?" he asks.

"Nothing," the tall one says. "We're going to the library to study."

"Let me make some introductions. This is my friend, Kristin, cross country runner extraordinaire," he says. "Kristin, these are the Sarahs: Sarah G, the math prodigy." He gestures toward the tall girl. "Sara S, who hails from Charlestown, South Carolina, and paints kick-ass portraits." She has bright red hair, like Liv. "And Susan, who wants to be a big animal vet." She is small with dark hair.

"Nice to meet you all," Kristin says.

"How did your calc exam go?" Eli asks the tall Sarah.

"Really well," she answers.

"Good to hear," he says.

Kristin watches Eli stroking his goatee as he asks each of them questions. He is so adorable, she thinks. What's wrong with her?

"Don't stay up too late," he tells them before saying goodbye.

"You're such a good RA," Kristin says after they go their separate ways. "Do you remember mine? Carol? She was writing a religious-studies thesis about captivity narratives, and she almost never came out of her room, except to fill her electric kettle. We used to joke that she was recreating the experience of having no freedom. I'm not sure she even knew who I was."

He shakes his head. "I have no memory of her. I don't think we were allowed on your floor."

This is an old joke. Their freshman dorm had single-sex floors. Kristin had requested this—she thought she'd have any easier time focusing—while Eli complained that the housing office had made a terrible mistake.

"You were allowed on our floor. You were in my room all the time."

"Was I?" he says. "I can't remember."

"Are you being serious?"

"I'm joking," he says, "though freshman year does seem like it happened eons ago. Don't you feel like a different person?"

"No," she says. "I feel like I'm exactly the same."

"Really? You're kidding, right?"

"No," she says, and she's not. "Are you saying I've changed?"

"What's wrong with you?" he asks.

"There's nothing wrong with me," she says.

"That's not what I said, Kristin," he says. He has stopped walking and stepped out in front of her so that she is forced to stop moving. "I asked 'What's wrong?'"

"Oh," she says. "Did you really say that?" She presses her lips together and pinches the skin between her thumb and pointer finger on her left hand. Her mom used to say you could get rid of a headache by doing this. She switches to the other hand. She doesn't exactly have a headache, but nevertheless the pressure feels good. It feels like she is keeping everything from spilling out.

"If you don't want me to keep asking you what's wrong, I'll stop," Eli says. "Just say the word, and I'll never ask you again. But if you don't tell me to stop, I'm going to keep asking because I'm your friend, and I'm worried about you, and I want to make absolutely sure that you know this, that you know how worried I am."

She presses her lips together harder now until her teeth get in the way, and her mouth feels like a jagged wound that been stitched together.

"I don't know what I want," she answers.

"That's a good start," he says.

"Is it?" she asks.

"I think it's better to admit you don't know than to pretend you do."

"Maybe if you're a dude," she says.

He cocks his head, laughs.

"I'm really struggling," she says.

"I can see that," he says. "I'm sorry."

"And I don't know how to fix it," she says. "I thought I did, I thought I could. I thought being alone would help. I thought telling someone would help. But I don't think it has. I'm still struggling. And I don't want to tell you because you're going to think I'm stupid."

"I promise I won't," he says.

"Well, now I don't believe you."

"Good point," he says. "But in general, I don't find you to be a stupid person."

FIRSTS

"HE THREW HIMSELF ON THE GROUND LIKE I WAS GOING TO ATTACK him," Kristin said, "like I was going to hurt him." Suddenly she started to giggle, and Eli found himself laughing, too, even though there was nothing funny about what she was telling him, and they both kept laughing until Eli panted helplessly, "Stop it. Stop it. I can barely breathe."

When he caught his breath, Eli said, "I'm sorry" and tried to hug her but she kept her arms at her sides.

"Don't say that," she said.

"Why not?"

"Because it makes me feel bad."

"But you have every right to feel bad," Eli said. "That's guy's a monster."

"I don't know about that," she said.

"He sounds like a monster to me," he said.

She got very quiet, and Eli realized his job wasn't to read the map; no, his job was to follow Kristin wherever she led him. He could try to do that.

Harriet called a team meeting.

Danielle missed a Monday practice. Rumor was she'd been nursing a two-day hangover from the Darlings' party the previous Saturday night. She could usually drink until the wee hours and then be up at the crack of dawn, looking totally put-together and ready to run, though sometimes she went too far. Freshman year, Harriet had slept on the floor of Danielle's room from time to time just to make sure she didn't choke on her own vomit or accidentally jump out her dorm window. Once Harriet woke to find Danielle climbing into bed with her. "Snuggle buggle, snuggle buggle," she sang briefly before passing out with Harriet wrapped in what they later coined the *gin grip* because that's what they'd been imbibing all night.

Gin, gin, it'll make you sin, but whiskey makes you frisky.

In a phone call with her parents, Patricia announced she was transferring.

"Patricia, why?" her father demanded.

"It's so small," she said. "Everyone's the same, except for me."

"But it's one of the best schools in the country."

Her father had a point, but still.

"Can I come home and go to UNM?" she asked.

"Absolutely not," her parents answered in unison.

Liv skipped class.

Feminist theory had been Harriet's idea. "Wouldn't it be fun to take a class together?" she'd written to Liv last spring from Paris. The postcard, the first of many, had been a surprise, since they were friendly but hardly friends. Harriet reminded Liv of Mel. They both had a taste for the dramatic. "French women are so chic, I want to fuck all of them," one postcard had said, and another: "I smoked a cigarette. Tell no one."

Just as Liv was making up her mind to skip—her first time at Frost, unless you counted when she was down with mono freshman year and slept for forty-eight hours straight—Harriet flashed through the door of the Emily and made a beeline for her. The Emily was not the actual name of the dining hall, but Harriet had renamed it for some obscure reason.

"Are you coming?" Harriet asked. Her eyes bright, her cheeks flushed, she looked like she had just come in from the cold, though she wasn't wearing a coat. Liv took a sip of water from her water bottle. The cafeteria glasses were inadequate.

"I don't think so."

"Why?"

Liv could have lied and told Harriet she hadn't done the reading, but instead she said she didn't feel like it. Henry still hadn't said anything about his trip to England. Harriet pulled out a chair and dropped into it. She planted her chin in her hands and studied Liv. The sunlight through the window caught silver threads in Harriet's hair. When did that happen? "You should get going," Liv said. "You'll be late."

Harriet didn't move. "Things are really fucked up," she said.

"That's one way of putting it," Liv said.

"*Mon Dieu*," Harriet said. "Have I offended your Midwestern sensibility?"

"Screw you."

Liv thought Harriet looked delighted, which only angered her more. Liv liked Harriet; she admired, and even envied, Harriet's swagger, her feminism, her patriarchy this and phallus that, which Harriet deployed to make them laugh, but not only for the sake of humor. And then there was Harriet's sweetness, which was like finding a crumpled-up dollar in the back pocket of a pair of jeans. But sometimes she could be too much. Just too fucking much.

"We need to do something," Harriet said.

"I did something," Liv blurted out. "I went to the dean. I almost called Kristin's mom." Why was she saying this? Was it because she had a nagging feeling that she had let Kristin down? It reminded her of Mel all over again, of being too afraid to know the truth, for fear that she could not do anything, or whatever she could do would be insufficient, like trying to repair a hole in a house with butcher paper and Scotch tape. She was the one who had lost her grip and dropped Mel in the middle of the freshman quad. But long before that, she was the one who lacked the nerve to tell Mel that she wasn't well, she needed help. Liv loved Mel so much, she didn't want to hurt her.

"Listen," Harriet said, her tone suddenly so grave that Liv wondered whether she'd misheard everything up until that moment. "Kristin was sexually assaulted this summer."

Chloe's roommate Kay had finally agreed to give her a sneak preview of her senior project—a ginormous canvas depicting Frost, though not the Frost of the glossy brochures, but the Frost of everything else.

Chloe stood in Kay's studio in the art building and studied it, this thing of wonder: the graffiti bathroom on C level of the library, and the vomitorium in the basement of Bates. The practice rooms in the music building where kids went to scream. The plundered artifacts behind museum glass. The dreams of animals reduced to specimens. Frost, if he were a rapper. A map of segregation past and present as it played out in the cafeteria. Nervous breakdowns by year. Overdue library books and the reasons they were late. A graph of loose change left behind in dorm-room desks and bureaus. Used checkbook registers. Overdrawn bank accounts. Sticky carpets. What falls out of windows. Portraits of the first class of women, not as they appeared to themselves, but through the eyes of the mostly male faculty. Flowering trees. Stained beds. Effluents. Joy. The snowball fight of 1989 between Frost and UMASS. The terrible chants: *"It's all right. It's OK. You will work for us someday."*

"Remember when someone from UMASS put a rock in a snowball, and that kid in our freshman class lost his eye?" Kay asked.

"That was really horrible." Then Chloe asked, "Is bad teenage boy part of it?"

"Oh yes, he's lurking somewhere along with all the ghosts as they'd like to be remembered."

"And Ken?" Chloe asked quietly. He was a guy who had lived in their dorm last year and hanged himself. Though Chloe didn't really know him, she had cried when she heard the news, the sadness swiftly turning to guilt because she wasn't sure what she was allowed to feel about someone who wasn't even an acquaintance. He had dark brown hair and bright friendly eyes. The crack of dawn often found him cutting across the dew-soaked quad, an early riser like her. Something about his lope made Chloe imagine he was from Alaska.

"There," Kay said pointing out a small figure. "That's his trench coat trailing behind him like a marvelous cape."

"Excellent," Chloe said. "Am I anywhere?"

"You're running," Kay said, gesturing toward part of the canvas covered in storm clouds of green leaves. "See. You're in the woods."

"Really?"

"Yes," Kay said. "You're running so fast you're invisible."

Chloe felt her head rise from her body like a helium balloon before she fell into an entirely new kind of darkness.

THERE YOU ARE

Kristin

When Kristin looks up from the book she's reading, there is Harriet and another girl who looks just like Harriet with shorter hair because she just let Harriet give her a crew cut. Kristin knows this, and much more about this girl, whose name is Karen, because Harriet went on endlessly about the thrill of having shaved her head on the drive to the last meet until Danielle politely told her to shut up. What she actually said through a sad tight smile was "Oh my god, Harriet's so in love," loud enough for Assistant Coach to turn around and give them all a goofy grin. Everyone laughed, except for Kristin, who was drowning in her own nervousness because she didn't know whether Danielle's advice would work: pretend you're running away.

"There you are," Harriet says in a loud whisper because Kristin has chosen a carrel at the end of a low row of books that only part with the press of a button in the sub-sub-sub-basement of the library. She's not hiding. She likes it down here, not just under her present circumstances, but all the time. The background noise is dependably the same—a soft hum that quiets her own mind and helps her focus on whatever she needs to do. Her shoes are off, and she's wearing a pair of thick wool socks over her regular ones and an oversized cardigan. The library gets cold as the night wears on. Not that it's terribly late. It's probably not even nine. All she wants to do is finish her reading and then go to bed. All she wants are for the days to flow by, like water through a ditch. Soon it will be the last meet of the season, the end of the semester, then a new year, the summer fading into the distance, the backpacking trip something she finds herself forgetting for hours at a time.

"We've been looking for you everywhere," Harriet continues.

"Why?" Kristin asks.

A frown dims Harriet's face before she recovers. *"Mon Dieu, it's not like I'm going to bite you."*

Kristin colors. Even though she knows that Harriet is just teasing, she feels the urge to apologize again, to try to explain something she doesn't really understand herself about why she needed to protect the rabbit, but Karen interrupts before she can say anything, sticking out her hand and introducing herself. "We haven't met," she says. "Hairy's manners . . ." Harriet playfully slaps Karen's shoulder. This is her love language, Danielle would say.

"You did great this weekend," Harriet says, sounding very much like Danielle.

"Did Danielle send you to spy on me?"

"Are you crazy?" Harriet says, her voice now louder than a whisper.

Karen purses her lips and presses her pointer finger to her

nose.

"I would never do that," Harriet continues, quiet again. "I'm just worried about you."

Karen nods in agreement.

"You disappeared . . ."

She waits for Harriet to ask the obvious: *Where were you?* It's weird that no one on the team has asked directly. Not even Danielle really, who said, "I get that you needed to take a break, but it would have been nice if you've told us where you were." But no one's asked her, because what could be worse than asking again and again and being ignored?

"Do you have time for a break?" Harriet continues. "We could get a coffee? Or we don't have to get coffee. We could get something else. We could get some ice cream?"

Ice cream?

She suddenly realizes what's going on. Harriet knows. Of course she knows, even though she made Danielle promise not to tell anyone, especially anyone on the team. How could she have been so stupid? She should have known that she couldn't tell Danielle without Harriet finding out.

"I don't have time," Kristin says.

BUDDY

BY THE TIME WE GATHERED IN HARRIET'S COMMON ROOM, THE DE-
tails of what happened to Kristin had circulated, becoming something serious, and also curious—as in *strange, unusual*. That was
the way of rumors: the bigger the drama, the more their actors
shrank until we could sometimes forget that we were talking
about real people, about our friends and teammates, people we
saw every day. About Kristin. We were furious with Danielle for
not telling us, and we were even a little pissed at Kristin, not that
we'd admit this out loud. We were her best friends, and we
wanted what was best for her, and she had a secret that she hadn't
shared with us. It stung a little.

Harriet clomped back and forth in her Doc Martens. Her
common room wasn't nearly as cozy as Danielle's. She and her
roommates had cool band posters, all of them black-and-white,
but beyond that, nothing that made it especially memorable.
Their desks, relocated from their bedrooms, were crowded along
two walls and covered in textbooks, stacks of borrowed cafeteria
dishes, and computers the size of small TVs. Along the third wall

were the college's standard-issue dorm sofas with the standard institutional-blue fabric that was supposedly stain and fire resistant. In the center, a pull-up bar was doing double duty as a drying rack for lace underwear. Was this another taste that Harriet had acquired in Paris? The faint smell of clove cigarettes hung in the air.

Kristin was not there. She had not been invited. Danielle was sitting alone on one of the couches, her arms pretzeled and legs crossed as though she were trying to fold her long limbs into the wings of an origami crane.

"I'm sorry for talking about Kristin behind her back," Danielle said, holding Harriet's gaze. "I was drunk."

"You should stop drinking so much," Harriet said.

Danielle shrugged. "I should stop drinking." She had said this before.

"You told some random dude that Kristin was raped," Liv said, "and you didn't tell us. Why would you do that?"

"Sexually assaulted," Harriet said in a professorial tone. "That's the correct term."

Liv shot a withering look in Harriet's direction.

"That's not what I said," Danielle protested.

"But you can't even really remember, can you?" Harriet pointed out.

"I know I didn't say 'sexually assaulted,'" Danielle said, stumbling over the words slightly, "because I do remember what Kristin told me and that's not what she said."

Down the hallway, a door opened. Moments later, Karen appeared, a pink towel turbaned around her hair. "Sorry," she said. "Am I interrupting something?"

"No," Harriet replied, patting the seat next to her. "We're discussing the Kristin situation."

"You told her?" Danielle demanded.

"She's my girlfriend," Harriet said.

"I am?" Karen said.

"This is a team meeting," Danielle said. "She's not on the team."

"Aren't you?" Harriet asked.

"I thought you found categories like *girlfriend* too bougie," Karen said, "but I'd love to be your girlfriend."

Harriet, who did not giggle, giggled. We almost missed the moment when Karen bent and kissed Harriet because of Danielle's face: an uncanny combination of all of our mothers' faces seconds before they lost their shit.

"I think I should go, Hairy," Karen wisely said. "I just needed some clean undies." She pointed to the pull-up bar.

"Hairy?" someone said. There was more inappropriate giggling as Harriet beamed. Then, Danielle brought her hands together with so much force, it sounded like the gun going off at the start of the race.

"It was that coffee-shop guy," she said. "You know the one she had a crush on? They were dating, and he behaved badly."

"*Mon Dieu*, Dani, '*He behaved badly*'? Just tell us what she told you," Harriet said. "There's no need to mince your words."

"Oh, stop," Danielle said. "You know exactly what I mean. She wasn't into it, and he was. Who hasn't been in that situation?"

The room grew quiet as we flipped through our memories of *that situation*. We shared so much—the fancy bottles of shampoo and conditioner that Danielle's mom sent because the locker-room soap was pink and grainy, safety pins, Band-Aids, pointy hip bones, bruised toenails, too much energy, cheerful dispositions except when we soured on everything and everyone, lucky lipsticks, our intense love of something we also dreaded, hunger pangs and a voracious appetite to be fast, even if we couldn't all be the fastest.

But what about *that*?

"He date-raped her," Harriet said.

"What does that even mean?" Chloe said.

Danielle glared at Harriet. "I don't think it was that bad," she said. "Kristin was fine. She was fine all semester. She was fine until he sent her a weird letter and then she freaked out. But she is fine. And what we need to focus on is making sure that she stays that way."

"It means he raped her," Harriet said to Chloe, ignoring Danielle. "It means . . ."

"That's not what Kristin said," Danielle protested. "And it's not that black-and-white. And besides, we need to—"

Harriet interrupted her. "If you say no, it means no."

"You've never said no and changed your mind?" Danielle's voice shook with anger.

"It's rape," Harriet insisted.

Liv turned so pale that freckles we never knew she had appeared across the bridge of her nose. Patricia mechanically unraveled one of her braids only to begin re-braiding it.

What were we thinking?

"It's not rape," Danielle said. "Rape is something else entirely."

"Why did she keep it a secret?" Chloe asked.

"You don't know," Harriet said.

"Because she was embarrassed?" Chloe said

"I am not talking to you, Chloe." Harriet sounded like she was addressing a toddler. "And for God's sake, why would she be embarrassed? It wasn't her fault."

"I don't know?" Danielle cried. "Are you kidding me, Harriet?" For a moment, she looked like she was going to burst into tears, but then she unfolded herself from the couch and went running from the room.

LOBSTER INVITATIONAL: OCTOBER 31

PL	NAME	TEAM	TIME
1	Alison Ackerman	Olin	17:40
2	Suzie Jackson	Sawyer	18:11
3	Chloe Brooks	Frost	18:12
4	Natalie Ybarra	Clapp	18:24
5	Charlene Zimmerman	Chase	18:34
6	Arianna Driver	Ladd	18:40
7	Audrey Fox	Crossett	18:47
8	Jenny Lynn	Miller	18:51
9	Meredith Henryson	Clapp	18:52
10	Sarah Hutchinson	Williston	19:00
11	Sarah Lyons	Miller	19:05
12	Liv Joiner	Frost	19:09
13	Caitlin Finnegan	Olin	19:11
14	Melissa O'Connor	Sawyer	19:14

15	Helen Wiggins	Chase	19:15
16	Michele Rhee	Crossett	19:16
17	Christine Liu	Chase	19:17
18	Stephanie Pendleton	Clapp	19:20
19	Juniper Joy	Sawyer	19:27
20	Elizabeth Woodman	Williston	19:29
21	Sue Campbell	Ladd	19:31
22	Laura Ivy	Sawyer	19:34
23	Danielle Ziegler	Frost	19:38
24	Dawn Underwood	Ladd	19:41
25	Rhonda Epstein	Sawyer	19:43
26	Stacey Alonso	Crossett	19:45
27	Heidi Beebe	Williston	19:47
28	Catherine Kwan	Ladd	19:50.1
29	Ina Burkhart	Clapp	19:50.3
30	Deb Kozlowski	Sawyer	19:52
31	Linda Honeycutt	Williston	19:59
32	Sarah Pickering	Crossett	20:04
33	Victoria Sanchez	Crossett	20:05
34	Suki Kim	Olin	20:08
35	Jennifer Jacobs	Ladd	20:08.3
36	Patricia West	Frost	20:10
37	Samantha Smith	Clapp	20:11
38	Jessica Valentine	Olin	20:13
39	Marcie Abramson	Williston	20:14
40	Leah Goldstein	Miller	20:16
41	Julie Irish	Crossett	20:20
42	Jennifer Summers	Miller	20:23
43	Michelle Rivera	Sawyer	20:24
44	Lisa Darling	Miller	20:27
45	Cheryl Wade	Chase	20:28

46	Andrea Sessions	Williston	20:29
47	Tanya Brooks	Miller	20:29.2
48	Jessica Lin	Williston	20:29.3
49	Cynthia Pike	Clapp	21:01
50	Harriet Quigley	Frost	21:25
51	Dawn Field	Chase	21:35
52	Tabby Reed	Clapp	21:57
53	Iris Choi	Olin	22:13
54	Anne Bergstrom	Ladd	22:31
55	Amy Cornwall	Ladd	22:47
56	Marcie Lyon	Crossett	23:07
57	Carrie French	Frost	23:30
58	Maria Delgado	Miller	24:10
59	Sue Barton	Chase	24:15.2
60	Katie Levin	Olin	24.15.4
61	Kristin Lapine	Frost	DNF

TALKING

Kristin

EVERYONE WANTS TO TALK TO HER.

She tells Liv and Harriet about the conversation about the bears: the difference between grizzlies and black bears, how to save yourself from a creature who doesn't speak your language. The fact that she liked Jed—What was I thinking?

Harriet responds, "You liked him. That's not your fault."

She does not tell them about the distant hazy mountains like framed nineteenth-century paintings or the blister on her left heel and how she told herself that the pain was clarifying. She does not tell them about the lake, a teardrop in the vast toothy peaks. The water so cold she could not breathe. She doesn't want them to know how many risks she took.

"He wanted me to pretend to be a bear," she says.

She sees the look that Harriet and Liv exchange. Bewilderment. She almost starts to laugh, just as she did when she was explaining all of this to Eli. Laugh—because it was weird? Or because she was embarrassed? The unspoken questions: How do you pretend to be a bear? Why did you do this? *Why didn't you know? How could you be so dumb?* Just because no one has asked these questions doesn't mean they aren't thinking them.

She tells Liv and Harriet that she played along, and then he acted like she actually was a bear, and he threw himself on the ground to save himself while she begged him to stop. She does not say that words are clumsy instruments, though they are. He said it was all a joke. She doesn't know why she keeps telling this part of the story.

"We were drinking," she tells them. "Maybe I was drunk, and I couldn't see that it was a joke?"

"Why are you talking that way?" Harriet scolds. "Don't do that. It's demeaning. And so what if you were drunk?"

Liv smiles at Kristin sympathetically.

Already she has forgotten the explosion of stars overhead, how the moon was missing until she found it impaled on a peak, just at the beginning of its journey across the sky.

She tells them they started to fool around, but she kept thinking about the weird bear stuff. She'd been expecting to sleep with him that weekend, she was so attracted to him, but they'd never had sex. This has become part of the story she tells because Danielle asked her about it. She's not sure how this fact is relevant, but she senses the question hovering at the edge of each and every conversation: *Were you already sexually involved? Were you sleeping together? Were you doing it?*

She wanted to, or she had wanted to, but not there, not right then, not under the circumstances. She tried to convey this to him, but he wasn't listening.

"You told him no," Harriet insists. "You didn't just *try* to. He ignored you."

"That's true," Kristin says, "but then I gave up."

Harriet snorts, and Kristin collapses under the weight of her judgment until she tunes back in to what Harriet is saying: "So typical."

Liv scoots closer to Kristin and takes her hand. "It's not your fault for giving up," she says. "I'm so sorry this happened to you."

The worst part wasn't having sex, her body a feral animal, but when she left later that night and somehow wandered off the trail and hiked for at least a mile before she realized she was lost. For a long time, she sat at the edge of the stream and sobbed because what if she never made it back, all because she didn't want to face him the next morning? Was dying a better option than having to deal with him? She was so weak. But she doesn't tell them this. Instead, she says: "While he was sleeping, or passed out," she exhales sharply through her nose, "I packed up and left."

"You are so brave," Harriet says, and all Kristin can do is laugh.

Though she doesn't admit to Patricia that she got lost, Patricia immediately understands how awful it was to hike back by herself. It was like heading out on a twelve-mile run and wishing it were over after ten minutes and then plodding along for another ninety without ever achieving a runner's high. She doesn't attempt to explain this feeling to anyone else.

Patricia is nodding yes. "Were you worried that he'd wake up and try to catch up with you?"

"No," she lies, because the answer is too complicated. When she was lost, she would have been grateful if he had rescued her.

"Huh," Patricia says.

"He was so slow on the way in," she explains. "He kept going on and on about how important it was to pace yourself and take small steps." Kristin makes herself laugh.

Patricia nods again.

"And he was hiking in cowboy boots."

At one point on the hike back, she gazed up at a high peak and saw on the final slope to the jagged top a solitary figure standing there that she mistook for Jed for a few moments until she realized it was a tree, the last one before it became too steep and rocky for anything to grow.

"I totally freaked out," she says, which is sort of true.

"The mind is a mighty trickster," Patricia says. "I have never once finished a long hike without thinking I was completely lost the last couple of miles."

"Have you ever actually gotten lost?" Kristin asks.

"Never," Patricia says.

"You're amazing,"

"Nah," Patricia answers. "I'm just very good at following blazes."

Kristin avoids Danielle.

It's not just that Danielle got drunk and told some dude what happened to Kristin (which she knows thanks to Harriet); it's not just that she has become the subject of gossip on their small campus (which makes her feel like the grasshoppers she used to catch and imprison in glass jars); no, the worst part, if she's being really honest, is the thought of her team talking about her. Danielle could have put a stop to the gossip by insisting that Harriet misunderstood her. She could have asked Harriet how much she had to drink that night. She could have said nothing. She could have teased Harriet for eavesdropping. Kristin's mom used to say *little pitchers have big ears*. She could have brushed the whole thing off as a silly mistake. She could have lied. She should have.

Danielle, the glass-half-full girl, Danielle, with a solution for everything. Da Da Dani. And Kristi. Tall Barbie and curvy Barbie.

Her friend from the second week of freshman year when she somehow intuited the depths of Kristin's homesickness and drove her to Duck Duck Bunny and met her for breakfast every Wednesday and invited her to the Darlings' parties and danced with her and kept inviting her to parties, even though Kristin always left early. Who introduced her to Champagne at the end of her freshman cross country season. Who regularly told her she was gorgeous and did her makeup before the holiday formal. Who felt like some combination of big sister and best friend, even though Kristin understood from years of drifting away from other girls in junior high and high school that she didn't have what it took to sustain a best friendship—that she didn't want to spend all her time with one person, that she was too stubbornly solitary, that she felt too different from most people.

Danielle told her she was strong. She told Kristin to keep doing what she'd done since the beginning of the semester: to channel her anger into winning races. Turning the negative into something positive. "Everyone has terrible things happen to them," Danielle said. "But your trauma doesn't define you. You can let that energy consume you, or you can harness it. Be burned or burn brightly." Kristin wanted to believe Danielle, and she did believe her, even though that's not exactly what she was feeling.

Kristin realizes she's furious not just because Danielle told everyone but even more because she doesn't want to become the girl she's becoming now, the object of everyone's pity. Danielle has no idea what it's like to wake up one morning in a place where you recognize nothing, not the language, not the food, not even the way to the bathroom. How utterly disorienting.

"The First Law of Running," Danielle likes to say, "is a body in motion stays in motion only if you ignore your thoughts."

Last weekend at the race, she felt something rising inside her, her muscular body suddenly an empty vessel being filled with something dark and putrid until it was choking her, and she had to stop running before she even finished the first mile, deep in the woods. She had to stop, and it wasn't because she was thinking bad thoughts, it wasn't because she was *letting her trauma define her* or whatever Danielle had said, it was because she couldn't breathe.

She's furious with Danielle for not understanding how that feels.

Chloe is Chloe. She sneaks up behind Kristin in the cafeteria and yells "Boo!" just as Kristin is turning around with three glasses of skim milk precariously wedged in the triangle of her hands.

"What are you doing?" Kristin cries as milk splatters around her. "You scared me."

"Oh, sorry," Chloe says.

They stand for a moment or two awkwardly as Frosties scurry around them, cafeteria-style eating the modern equivalent of hunting and gathering. Someone hands them a bunch of napkins and Chloe pushes them around with her toe. She shouldn't care that Chloe beat her last weekend. It's hardly a competition if you don't finish the race. But Kristin thinks she can sense Chloe gloating, her expression almost a smirk. Someone bumps into her, and more milk sloshes onto her fingers.

"I should go put these down before I spill any more."

"Definitely," Chloe agrees.

"Well, I'll see you later," she says when Chloe says, "Wait."

Kristin peers at her as Chloe plucks at her lips.

"I'm sorry about—you know—whatever happened," she whispers. "And I just want you to know that I forgive you for punching me in that race. I know you were having a hard time."

She lets out a laugh. "Thanks a lot," she says, because the last thing on her mind is apologizing to Chloe, especially right then. She has the feeling that everyone is staring at her, the penny-loafer girls and the New Wavers, the beefy football players and the blue-blazered boys who belong to not-so-secret underground fraternities, all the shoulder pads and feathered bangs, rugby shirts and cable-knit sweaters, L.L. Bean and Land's End, they are all are staring at her not because she was Tubs athlete of the week, not because she's from Boise, Idaho, not because she's a skinny girl with big boobs, but because she is so stupid, and she is sure they can all see this. Suddenly without thinking, she lets go of the three glasses of milk—or do they slip?—and there's a loud crash, at least it seems this way to her, and she's standing in a circle of spattered milk and big chunks of broken glass, and Chloe materializes back at her side with more napkins, and the communal din in The Terminal, after dying down briefly to take in Kristin's accident, quickly returns, growing louder and louder, until Kristin can barely hear Chloe when she says, "We looked for you everywhere. Patricia and I did. Everyone else thought you'd gone home, but I knew you wouldn't do that to us. Where were you? Were you hiding?"

"I wasn't hiding," Kristin answers.

"Then where were you?"

Oh, Chloe. She's the only one who has asked her this question directly.

"I'm just curious," Chloe continues.

"I was at the farmhouse. The one at the top of the orchard." Who cares if Chloe knows?

"I thought so," Chloe says.

THE SAFETY DANCE

Danielle

WHAT DANIELLE KNOWS IS THAT THE QUALIFYING MEET IS TEN DAYS away. Her last college cross country race if they don't win. Everything seems especially tragic since last week she ran the best race of her college career—top twenty-five! Third for the Poets!—and Kristin didn't even finish, and because of this, they placed sixth out of nine teams. Afterward, when Danielle went looking for Kristin, she found her bent over a stump just before the first mile marker, making little gasping noises that sounded like crying.

"Kristin," she called out.

And then something happened that Danielle still can't understand. Kristin looked over her shoulder, saw Danielle, and shrieked before bolting into the tangle of small bushes and trees, and though Danielle thought she should follow Kristin—at the very least, she could tell Kristin she'd been drunk, she was so sorry, and she wasn't trying to downplay what had happened, she was only trying to be true to what Kristin had told Danielle, attempting to set the record straight when Harriet had called what happened *sexual assault* and *date rape* but of course it was her fault for getting drunk, she was so, so sorry, she was sorry, she was sorry, she was sorry, for getting drunk, for everything—she couldn't move, paralyzed with something that felt very much like fear.

It's Wednesday, and they've just come in from running mile repeats, the last hard speed workout before they start tapering. The trail through the woods is covered in leaves—Danielle thought practicing there was dicey, especially since Patricia tripped over an invisible root on the first mile and fell, but thank God she was fine, just annoyed because she ripped the knee of her lucky tights. After the second one, Assistant Coach quizzed them: How do you spell "genuflect"? "Hyperventilation"? "Anaerobic"? *A* word starting with a W that Danielle can't remember that Patricia got right because it was a kind of hut that Southwestern Indians had once constructed. They weren't running hard enough, he said too gleefully. They should run so hard they couldn't spell the simplest words. Coach looked perturbed. They all sort of laughed while gulping down as much oxygen as they could. Kristin was still avoiding Danielle, and Liv and Harriet glued themselves to each other at the starting line, even though Harriet quickly fell behind and became an obstacle they had to pass to hit their marks. Harriet had no right putting herself at the front of the pack. "You should let Chloe and Kristin start with Liv," Danielle said, and Harriet snorted loudly.

Danielle takes a boombox out of her locker.

No one can accuse Danielle of giving up. Acting oblivious, yes, but only because they don't have a clue—not about her, not about the effort she has invested in the team, not about the weekly meetings with Assistant Coach, how maddening it is to sit there watching him wolf down three or four of his homemade muffins while she breaks hers in half and then in half again and again, trying to make it last as long as possible. She could eat a half-dozen of his muffins—her favorites are bran, little bombs of sweetness made with dates and coconut—but he only ever offers her one. One! She can hear Harriet's critique of how Assistant Coach is testing her, surveilling her appetite, the same way he and Coach surveil the team's bodies, how both are tools of the patriarchy to distract women from focusing on what's really important. Right. And what is she supposed to do about that? Snatch a muffin right out of his hands?

Harriet won't even eat a cookie from the cafeteria. Once, Danielle saw Chloe take a bite of a brownie and spit it out.

She pushes the play button, jumps up on the wooden bench, wills herself to laugh light-heartedly, and shakes her hips to the opening notes of "The Safety Dance."

"Spontaneous dance party," she cries, as she struts carefully back and forth across the bench, avoiding their piled-up clothes, Patricia's blue bottle of Dr. Bronner's 18-in-1 soap, Kristin's cowboy boots, Harriet's burgundy Doc Martens.

There's no enthusiasm on their faces. Harriet raises one eyebrow skeptically, Chloe looks confused, and Patricia says, "This is literally the dumbest song. Have you seen the video? There's an elf dressed like a medieval jester in it."

An elf? Danielle sighs, and for a moment, she's back in junior high, not just the tallest girl on the dance floor, but the tallest person in all three grades, and she's pretending that she's not self-conscious as she tries to shrink her body so that she is smaller than the short boy with whom she is slow-dancing. Doesn't anyone care how hard she is trying? How she would do anything for them? How she has done everything? How, if she could have, she would have cut off her legs back when she was thirteen?

Well, fuck it. She's about to jump down and give up when Liv sweeps back her red hair in a very un-Liv way, blows a huge pink bubble, and skips around their row of lockers once and then twice, waving her hands in the air and making loose geometric shapes with her hands.

Danielle allows herself a deep breath. Then Patricia comments, "Liv, you nailed the lead singer."

"I like this song," Danielle protests feebly. "It makes me feel hopeful about our strength." She raises her hands. "We can dance. We can run. There's such power when we stick together. Will you just try?"

Everyone's silent until Harriet lets out a laugh. "Let's dance to Danielle's cheesy song. Let's all get drunk and jump up and down like pogo sticks and dance our hearts out and pretend like everything's fine."

It takes Danielle a moment, but then she realizes that Harriet is mocking her.

"What should we drink?" Harriet continues in her loud strange voice. "White wine? Red wine? Gin? Whiskey?"

Ignoring Harriet, Danielle turns to Kristin. It's awkward because she's still up on the bench, and she has to crouch down so that she's not looming above her like a giant. "I'm sorry, Kristin," she says. "I'm the one to blame. I got drunk and I told someone what happened to you, and Harriet overheard me."

"One drink, two drinks, three drinks, four?" Harriet continues, a mixture of pleasure and pity conveyed by her small, tight, toothless smile. Her eyes flash, her nostrils flare and the small purple stud winks. "Twelve drinks?" Suddenly Danielle knows what's happening. Harriet's going to tell them. Danielle thought Harriet had already humiliated her enough at the team meeting. But no. Now she's going to tell them everything. About freshman year. And the bats. Not just two, but three. And why they attacked her. Why she deserved it. Harriet has been helping her carry the weight of a secret she couldn't possibly bear by herself, and now Harriet is going to drop her end of it.

Danielle is holding her breath, waiting for the moment when everything comes crashing down, and everyone knows the truth, when suddenly Kristin is jabbing a finger in her face.

"You told everyone," Kristin says. "I told you what happened, and then you told everyone it wasn't a big deal."

"You said it wasn't a big deal." Danielle hops off the bench as she tries to recollect what Kristin said exactly. "You said you were fine. You said you could have run from him if you'd known . . ."

"It's called date rape," Harriet declares. "It doesn't matter whether she could have run away from him, whether she was faster than him, whether she was bigger or stronger than him. It doesn't matter that she knew him or that she went backpacking with him. Kristin said she didn't want to have sex, and the fucker ignored her. That's what sexual assault is."

They're all talking over each other at this point.

"It was still a big deal," Kristin says to Danielle. "I almost got lost trying to get back to the transfer camp."

"I just wanted you to be OK," Danielle says, close to tears. "I don't want you to lose everything you've worked for just because some guy was a jerk to you. You were running so well."

"She was sexually assaulted," Harriet insists in an even louder voice that Danielle can no longer ignore.

No one's going to blame Kristin for what happened to her on the backpacking trip, but Danielle on the other hand? Danielle can hear what her friends are going to say: You know how she is. You know how she gets when she's been drinking. She can be such a slut. The realization is like a sudden stitch in her side, making it difficult for her to breathe. All this time, she felt better believing that Harriet still loved her. *Loved.* What an odd word to describe what she thought Harriet felt for her. Harriet loves Karen. She doesn't love Danielle.

"Will you please stop talking about me like I'm not here," Kristin says. "That's part of the problem. I feel like no one's listening to me."

"I'm sorry," Harriet says. "I'm really sorry, Kristin, but I think it's important that we are clear about what happened to you."

Liv, who has been quiet this whole time, says, "And maybe talking about it will actually make you feel better."

"It's not making me feel better," Kristin says. "I actually feel worse."

"Most women don't think they were raped," Harriet continues. "Most men don't think they've committed rape. It's sewn into our culture. Men think they have to be aggressive, and women think men have to be aggressive."

"Just leave her alone," Patricia says.

"I think you're in denial," Harriet says to Kristin. "I don't blame you. We're all in denial on some level. If we weren't, we would lock ourselves up in our houses. We would never go out. We would never do anything."

"I know he was being aggressive. I'm not stupid," Kristin says. "But he didn't rape me. Stop saying that. I wanted to have sex with him, that's why I went backpacking with him, but then he was so weird."

"Wait—he did rape you," Harriet says as Liv nods her head in agreement. "It's not your fault."

Denial? Danielle's mind is stuck on this word. She has to do something, even though she feels crippled by her fear of Harriet hurting her more "Are you accusing Kristin of having a false consciousness?"

"Oh, Danielle." Harriet makes a *tsk* sound like a chipmunk as she steps forward, her hand raised, her wrist cocked, her palm facing forward. "Listen to you and your fancy psych jargon."

"Don't hit me," Danielle says as Harriet's hand is moving toward her. It stops. "If you ever hit me again . . ." She suddenly feels breathless, like she's in the last hundred meters of a race. "If you ever hit me again, I'll beat the shit out of you," Danielle hisses, her heart now beating so hard she can barely speak. Harriet freezes. As soon as the words are out of her mouth, Danielle wants to snatch them back. There's no way to undo them, no apology that can make it all better. At the same time, though, she means it. Or she thinks she does, though she has never hit anyone in her whole life.

Harriet's hand suddenly drops like a stone to her side, and Danielle takes a sharp breath, and they remain frozen there, Danielle trying to unscramble her thoughts, her eyes moving from the floor to the ceiling, then pausing on the red shirt of the Tarahumara Indian runner, the poster that Kristin recently taped up on the inside of her locker door. The shirt looks like a priest's cassock. The man is wearing sandals, a piece of string snaking through the space between his big toe and the next one. What crazy shoes to run in. She couldn't run a half-mile in shoes like those. She doesn't want to meet Harriet's eyes, and when she finally brings herself to look in her direction, Harriet's chin is pressed against her chest, her head bent in submission or anger, both possibilities mortifying to Danielle. Maybe she is a monster. Maybe she is to blame for everything.

"I'm quitting," Kristin announces.

"No." Danielle is shaking her head. "No. No, no, you can't."

"You're not my friends," Kristin continues. "You're not listening to me. Well, fuck you," she says. "You're on your own. Good luck at the last meet."

"Please," Danielle pleads, joining the chorus of her teammates' *pleases*. Look how easily the pendulum swings from vitriol to civility. Is this the essence of what it means to be a girl?

She has failed and is failing and will fail again. But failure makes us stronger. Such nonsense, though it's nonsense she still believes. The boombox sits on the bench, already an artifact. She will have to find the strength to carry it back to her dorm room, but not now. Now, Harriet is crying quietly, her shoulder curling delicately in, revealing the fragility she tries so hard to hide, and Kristin is quitting.

"If you quit, I'm quitting," Patricia threatens, planting her hands on her hips, her pointy elbows sticking out.

This would be the time to tell them what happened to her, but she can't bring herself to do it. Do they share anything at all, except for a little discipline, a big dose of masochism? She can't even bring herself to apologize to Harriet. Somewhere deep in the bowels of the gym the furnace cycles on, and there's a sudden gust of warm air from the vents above them, but nothing can thaw the self-hatred that Danielle feels right then.

NOT NOW AND NOT BEFORE

Kristin

WHAT HAS SHE LEFT OUT?

Breakfast at the lodge, the sign that read, "What happens at the lake stays at the lake." The chandeliers constructed from antlers that hung in the dining room and now seem monstrous. The early-morning mist rising from Redfish and the boat ride across it, the gas outboard profane and stinking against the fathomless sky and godly spires. The hike, rocks crunching underfoot like potato chips, the puzzle bark of the Ponderosa pines that smelled of butterscotch and caramel, the rarer strawberry- and chocolate-flavored ones, something she'd never known until Jed told her to press her nose into their crevices, the places where trees lay scattered across the slope as though someone had thrown a tantrum and broken them to bits, the sudden chill when she and Jed passed into shadow, and back in the sunlight the raucous whirr of grasshoppers.

Her desire. Her longing. How when she sat beside him on the

hill at Camel's Back, she could feel heat radiating from his body, and when they did touch, pressing herself so firmly against him, she wanted their bodies to merge.

That she prided herself of never getting lost. When she was running in a new place, she had a system. At every intersection, she continued straight, and if the road came to a T, she went left, so that when it was time to turn around, she knew exactly which way to go to carry herself safely home.

At what point had she taken a wrong turn?

After sitting on the boulder beside the stream while she cried, she splashed water on her face and said aloud, "Get a grip, Kristin," and then she got up, shouldered her pack, and tried to retrace her steps back to the trail, but the path that had seemed so obvious to her earlier kept disappearing, and she was afraid of getting more lost. If you were already lost, was this possible? Hadn't she read stories of people perishing within one hundred feet of the path from which they'd wandered?

She took off her pack, and she drank some water so cold it made her chest ache, and she watched the sky lighten to the east. She had a headache, and she wanted coffee, but she didn't have any. Jed had all of the food in his pack.

If she couldn't find the trail, then maybe she could follow the stream down to the lake. If it was the same stream as the one that they'd crossed yesterday, then eventually she would come to the bridge, and she would know that she's wasn't lost.

But what if it were a different stream?

Well, then she could follow it all the way back to Redfish Lake. It had to eventually end up back there, unless she was more lost than she knew—she tried not to dwell on this possibility—and the stream drained into a different lake. Or what if it dwindled until it was nothing more than a trickle of water, like the ones that had occasionally crossed the trail and muddied their boots on their way up?

Yesterday seemed so long ago.

She wasn't sure how much time passed while she was trying to decide what she should do, though eventually the sun appeared, lighting the peaks of the mountains behind her. It would be hours before the warmth reached her, and maybe it never would. She thought she could just make out the switchbacks of the trail she'd descended, like scratches across a woman's pale body, and she considered whether she should climb straight for them, even if it meant losing all the time she'd gained. But what if the closer she got, the harder it was to see them? What if they also disappeared?

She lay back on the rock, letting its cold seep into her, closed her eyes, and listened to the stream. Then she got up.

Leave no trace, Jed had told her when she asked him what she was supposed to do with her dirty toilet paper. Pack it in, pack it out. Because she knew she was going to have to jump from rock to rock and maybe even walk across a few logs, she was tempted to leave the backpack behind. But it had belonged to her dad, or so she thought, and she needed all the luck she could invent.

What else?

They can't possibly understand what it was like to follow the stream with no idea whether she was heading in the right direction and no one to blame but herself.

Instead of going to practice, Kristin runs through town by herself, past the bookstores and the boutique where she bought her ironic cowboy boots and the Purple Ewe where Chloe's latest crush works; past Merts, the best ice cream in New England, and

Odyssey, purveyor of life-enhancing dorm décor; past two pizza parlors and a Chinese restaurant with delicious steamed vegetables, past the package store where Danielle picks up red wine and Riesling for special team dinners and Kristin planned to buy a bottle of Champagne at the end of the semester when she turns twenty-one, except now there is nothing to celebrate.

She thinks about the possibility that Danielle and Harriet are both right. And wrong. It's exhausting to hold two opposing views in her head at the same time, to keep running when she has come to learn that being the fastest will not save her, that it hasn't, not now and not before. What is the point of running except that she still loves it?

SOMETHING BURNING

Danielle

DANIELLE'S EATING BREAKFAST IN EMILY DICKINSON. THIS IS NOT something she normally does—most mornings start with a cup of tea and an English muffin in her common room with the Darlings. But Chloe has asked to meet her—for what reason she doesn't know.

Harriet has renamed all of the buildings on campus after famous women, which once upon a time delighted Danielle, because how lame was it that all of the buildings at Frost were named after rich and famous men? That this practice seems to continue up to the present day? Though right now, the thought of Harriet, or anything associated with Harriet, makes Danielle feels like someone is stomping on her heart.

At 7:30 on the dot, Chloe comes scooting through the door in her oversized red parka with a fur-edged hood. She's like Little Red Riding Hood, except instead of carrying a basket on her arm, she's pulling a rolling purple suitcase behind her. It's difficult to conjure what the Big Bad Wolf would think of Chloe, the trickster. He might actually turn and go loping the other way.

Danielle waves, then joins her at the coffee station.

"Good morning," Chloe says brightly, before taking a noisy sip of her coffee.

"Good morning," Danielle says.

"Shall we sit?"

"I have a table over there." Danielle points.

"Oh." Chloe sounds disappointed. "I like to sit by the windows."

Danielle mentally rolls her eyes. Why must Chloe always be so difficult? Then she scolds herself: *Why do you let yourself be surprised?* "OK," she says, "Let me grab my stuff."

Once they're seated, Chloe finally lowers her fur-lined hood and with one hand gathers a handful of damp hair, scrunching it into a ball and pressing it against her scalp. She repeats the action, releasing the smell of lavender. She could be pretty, Danielle thinks, but she always looks so serious, almost to the point of seeming sour. Chloe takes another slurp of coffee.

"I know where Kristin was hiding out."

"What?" Danielle asks, confused. Is Kristin gone again?

"When she disappeared."

How is this relevant, Danielle is thinking, *after everything that has happened in the past three days?*

"Do you believe me?"

Danielle sighs. She has wandered so far away from the route she thought she'd be following this semester, and all of the landmarks that would help her find her way back have become unrecognizable. This is what she knows about Chloe from years of observation: she is unpredictable, not because she chooses to be, but because she knows no other way of being. She's like a bird migrating north when all the other flocks of birds instinctually know that it's time to fly south.

The *Sesame Street* birthday cake comes swimming into Danielle's head. The twenty-one trick candles that kept maddeningly reigniting each time she blew them out. And Danielle's distress because she thought there was a guy from the lacrosse team there. Just a freshman, but still, she was trying to avoid everyone on the men's lacrosse team. Why on earth would Chloe throw a fake birthday party for her?

"I honestly don't know what to think," she says at last.

"I thought I saw her," Chloe insists, almost whining. "And then she told me. She was hiding in the farmhouse."

"The boarded-up one in the apple orchard?" Danielle asks. "Why on earth would she go there?"

"I'll show you," Chloe continues. "We'll go to the farmhouse."

"What is the point, Chloe?" she asks. "She quit."

"Because then you'll know for sure."

"Know what? That our season's fucked. That I screwed up." This has become her mantra.

"You'll know where she was."

Danielle can't believe it. All their hard work is going down the drain, and this is what Chloe is worrying about?

"Just a sec," Chloe says. "I need more coffee."

Outside, the campus is still deserted, except for a small cluster of people doing karate in slow motion on the quad. When Chloe returns, she has a tray with two bananas, three hard-boiled eggs, a bottle of Tabasco, and two cups of black coffee.

"What are they . . . ?"

"It's Qigong," Chloe says. "My mom swears by it, says it's the best workout she's ever done." After peeling her egg, she carefully slices it in half lengthwise and forks out the yolk.

Danielle watches this, trying to keep her face neutral. Trying to have a normal meal with anyone on the team is almost impossible.

"My mother is also a little fat," Chloe says.

"Everyone's mom is a little fat."

"Except for Harriet's."

Danielle's heart starts to beat faster.

Chloe raises her left eyebrow.

"I suppose it's not Harriet's fault she's so neurotic," Danielle says. How many times has she said this? "I'm just glad I have a mom mom."

Chloe cuts half of an egg white in half, shakes on a few drops of Tabasco, and pops it into her mouth.

"Like a normal mom," Danielle continues. "What's your mom like?" she asks, making small talk out of habit.

Chloe forks in another sliver of white. "My mom believes you should make your bed every day because if you accomplish nothing else at least you've done one thing."

Danielle laughs. "Does that mean you make your bed?"

"Of course," Chloe says. "I iron my own clothes, too."

"I love ironing," Danielle says.

While they have been talking, Chloe has eaten all of her egg whites and left six hemispheres of yolks. Danielle inwardly shudders. Chloe slices off the top of her banana, then makes incisions going the long way with her knife. She removes the peel in four separate sections. Danielle thinks there is an article about the way women interact with their food, what it says about their personalities. Next Chloe slices the banana into thin disks, dividing them into two little pyramids. They keep falling apart when she spears them with the tines of her fork.

"My mom paid me five cents a day to keep the floor of my room clean," Chloe says. "And just like that—it became a habit."

"That's effective," Danielle says. She thinks of Pavlov and the other behaviorists. "Rewarding good behavior."

"I don't think my mom really wanted to be a mom," Chloe says, eventually getting a slice of banana to stay on her fork. "I think she had to learn strategies for doing it." She eats it in three or four tiny bites.

"I'm sorry," Danielle blurts out, this time with genuine emotion. Harriet floats back into her mind as she remembers all the times Harriet came to Providence their freshman and sophomore years. Her home away from home, Danielle always said. *Mi casa es tu casa.* And Harriet always added, "My chosen home." She has tried to be a friend to both Harriet and Kristin and look where it has gotten her.

"For what?" Chloe asks.

"That you think your mom didn't want you."

"I don't feel bad," Chloe says matter-of-factly. "I don't take it personally. I just don't think it came naturally to her. She probably loves me."

This almost breaks Danielle's heart. She can't imagine wondering about her mother's love for her. That's been a constant: no matter what she does, no matter how much she falls apart or fucks up, she knows that her mother will always love her. Even if she did something really bad, even though she's done something really bad.

Chloe is still speaking, and Danielle almost misses what she says but then catches it.

"You're joking?"

"I'm joking," Chloe repeats, waving her fork around. She's smiling stupidly.

"It's not funny," Danielle says, surprised by how intensely she's feeling right then.

"I can't believe you would believe that."

"Why wouldn't I believe you?" Danielle says. "I like to assume that most people tell the truth."

"It was a joke," Chloe says again. "Come on. Of course, my mom loves me. Whose mom doesn't love them?"

Yours, Danielle is thinking. She's so angry she is almost shaking.

"Puh-lease," Chloe says, rolling her eyes. "It's a joke. Lighten up."

Danielle's plate sits in front of her, the food untouched. The scrambled eggs look like dirty cottage cheese. She picks up a cold piece of bacon, then puts it down again. Chloe is staring at her.

"Why did you have a birthday party for me when it wasn't even my birthday?" Danielle asks. "Why on earth did you do that?"

Chloe looks surprised. "You mean freshman year?"

"Yes," Danielle says curtly. "Your freshman year. My sophomore year. You didn't even really know me." She remembers the third time the candles relit themselves, how she kept licking her fingers and trying to pinch out the flames while the guy from the lacrosse team—she was sure of it—kept smiling at her in a weird way. She had to get out of there. If she didn't, she was going to lose it. *You're such an ass*, Danielle is thinking, *such an ass*. This is not a word that Danielle has ever used to describe a girl—woman, she hears Harriet say, *woman, woman, woman*, scolds Harriet, who has wormed so deeply into Danielle's subconscious, she's like a ghost there, a poltergeist. *Sleep it off*, Harriet said. *If you keep one foot on the floor, that will help with the spins. Oh, and I told the boys to get lost*. Danielle shakes her head to free herself of Harriet while Chloe studies her, doing that thing with her hair again. There's the lavender, and the smell of being freshly scrubbed, of Chloe, hazel-eyed and lively, clean, and alive in Emily Dickinson just about a week out from the qualifying meet. *Fuck Harriet, too*, Danielle thinks. *Fuck them all*.

Chloe sticks out her bottom lip, pouting. "I liked you," she says finally. "That's why I did it."

A laugh bursts out of Danielle. "You had a fake birthday party for me because you liked me?"

"Yes!" Chloe exclaims. "I thought you were perfect. You always believed in us, even though we sucked back then. Like bigtime. You were so positive. And you had those parties. Remember? The blue party? And the cookie exchange? The drinks potluck?"

Danielle can barely believe what she's hearing. Her expression must betray this.

"I'm serious," Chloe says. "I'd never had a glass of wine until I met you. Like wine in a real glass. And you're the one who first took me to Duck and Bunny."

What a weird world, Danielle is thinking as she watches Chloe press the back of her fork into the abandoned yolks, smearing them across her plate. She seasons this with egg shells. The banana peels already browning on her tray are the final touch. Danielle has watched so many girls try to disguise how little they've eaten so many times, and yet it still makes her feel sick.

"Now I know you're not perfect," Chloe says, "but I still admire you so much. Maybe even more."

At this point, nothing should surprise her. And yet Danielle is surprised when they get to the farmhouse and Harriet is leaning against the front door. Her eyes are closed, and her face is turned to the sun that is just breaking above the trees.

At the sound of their voices, she blinks.

"What the fuck," Harriet says, which is exactly what Danielle is thinking. Her heart leaps into motion, urging her to turn around and sprint back toward campus.

"Surprise," Chloe says.

"Chloe!" they cry out at exactly the same time.

"You two have to be friends," Chloe says. "You have to make up."

Make up?

"Kissy kissy," Chloe adds with a laugh.

Danielle is silent. She knows that Harriet won't be the one to make the first move, she's too stubborn. She never admits she's wrong, especially not in the heat of the moment. A truck roars past on the road below them, and then it's mostly quiet again except for the riffle of a few remaining leaves.

"I'm sorry," Harriet starts, surprising Danielle. "I'm sorry for always hitting you. It really is a form of affection, but I can see how it would be annoying."

Harriet sounds so sincere that Danielle can almost forgive her for not apologizing for what's really wrong. And then from habit she says she's sorry, too, because *I'm sorry* is always followed by its twin, something warped and broken facing itself in a mirror. Her own tears surprise her. She doesn't feel like crying, and yet her eyes are wet because she doesn't know any other way. This is what girls do. They smooth things over.

Harriet steps close to hug her, and they press their flat chests together. Harriet is a bag of birdlike bones, and so is Danielle, just taller. No wonder they're always breaking. Both of their bodies quake. "I'm snotting all over you," Harriet says, and Danielle laughs.

"Now we can go into the house," Chloe declares.

"*Mon Dieu*, haven't you gotten what you wanted?" Harriet asks. "We've made up. Do you want a snotty hug, too, Clo Clo?"

"Ugh, no thank you," Chloe yelps, taking a step back from them.

"Can we please just leave?" Danielle asks. At the very least, Danielle and Harriet can now be united against Chloe.

"But we're all here," Chloe says, slipping her hand through a loose corner of the screen and unlatching the handle from the inside. Then, she pulls out a bobby pin that is holding her bangs back and effortlessly picks the lock of the scarred front door. "Let's just look around."

Danielle and Harriet exchange a look. Danielle is not going to praise Chloe, even though she's sure that Chloe is waiting for it. Danielle is still smarting from Chloe's earlier blow. The things girls say to each other: *I like you even more for being not perfect.*

"*Merde,*" Harriet says. "If I'm ever locked out, I know who to call."

Chloe smiles triumphantly. The door swings open. The house smells like wet shoes and something sweet that Danielle can't quite identify. Old cheese? The light leaking along the edges of the curtained windows shows a mostly empty room: there's an old floral couch, a newish coffee table with a few candles scattered across it, a pack of cigarettes, a paperback. Chloe flips the switch next to the door but nothing happens. "I guess they turned off the power," she comments.

The three of them move into the kitchen, which is brighter, daylight pouring through the uncovered windows. There's a Gatorade bottle on the top shelf next to an apple in the refrigerator. "Ah ha," Chloe says. "Kristin loves Gatorade." Danielle is not convinced, but whatever. She looks at Harriet for confirmation that she's right, but Harriet's face is placid and unreadable right then. The oven door is open and inside is a pair of running shoes.

"Those are Kristin's," Harriet says as though she can't quite believe it.

"See, I told you I was right," Chloe says with glee.

This time Danielle can't disagree. Kristin wears white Nikes with red stripes. She has two or three pairs, all of them miraculously clean.

"But why would she put her running shoes in the oven?" Danielle asks.

"Maybe she was drying them?" Harriet says.

"Isn't the power out?"

"It's gas," Chloe says, pointing to the box of matches. She strikes a match, and the oven lights with a loud and sudden whoosh that makes Danielle worry for a moment that the house will explode. "Whoa," Chloe says, quickly turning it off again.

"I guess you're right," Danielle says.

Harriet sneezes, then points to the floor. Mouse droppings litter the linoleum like spilled brown rice. "Do you think she actually spent the night here?"

"I hope not," Danielle says.

"Do you think she's going to be OK?" Chloe asks looking from Danielle to Harriet.

Of course, Kristin will be OK, all of them will be OK, every single girl on the cross country team, and all the girls at Frost, all of them, all of them, they will all be OK because what other choice do they have? This is Danielle's ready answer. But she can't bring herself to say it.

"I think we should do Take Back the Night," Harriet says.

"Take Back the Night?" Chloe asks blankly.

Danielle's heart sinks.

"Clo Clo, has your head been buried in the sand?" Harriet says. "It's about women gathering and reclaiming their right to walk around safely at night. But we'll do it in our own way and go for a run after dark. And then when we're done, we can all share our stories of, you know, things that have happened."

"What do you think, Danielle?"

Why is Harriet doing this to her?

"It wasn't my fault," Danielle blurts out. She has no other choice.

"What?"

"It wasn't my fault." She leans heavily against the counter. "I know I was drunk, but it wasn't my fault."

"Dani?" Harriet says. "What are you talking about?"

"I'm talking about what happened at the end of freshman year."

Harriet's gaze narrows, and Danielle closes her eyes to protect herself against the blow that she's certain is coming. Harriet is going to say she got what she deserved.

But instead, Harriet asks, "What happened?"

Her body starts to tremble. All she can remember is riding the bike up and down the hallway of the Monastery, falling off, the guy she liked lifting her pant leg, kissing her scraped knee, applying a Band-Aid. They're walking her back to her room—the guy and his friend—but she keeps falling down, so they join hands to make a swing for her. It's very dark, and she's being carried across the freshman quad by the guy she likes and his friend, her arms around each of them, and they laugh and call her *my princess* and joke about chariots and ladies in waiting. *We are the knights of the square table.* No one has ever called her princess. She's always been too tall. "I wish you were my boyfriend," she cries out drunkenly, happily because *there's a shooting star, make a wish,* though it's long gone by the time she tilts her face up to the sky to see it. And then it's the next morning, and her head is too tender to rest on the pillow, and the whole room rocks every time she tries to sit up. Harriet marches in and moves the garbage can right next to her bed and says she sent the boys packing, and her body hurts all over, not her skinned knee, but parts of her that she cannot see. Like someone has jammed a spoon in her and scraped out her guts.

"Danielle?"

"Do you think I asked two guys to fuck me while I was passed out? I know I was drunk . . ." She starts to cry for real this time. "Who knows, maybe I did, but I certainly didn't want it."

"Oh my god, Dani," Harriet says. "Of course not. I had no idea."

"Yes, you did," Danielle says. "You were the one who scared the guys away the next morning."

"Are they still at Frost?" Chloe asks. "Is it awkward to see them every day?"

"But I didn't know what happened." Harriet is at Danielle's side.

"What did you think happened?" she sobs. "That I decided to go to bed with Brian Donner and Jake Levingston?"

Chloe says something that Danielle misses. She's pointing to the range. "I think the oven's still on."

There's no smoke, but the smell of melted rubber is unmistakable.

"Shit." Harriet springs forward and twists the knob hard, and it flies off, skittering across the floor. "Oh my god, did I just break it?"

"Just a sec." Chloe retrieves the knob, sticks it back on, fiddles with it, checks the oven, and then fiddles with it some more. "There," she says. "Now, it's off."

This whole time, Danielle hasn't moved.

And the shoes? Kristin's shoes?

Harriet goes to grab them from the oven.

"Careful," Chloe says, "they could be hot, you don't want to burn yourself."

When Harriet turns back to them from the open oven, she's holding two white shoes that are missing their soles. They seem like a symbol of something, though of what Danielle isn't sure.

"Oh Dani," Harriet says, "I didn't realize. I'm so, so sorry."

JUST HANG UP

Kristin

SOMEONE IS KNOCKING AT HER DOOR. COULD IT BE? HE HAS CALLED her three times over the past two days, once in the morning, and twice just after midnight when she's lying in bed, moving across a map of the United States in her mind, trying to picture where each state fits. Her heart pounds. This is the last thing she needs. The answering machine picks up, and he says the same thing every time: *Kristin, it's Jed. Give me a call. I really need to talk to you.* He repeats his number twice. His voice sounds strange—nicer and more normal than the way she hears it in her head—and with a start, she realizes that she has never talked with him over the phone. Last summer, he just kept showing up, at the coffee shop and late night in her backyard, or he left notes under the pot of geraniums on the front stoop of her house. It seemed romantic. How did he get her number at college? In his last message, he adds *please.* She's dismayed with herself for listening so closely.

"Kristin?"

It's Danielle's voice. Kristin stops holding her breath.

"Harriet and I are here. Are you in there?"

She's sure they've come to try to convince her to race in the championship meet. She's angry at both of them.

"Hey." Her room is mostly empty because she still hasn't bothered to retrieve her belongings from the basement. There are a few objects on her dresser—her talismans—a photo of her father, one of her mom and grandma wearing identical red lipstick and black witch hats and laughing in a way that always makes her smile, a pine cone, a rusty horseshoe that Jed gave her. She doesn't know why she hasn't thrown it away except that doing so seems like bad luck. Pinned to her bulletin board is the bib from her first race at Frost. She placed in the top twenty-five, surprising everyone, including herself. She had no idea what to expect when she started college. Her speed astonished her.

For a second or two, the three of them stand awkwardly just inside the door. Danielle and Harriet smell like rain, tiny drops clinging to their hair and jackets. Danielle's forehead is tight with worry. When Harriet leans forward and kisses Kristin's left cheek and then her right, her lips are shockingly cold. No one has set foot in Kristin's room all semester, except for Eli. She's forgotten what she's supposed to do.

"Can we sit down?" Harriet asks.

"Yeah," Kristin says, though there's no place to sit really, except her bed and desk chair. Harriet and Danielle drop to the floor, and Kristin joins them.

"I love what you've done with your room," Harriet says.

Silence.

"It's a joke." Harriet's eyes flash.

Silence.

"I'm sorry." They both say it at the same time.

Kristin lets out a little laugh.

"I wanted you to be strong because it's what I wanted for my-self," Danielle says.

"What are you talking about?" Kristin asks.

"Something happened to me." She looks at Harriet. "At the end of freshman year."

"What? What are you talking about?"

"I can barely remember. I was really drunk."

Kristin has never seen Danielle look so sad before. Her face is pale, and her eyes look cloudy. She realizes with a start that Danielle is barely a year older than she is.

"I was completely out of it. Like blackout out of it. Maybe I was even asleep. And these two guys—I had a huge crush on one of them." She shudders. "Brian Donner. He was the captain of the lacrosse team. And." Danielle stops suddenly and covers her face with both hands.

"Why didn't you tell me that day at the track?" Kristin asks.

"I don't know," Danielle says.

"You said I was going to be fine," Kristin continues, feeling angry all over again.

"What did you want me to say?" Danielle says. "That you weren't going to be fine?"

Kristin considers this: "What about you? Are you fine?"

As Danielle's bottom lip begins to quiver, Kristin finds herself thinking back to the baby rabbit on the trail: how quick Harriet was to pick up a rock and announce she was going to dispatch it with a good hard blow—and how much this enraged Kristin, though she didn't exactly know why. Now that rage is back. It feels like a foreign object in her body, like something she has swallowed that will slowly choke her if she doesn't figure out how to expel it.

"I'm sorry," Kristin says, trying to keep her voice calm and even. "I'm sorry those guys had sex with you."

"It's called rape," Harriet says.

Danielle whimpers, and then there is silence.

"I need to make a phone call," Kristin announces.

Harriet looks confused. "Do you want us to leave?"

"No," she says, moving to the desk where her answering machine sits. There's his voice again, so small and normal it's shocking, and she scribbles down his number while something passes between Harriet and Danielle that Kristin doesn't have the attention to decipher.

"Is that Jed?" Danielle asks.

"Do you think this is a good idea?" Harriet adds.

"No." she repeats. Her hands shake as she dials and she has to start over, as in an anxiety dream where the simplest tasks are impossible to complete. But then the number is ringing and ringing. For a moment, her resolve wavers. Maybe trying is enough? Harriet's lips are pressed together, her nostrils flared. Danielle hugs herself. They both look serious and a little sick, just the same as when they're sitting in the padded wrestling room waiting for Coach to call their names and make them mount the scales. Is this what it takes? Is this the price? After a few more rings, she lifts the receiver from her ear but then there's the magic click, and a door creaks, and someone is standing at the end of a very long hallway on the other side of the country. She imagines the wire stretching between them. *Hi. Hi. Can you hear me? I can hear you. Can you hear me? I can hear you.*

"Hello." It's a woman, her voice warbly and old. Could this be Jed's mother?

"Umm, is Jed here?" she says. "I mean there." Her nerves are still jumping around.

"Jed?"

"Jed?"

There's silence, probably no longer than the time it takes to tie a shoe, but every second pinches.

"Do I have the wrong number?" Kristin asks.

The woman growls, and Kristin considers hanging up until she realizes this is just the woman clearing her throat.

"Jed?" A little laugh. "You mean Jebediah?"

"Yes, Jebediah." She says it as though her mouth is full of pebbles. So many stunted syllables.

The woman growls again. There's a strange sound like wrapping paper being crumpled up. And then faintly: "Jebediah."

Someone says something, though she can't quite hear it.

"It's the telephone for you."

She imagines the creak of his scuffed cowboy boots across a wooden floor. The same boots that he backpacked in. She teased him, asking him whether they could possibly be comfortable. "Don't interfere with something that ain't botherin' you none," he said showily.

"I don't know," the woman says. "You want me to ask?"

And then suddenly, it's Jed saying hello. Question mark. As though he's already forgotten that he's called her three times. Who does he think it could be?

When she doesn't say anything, he says hello again, irritation now infusing the demand.

"Hey."

"Kristin?"

"The one and only." Harriet's laugh suddenly reminds her that she's not alone.

"Oh hey. Just a sec."

She hears footsteps, a door opening, and then closing. "Are you hiding in the closet," she can't help but ask.

"Close," he says. "The bathroom."

"Jebediah? Is that your actual name?"

"Yep," he says. "Beloved son of Jehovah. A real prophet."

"Was that your mom?"

"My grandma."

"I thought you said you lived with your parents—in their dingy basement."

"Nope," he says.

"Is anything you told me true?" Her chest is tight.

"Well," he says, "let's see. My grandpa really is a ghost. And I do think it's cool you're a real fast runner."

"Was," she says. "Was a fast runner."

"I'm sorry," he says with what sounds like real concern, but who can know. "Dry spell?"

"I guess you could call it that."

"It'll end," he says. "Feast always follows famine."

"Except when it doesn't," she says. "Sometimes people just die." Danielle and Harriet are suddenly next to her, their bodies pressed close, their hands on her arms and shoulders as though they know they might need to grab her and keep Jed, or Jebediah, or whoever he is, from dragging her all the way back to Alpine Lake. She recalls how willingly she dove into the cold water, how far she leaned into the open window of his car.

He sighs. She won't fill the silence.

Danielle and Harriet anchor her.

He sighs again.

"Are you even a river guide?" she finds herself asking.

He says *hmm, hmm, hmm.* She can picture his smirk, his habit of introducing long, awkward pauses into conversations. Eloquence is an art, but silence is a weapon. "That is the question."

"How can you not know?"

"It's fall," he says. "No one on the river now except the bears. We'll have to see what the next season holds." And then: "Can you hang on a sec?"

How dare he bring up bears?

She listens. "Just use the bathroom in the basement." Then angrier. "Just use that bathroom." And then he's back, at least she thinks she hears the rasp of his breath in the receiver. If Danielle weren't gripping her arm so tightly, she could so easily get lost again. She feels Jed's pull, but more disturbingly she senses something in herself—something irrepressible and good, but also too eager to please—moving toward him. As though his present silence is a puzzle worth solving.

"Just hang up," Harriet whispers.

"Grandma had to take a dump," he says. "What a lady." His laughter sounds forced.

Danielle kneads her bicep, drawing Kristin back into her senses. Her hand aches from clenching the phone. She will not say another word. She will not. She will not. Not after he just mentioned bears.

Shaking her head, Danielle mouths the same thing: just hang up.

She hears what sounds like a sharp exhalation. "Why did you call me?" she asks. "Why did you write me?"

"Why did I call you?" He pauses, as though he's turning the question over in his mind. "*Hmm, hmm, hmm,*" he says. "Why did I write?"

More silence.

She can almost see him twirling the telephone cord around his finger, gradually cutting off the circulation, the tip turning bright red, then purple, and finally black.

"Penny for your thoughts," he used to ask during the awkward quiet stretches on top of Camel's Back when she was desperate to kiss him, or at the coffee shop when they ran out of funny stories to tell each other. She found the question romantic, even though when she looked inside her head, she discovered her thoughts quite wanting, all of them wriggling away the moment she tried to pin them down.

If she hung up . . . ? That's what she's thinking now, though the idea doesn't even fully belong to her since it's Danielle and Harriet who keep whispering it, like a mantra or a bit of encouragement. It's not a big deal, not an order like *Hang Up!* but a reminder of what she's capable of doing: *Just Hang Up.* A first step. How many times has she run a little faster because she was surrounded by women who believed she could run a little faster, and about whom she also believed the same? This was the nature of competition, yes, but it was also woven into the fabric of friendships: seeing the best in others who also saw it in you. It was beautiful and terrifying, and it often led to defeat and disappointment, and it occasionally carried you farther than you could ever go on your own.

Just hang up.

Jed is not her friend, even though that would be a happier ending, even though that is the ending she has been pursuing by imagining that if she had not hiked out of the wilderness all by herself, without the pump to purify water, without a Band-Aid for her blister, without coffee which he had convinced her to start drinking, if she had not gotten so lost she had started to doubt whether she would ever find herself, then somehow they would have woken together in the clarifying light of a new day. Never mind that she got up early and left to avoid just this. But if she had stayed, then maybe all of the awful mysteries of the night before would solidify into a stump and a sideways-growing tree, her pack leaning against a rock, the small curled-up creature his forgotten fleece, the monster across the lake a lichen-covered boulder, the bear jokes really, truly a misunderstanding, it wasn't like he was threatening her by pretending he was a grizzly, he'd made her the powerful creature, and didn't she see him wink?

She had good reason to leave, and yet if she'd stayed, and he'd kissed her. If he'd said she looked cute with messy hair. If he'd joked about an early-morning plunge. If he'd said *I'm not sure what happened last night.* If he'd said *I'm sorry.* If he said, *Look . . .* If he'd started to sing, *The ants go marching one by one.* Or told her a story about picking whortleberries as a child, driving his mom and dad crazy because the fruit were smaller than blueberries or huckleberries, barely bigger than a grain of sand.

She knew she was right, and yet, if he'd given her any reason to doubt herself, how easily she would have done so. She almost feels good that she left.

Just hang up, her friends whisper.

"That letter I sent you was fucked up," Jed eventually says. "I was pretty wasted when I wrote it." Hmm, hmm, hmm, he says or doesn't say. She's still listening too closely. It's a weakness. Her body feels like a hollowed-out log.

Some part of her aches to hear more about the letter and what he'd take back and everything else he wants to say to her for as long as he wants to speak, but instead she does it. She finally hangs up.

And here are Danielle and Harriet, and Kristin is still enraged. It sucks.

"I can't believe I got involved with him."

"It's not our job to be on the lookout for bad guys," Danielle says, stroking her arm.

"Isn't it?" Harriet says in a dry academic voice. "Isn't that why all our mothers are so scared for us? Isn't that exactly what women are taught to do?"

TAKE BACK THE NIGHT

WE WERE RUNNING THROUGH THE WOODS IN THE DARK, POOLS OF light barely bigger than dinner plates bouncing around on the path three or four feet in front of us, illuminating patches of the leaf-covered trail, a tree root here, a puddle there. The flashlights that Danielle had presented to us were slender and elegant. They came in two colors—gold or green, the closest she could find to Frost's—and we got to choose whichever one we liked the best.

"I would've bought bigger flashlights but I didn't want us to feel encumbered," Danielle said when Patricia started in on what a terrible idea this was. Patricia had tripped last week in the very same woods. Did Danielle want us all to wind up with broken ankles two days before the New England championships?

"Of course not," Danielle said from somewhere in the middle of the pack. "We're doing this because . . . umm . . ."

"Just say it," Harriet urged.

". . . because girls, I mean women," she said before Harriet had a chance to correct her. ". . . women shouldn't be afraid of being out at night."

The run had started at Danielle's dorm where street lamps stood every few feet on both sides of the road. After the physical plant, with its single phallic smokestack, the lights disappeared, and the road petered out in the gravel parking lot in front of the tennis courts. This was where we all flicked on our flashlights and plunged into the woods.

Harriet quickly took over. "We're doing this as an assertion of our power," Harriet declared. "We're doing this in support of victims of sexual assault. And we're doing this to show that we refuse to be second-class citizens who fear the night. And we won't be controlled by the possibility of bad things happening to us."

Kristin was quiet, and so was Danielle.

"You know what Henry said the other day?" Liv suddenly piped up. He had still not told her about his trip to London, and she had still not asked. "He said he was going to go into his Goldman Sachs interview with quote unquote his big dick swinging and he was going to knock it out of the park. And then he laughed."

"Where do guys come up with that shit?" Patricia said.

"Liv, may I offer you some advice?" This was Harriet. "Even if Henry has a big dick, you should definitely dump him."

Liv sighed. "Why do we have to symbolically assert anything," she asked, in a wondering tone. "Why can't we go in with our big boobs swinging . . ."

"And our big butts bouncing . . ."

"And slay those motherfuckers."

Metaphorically, of course, since we all, except for Kristin, had figures that neither moved nor grooved.

We whooped.

That was when Patricia did, in fact, stumble, almost going down. "Jesus. We'd have better luck navigating with our natural night vision."

"Maybe if we were cats," Harriet said. "But human eyes are piss-poor at seeing in the dark compared to most animals."

"We could try it," Patricia suggested.

"If we do, we'll have to stop and let our eyes adjust to the dark," Harriet said.

"I don't want to stop." This was the first time Kristin had spoken all night.

And so we slowed down instead. We were like a group of children tied together with twine trying to run from one side of a field to another. We kept bumping into each other and squealing. Screaming theatrically when we encountered something unexpected: a red mitten that at first glance appeared like a bloodied animal. A stick that might have been a snake. Something mysterious just beyond the edge of our vision that kept vanishing.

It was cold, but not bitter, and the woods were quiet, except for our distinctly human noises. Our hands were tucked into the sleeves of our shirts to keep them warm. Overhead, invisible clouds smothered the stars and moon. The smell of dried leaves hung in the air.

"Where do you think Chloe is?" Danielle asked. Chloe had not shown up at the appointed time at Danielle's dorm room. After waiting fifteen minutes and leaving three messages on her answering machine, Danielle had decided we had to get our show on the road without her. Whatever our show would be.

"I don't know," Harriet answered. "It's weird. I thought she liked the idea of the Take Back the Night run."

It wasn't so bad running in the dark. Though we were "reclaiming the night," we'd never really given it up in the first place. Patricia waited for the sun to set to head out on training runs because New Mexico summers were griddle-hot and heat stroke was a real threat. When faced with the option of getting up early or running late, Harriet often did her workouts after she finished at the lab. She needed every bit of sleep she could get, especially between seven and eight a.m. Kristin had loved the foothills above Boise at dusk, a bit of water trickling through a gully, the balm of the moist smell of cottonwoods after a scorching day. She hoped that would not change. The only one of us who'd sworn off running after dark was Danielle, who had once believed, and maybe still did, that she'd been bitten by two, if not three, bats the summer after her freshman year because she deserved it.

But it turned out that running during the day couldn't save you. Danger was closer than you thought. Indeed, it could be right in your bedroom. That was where Danielle had been the last time, the third time, when she might, or might not, have been bitten by a bat. She'd woken up, and there in the corner where the wall met the ceiling was a small creature. She hoped it was a trapped bird. Or even a big hummingbird moth. Anything except what she knew it surely was. She crept up to it, keeping her distance. It was hanging upside down, its small leathery wings tucked into its brown furry body, two tiny feet with five claws apiece defying gravity. A miracle, a nightmare.

Was there a lesson to be learned from this?

If you woke up with a bat, then it was possible you'd been bitten, even if you had no memory of it.

A girl drinks too much, and two guys walk her back to her dorm room . . .

What was the punchline to that joke?

"It's actually pretty nice out here," Liv said before pressing her thumb to the side of her nose and shooting out a string of snot. Members of the men's team did this all the time, and we found it universally repulsive.

"Dude, I'm downwind from you," Harriet screeched. "And it's dark."

"Oh, I'm sorry," Liv said.

The rest of us giggled.

"Just use your sleeve," Harriet continued.

"That's disgusting," Patricia said.

"You're not getting a cold, are you?" Danielle asked. "Don't get a cold."

"You're making us run at night," Patricia said. "What do you think's gonna happen?"

"You don't get colds from being in the cold," Harriet said. "Karen says . . ."

If it weren't dark, we would have seen Danielle roll her eyes.

"Well, it sure doesn't help." This was Patricia again. "It takes all your energy to stay warm, and that's when the germs sneak in."

"I wanted to try it, just once," Liv explained. "I just wanted to see how it felt."

"And how did it feel?" Kristin asked.

"It felt good," she said. "It felt liberating. Next time the only thing I'd do differently is blow harder."

And just like that we'd fallen back into our usual banter.

The only tricky part was that the trail was covered in leaves, barely distinguishable from the ground around it. This was also true during the day, but it was worse at night. The space between the trees could be the path winding through them, or it was just the space between the trees. Kristin tried not to worry. In the dark, it was easy to forge our own way without fully knowing how far we had strayed into uncharted territory. We kept stumbling off the path, shrieking, turning around, and retracing our steps. The only clues that we'd drifted from where we were supposed to be were the sticky spiderwebs strung from tree to tree or an ankle-breaker that could send one of us crashing to the ground. Suddenly Liv and Patricia, who were in the lead, came to a quick stop. "What is that?" A muddy magazine lay on the ground.

"It's a magazine," Danielle said, stating the obvious.

Our flashlights flicked over the cover. The title was obscured by leaves and dirt. Beneath it was a photograph of something wearing a satiny red leotard with a plunging neckline.

"Is that a . . . ?" someone asked.

"I think it's a porno," Danielle said.

Harriet strode forward and kicked leaves and mud over it. She and Danielle waved their lights back and forth in front of them. What would happen if we saw a pair of shining eyes out there, a shadowy form, or heard running footsteps? Threat was always simultaneously theoretical and real, random and personal. Who would be out there, and why would they want to hurt us, except to show us that we should be afraid?

"Let's get out of here," Kristin said. She and Harriet assumed the lead. Back on the trail, or what we hoped was the trail, we lurched on.

Where was Chloe, we wondered as we started running again? Actually, we were moving no faster than a jog. Was she short-sheeting the president's bed, someone joked? Toilet-papering a professor's house? Filling our lockers with jellybeans or inspirational quotes? Stealing books from the library?

"I don't think stealing is her style," Kristin offered. "She likes pranks."

Danielle snorted. We all knew that Chloe drove Danielle crazy, especially because Chloe had pulled an elaborate joke on her once, inviting her over for tea where a bunch of kids Danielle did not know jumped out and screamed surprise and acted like it was her birthday.

"Poor Clo Clo," Patricia said, because she understood the depths of Chloe's loneliness.

Later on, we would look back with wonder at the young women we'd been—how swift and strong; how often we came through the first mile of a 5K in under six minutes; how hard we pushed to hang on to that pace until the end of the race, how many miles we logged in a single week; how many days we went without taking a break; how long we lasted on diets of salad and egg whites, bowls of brown rice and cups of Grape-Nuts, low-fat cottage cheese and skim milk; how much we drank; how little we slept. The miracle of our young bodies. The tragedy. Later on, not that we knew this, we might look back and see how much was wrong in the midst of so much that was good. How quick we were to reassure ourselves that everything was fine. How slow we were to notice what was seriously fucked-up. We might think we were lucky to look back. Period. To come out of these woods alive.

The meet was so close, and though we were all running stupidly slow, because even if the flashlights did illuminate the surface of the leaves, they didn't reveal what was underneath—rocks, roots, any number of small things that could catch a toe, make a foot roll—we were all actually feeling pretty good. Even Harriet, who was jittery with a secret. She and Karen had not yet consummated their relationship. It would be her first time with a woman, and she was waiting for the end of the season. She wasn't sure why. Maybe she was a little superstitious. And Kristin, who had so many reasons to flounder, knew it in her bones that running was better than not running. Tucked right behind Harriet, she was loose and easy and a little blank. Strong enough. She tried to imagine sewing herself to Liv or Chloe on Saturday, not thinking, just being there, floating along behind them, like a child's kite or Superman cape. She still wanted to beat Chloe, even though her reasons for wanting to beat her had changed. She wanted to be the best because that's what we all wanted. To run fast and win.

We were fine. We were strong. We had tapered. We were peaking. We loved to run, and we hated it. But that was the nature of love. The moon emerged from the shadow of the clouds, and the sky looked bruised but beautiful.

Eventually, we made it to the fork in the road.

Two roads diverged in a leafless wood, and one of them led around the pond and through the forest that stood at the bottom of the campus. This way was generally less known, and yet we knew it as well as the routes we'd walked to elementary school, we'd know it for the rest of our lives. If we went this way, we'd be back in Danielle's dorm in fewer than fifteen minutes. But we weren't ready to go home, not just yet.

The other path led to the orchard. Down the hill was a road we often ran along during the day, but going there at night would be pure madness, even with our flashlights. There was hardly any shoulder, and the tunnels under the old train bridges were narrow and treacherous.

Surging forward, asserting her position as captain, Danielle took the lead.

And then we were there. At the house at the top of the apple orchard. Danielle jogged to a stop. Something ticked steadily like a clock. The light above the front door was burning brightly. A single moth fluttered hopelessly next to it. Liv puffed out her cheeks. Patricia rubbed her arms. Harriet jumped from one foot to the other. Kristin pulled up the hood of her sweatshirt. The cold moved swiftly in.

"Dani," Harriet said.

"Hair," Danielle said.

"Are you ready?"

"I'm ready."

"Do you even know how to get in?" Patricia asked Danielle.

"Of course I do," she said, slipping her hand through a hole in the screen, just as she'd seen Chloe do. The door swung open.

Kristin stood at the threshold. "I don't know if I want to go in."

"But you've already been here," Patricia said.

"That doesn't necessarily mean I want to go back in," Kristin said.

And that was fine. As long as she said yes to running, Kristin could say no to everything else.

STAYING CLOSE

Danielle

LIGHT SPILLS FROM THE OPEN DOOR, THEN A PUFF OF HEAT AND THE smell of matches, hot wax, burning wicks, perhaps a hint of lavender, and something else, something slightly rotten: wet carpet, a tangle of seaweed steaming in the sun? Because Danielle's surprised, it takes a moment for her to absorb everything: the tea candles carefully arranged on the coffee table and mantel, the lit candelabra in the fireplace itself, the glow of yet more candles from the corners of the room. The couch is covered in a pink sheet. There are two chairs that she doesn't recall seeing before. Both look like they belong in the library.

"Did you do this?" someone asks. "This is very you."

"No," she says, still frozen near the front door. It's so beautiful, it's almost perfect.

"Look." Patricia points to the candles on the coffee table. "They spell FROST."

Chloe, Danielle thinks. Of *course. That's why she didn't show up.*

She swells with irritation and affection. "Chloe," she calls out in a singsong voice. "Chloe, come out, come out, wherever you are."

"Chloe," they call out in a chorus of voices. "Chloe?"

"Let's split up and look for her," Danielle proposes.

Harriet and Danielle will search the kitchen, Patricia and Liv the bedroom. Kristin shakes her head. She's not going anywhere. That's fine. Danielle's just grateful she agreed to come at all.

Danielle and Harriet go down the hallway, moving farther from the light, pausing at the threshold of the dark kitchen.

"Where is she?" Danielle repeats.

"It's just Chloe being Chloe. Why do you let yourself be surprised every time?"

This is Harriet. Too cool for school.

"I don't want anything bad to happen to Chloe," Danielle says. "And we're also screwed without her."

"I know you care; I just said you shouldn't be surprised."

Harriet flips the light switch on but nothing happens. They both turn on their flashlights, the beams skittering around the room, briefly illuminating the gaping mouth of the oven, the doorless refrigerator, the sink without water. Danielle moves closer to the oven, shining her torch directly inside. Kristin's soles are gone. Chloe has certainly been there.

Danielle's irritation flares. All they need to do is stick together. All they need is to run as a team, staying close to each other as they've done day after day in practice and at nearly every single race. If Kristin is really back, if Chloe tries to beat Kristin, if Liv is as dependable as always, if Patricia goes to her happy place and pictures herself running through the endless vistas of New Mexico, whatever that looks like, if she and Harriet just hang on, if they hang on for dear life like water skiers being dragged behind a speedboat, if they stay as close as they can to the fast girls on their team, drawing on their reserves of pride and competition, loyalty and love, then surely they have a chance of winning. But without Chloe? Forget it.

"Can I ask you something?" Harriet says.

Danielle nods, and Harriet asks again.

"I said yes," Danielle says.

"No, you didn't."

Danielle suddenly laughs. "I guess you can't see me nodding my head in the dark."

"The dark does make it difficult," Harriet agrees. "Why didn't you tell me?"

"What?"

"About what those guys did to you."

"I really thought you knew what happened," Danielle answers.

"But if you thought I knew, why didn't we talk about it?" Harriet asks. "Were you waiting for me to bring it up?"

Danielle shakes her head. No. Of course, Harriet cannot see this in the dark, no more than Harriet can read her mind, no more than Danielle can tease out how she feels. This is what she understands: her faith that Harriet knew the absolute worst thing about her, and did not abandon her, made her survival possible.

"Dani," Harriet says, "it wasn't your fault."

Danielle's tears fall silently.

"I wish I could have told you that," Harriet continues.

"Whose fault was it, then?" Danielle blurts out. "I was drunk, and they were drunk."

"It was their fault," Harriet says firmly.

Danielle wishes she could believe this, but she can't. She had a huge crush on Brian. For the past two and a half years, she has succeeded in not saying this name out loud, as though she could will herself to forget him—and it. She was drunk, and she still gets drunk. She promises herself that she won't, but then she does, and once she starts, she doesn't want to stop, even though she sometimes ends somewhere dark and tragic. Maybe if she could stop drinking. Maybe if she had stopped. Maybe if she had never started. Anyway. She doesn't remember. Maybe her body does, but she doesn't. And it's not like she's going to ask Brian. Or would have asked him in the weeks after it happened, or Jake, whose name she hadn't known until she found him in the hockey picture hanging in the hallway of the gym. She had to walk by that picture almost every fucking day. And there's this: If they were as drunk as she was, what would they even remember?

Then there was feeling scraped-out inside, and the slick stuff that ran down her leg—

Before she can say any of this, and she's not sure she could, someone calls out *Chloe!* In a tone of voice that suggests that Chloe has appeared in some strange form. *What has she done now?* Danielle wonders. Dressed up like a cross between a ginormous bat and a rabbit—powdery black wings and pert bunny ears—the imaginary creature they become when Coach chooses one of them to be the one who is chased, the one who runs away in terror? Launched herself from the second floor? Danielle freezes until Harriet grabs her hand and leads her back to the living room.

And there—

Danielle draws in a breath.

Well, there is Chloe standing in the middle of the candlelit living room, dressed in yellow tights and a green Frost sweatshirt that hangs down halfway to her knees. Patricia stands next to her. Liv is sitting on the couch, with her knees drawn to her chest. Kristin has moved far enough into the house to allow the door to close behind her.

"I'm sorry I missed running with everyone," Chloe says, "but I had to do this." She spreads her arms as though unfurling a pair of wings. "Do you like it?"

Oh Chloe, Danielle thinks.

"I wanted to do something special for the team," Chloe continues. "Do you like it?" she repeats.

"You're like Pop Rocks," Patricia says, "A little crazy, a little surprising, and way too sweet," and Chloe's face lights up, and she starts to vibrate like a small excited child.

"It's nice," Kristin says.

"Though I don't know whether it's in the spirit of Take Back the Night to abandon us for a home-decorating project," Harriet says, because this is what she must say, and then Danielle adds, "And we were worried about you," because she is also playing her part. "I was worried something had happened to you." Harriet squeezes her hand.

"But I'm fine," Chloe insists, "and I just wanted this to be like your room, Danielle. Like the night before the meet, even though it's the night before the night before. You know what I mean. I wanted it to be like that." Chloe looks at her expectantly.

"It's really nice," Danielle says. "Thank you."

There's a pause. They have navigated the woods by flashlight, survived them, and even rediscovered some of their own weird dark humor, the glue that holds them together. Danielle has led them here, and yet she doesn't know what comes next.

"What are we supposed to do now?" Liv asks, glancing down at her watch.

"Are you in a hurry?" someone says.

"No," Liv insists. "I'm glad we're together."

"Is Henry waiting for you?"

"No," she says more firmly.

"Wait a sec," Harriet says, letting go of Danielle's hand and kneeling to remove something from the key pouch laced to the top of her running shoes. As Harriet unfolds a small rectangle of paper, Danielle's heart churns. Is now the time when she's going to ask them to share their stories?

Harriet steps closer to the light. "I have something to read." She clears her throat. "We must use our bodies to say 'Enough'—we must form a barricade with our bodies, but the barricade must move as the ocean moves and be formidable as the ocean is formidable."

Danielle pictures the starting line of their cross country races. She has been there so many times, always in such a heightened emotional state, that she can feel herself standing there now, her left foot forward, her right foot back, her hands tightened into fists, one sharp elbow pointing to the left, the other jutting out back and to the right, readying herself to use her size and will to create a pocket of space for her teammates behind her.

Harriet continues: "We must use our collective strength and passion and endurance to take back this night and every night so that life will be worth living and so that human dignity will be a reality." Pausing, she looks at each of them, though Danielle senses her gaze lingering for an extra second or two on her and then Kristin. "What we do here tonight is that simple, that difficult, and that important."

"Did you write that?" Liv asks. "It's really powerful."

Harriet laughs. "Oh God, no. I wish, but no. It's Andrea Dworkin. She wrote it for a Take Back the Night march in New Haven."

"Danielle?" Patricia asks. "What are you doing?"

Oh. Without knowing it, she has assumed her starting-line position. "I was thinking about the beginning of our races—" She shakes her head. "—and creating a wedge."

"The way we use our bodies to say 'Enough,' Harriet adds. "The way we form a barricade."

"Except we're doing it to beat every other girl out there," Patricia says, and Danielle's inner Harriet says *woman, not girl, woman,* though Harriet doesn't actually correct Patricia this time.

"That's true," Harriet says. "But there's also a lot of power in all of us out there together. Our mothers didn't get to run cross country."

"We're going to win," Chloe says. She does a little skip and almost knocks over a candle. "Is it time for our stories?"

What more can Danielle share when she knows so little? Is there any power in telling a story about her own powerlessness, her own failures?

"I don't want to," Danielle says.

She watches Kristin take a step toward her. For a moment, she worries she has let Kristin down again. But then Danielle hears this: "I have nothing more to tell you," Kristin says. "I want to get ready for the race. Unless someone else wants to go."

But no one does. Danielle glances at Harriet, watching her run her fingers through her curly hair which will be gone by the time they race on Saturday. Shaved off by Karen, or one of her roommates in some kind of rowdy feminist ritual. Danielle would like to be there in Harriet's common room, listening to an all-girl punk band belt out all the words that have been used against them: *Slut. Cunt. Bitch. Whore. Dyke.* She'd like to be the one to flip the switch on the clippers. Jokingly brandish them like a weapon. And then work her fingers through Harriet's unruly curls, palm her beautiful head. Danielle knows, though, that Karen should be the one to do it. She also knows that she loves Harriet with her whole heart.

"We can certainly talk about our badassery," Harriet says. "That's a very worthy project. We can't fight the patriarchy if we don't remember how strong we are."

"When did you first know you loved to run?" Kristin says.

"Me?" Danielle is surprised that Kristin has asked her. Is it possible that Kristin will eventually forgive her?

Danielle presses her hand to her chest. Her heart is still there.

"Yeah, you," Kristin says, rubbing her arms as though she has just come out of the cold, "but then everyone. When did you know how much you loved to run?"

NEW ENGLAND DIVISION III
CHAMPIONSHIPS

November 14

HERE WAS THE THING ABOUT CROSS COUNTRY: THE RACES DIDN'T add up to anything, and yet we had to run every race like it was the last one, like it was the qualifying meet or the championship. Every Saturday, we had to put everything on the line and push ourselves to get stronger. We had to invite suffering if we wanted to get faster. Setting a PR one week might mean we could do it the next, each competition an opportunity to lay down new slow-twitch muscle fibers and build anaerobic lung capacity; to overcome the mighty tricks the mind deployed to make a girl want to quit.

But let's be honest: just because we'd learned to hold out our arms and pull pain and fear into a tight embrace, we still might someday cross these very same too-skinny arms across our chests and turn away.

We just might.

And yet, we'd made it to the qualifying meet, all of us, even Kristin. Assistant Coach had driven the van through a drenching storm, and Coach hadn't smiled once because he thought the rain would slow us down, and worse, give us all a million excuses for fucking up badly, but just as we pulled up, the rain stopped and the sun came out.

"I knew the weather would improve," Patricia said.

We warmed up. Chloe complained that her socks were getting wet.

"Did you not bring an extra pair?" Danielle asked.

"Patricia told me it was going to be a nice day," Chloe whined

"And it is," Patricia answered. "The sun's out. It's not too cold."

"I've got extra socks," Liv said. She blew a bubble and popped it noisily.

"What's our strategy, Dani?" Harriet asked.

"To win," Danielle answered, and we all laughed.

We stretched. We changed into our spikes, because the course was wet, and it would be slippery. Danielle dabbed pink on all of our lips. Harriet had to pee. Liv accidentally swallowed her gum.

"Ugh," she said. "I hate it when I do that."

The more nervous we were, the more sober. Danielle wouldn't even talk to her parents when they swung by to wish us all good luck.

Then it was ten minutes until the race began, and we circled, stacking our hands on top of one another, and Danielle said, "Listen, I want Chloe, Liv, and Kristin on the starting line. Patricia and

Hairy will go right behind them. And I'll bring up the rear."

"What?" Harriet said.

"It's just a variation on the wedge," she said. "You three will clear the way."

"Are you sure?" Kristin said.

"Totally," Danielle insisted.

Assistant Coach, who was hovering just outside our circle, piped up, saying he'd brought homemade muffins, and he'd give us some if we won. Danielle rolled her eyes. Harriet said, "How 'bout you give us some if we do our best?" Assistant Coach laughed nervously.

We raised our arms. We shouted *Go Girls*. Harriet said *Go Women*. The word *poets* did not come out of our mouths. Chloe squeezed Patricia's hand but made sure she was the first to let go. Liv tried not to think about Henry. Harriet touched her deliciously prickly scalp. Patricia wondered whether she'd gotten good enough to run for Stanford, which was a lot closer to home. Kristin pulled Danielle into a loose hug and whispered something that we all wanted to hear but couldn't.

And then we took our new places on the starting line.

ACKNOWLEDGMENTS

TK
TK

ABOUT THE AUTHOR

STEPHANIE REENTS is the author of *The Kissing List*, a collection of stories that was an Editors' Choice in *The New York Times Book Review*, and *I Meant to Kill Ye*, a bibliomemoir chronicling her journey into the strange void at the heart of Cormac McCarthy's *Blood Meridian*. She has twice received an O. Henry Prize for her short fiction. Reents received a BA from Amherst College, where she ran cross country all four years, a BA from the University of Oxford as a Rhodes Scholar, and an MFA from the University of Arizona. She was a Stegner Fellow at Stanford University.